THE
LAST
WIFE

BOOKS BY NICOLA MARSH

The Scandal

THE LAST WIFE

NICOLA MARSH

bookouture

Published by Bookouture in 2019

An imprint of StoryFire Ltd.

Carmelite House
50 Victoria Embankment
London EC4Y 0DZ

www.bookouture.com

ISBN: 978-1-83888-052-1
eBook ISBN: 978-1-83888-051-4

For my boys, with love.

PROLOGUE

Hatred is a living, breathing entity. It festers, sometimes for years, and if allowed can take on a life of its own. At least, that's what I think happened. I let my hatred grow to monstrous proportions, until I lost control of it.

That's where I am now. The point of no return as I watch her stroll toward me, completely and utterly clueless.

I don't want to hurt her.

But I have to.

I like to think I'm an open-minded person. Generous, almost. I see the good in people, until the inevitable bad rises to the surface and obliterates everything.

We're all the same, liars at heart. Wearing masks. Uttering falsehoods. Pretending to be someone we're not.

She catches sight of me. Her step falters, like she's unsure. Then her stride quickens as I call out to her, injecting the right amount of urgency into my voice.

She doesn't see me smile.

I've hidden a lot behind that smile over the years.

Rage.

Jealousy.

Derision.

Loathing.

My smile broadens. This isn't about revenge or vindictiveness or hatred. It's about one thing.

The only thing that matters to me.

Family.

CHAPTER ONE

RIA

Adrenaline makes my fingers tremble as I bring up the screen to submit my third article for the day. Nothing beats the buzz of seeing my byline in the *Chicago Daily News* and I work longer and harder than everyone else to ensure my name is prominent in one of the city's biggest online news channels.

I have little doubt this article will be accepted and published like all the rest. I'm good at my job, one of the best freelance journalists in the city, and I'm paid more than the average, which is just as well. The money helps keep the doubts at bay when I lie awake at night in my renovated terrace house in Brunswick, a trendy suburb on the fringe of Chicago's Central Business District, wondering how my life has come to this.

I had it all planned out once. Marry the perfect guy, raise the requisite two perfect kids, live the perfect life. Pity Grayson Parker, my ex-husband, didn't get the memo.

"Focus," I mutter, annoyed I let my concentration lapse for a moment. Thinking about Grayson and how he abandoned me five years ago isn't conducive to good work practice.

I'm over it. Almost.

My fingers fly over the keyboard as I edit an article about flimsy firewalls, then move onto the final proof. The owner of a large private investigation firm had been more than forthcoming with answers to my questions considering the sensitive client information they store. Surprisingly, their cyber security had been woeful. I'm no computer whiz so I paid one of the newspaper's IT guys to see if he could breach the firm. It hadn't been difficult to hack into their client database and my article will highlight the vulnerabilities of companies like this.

I love writing articles emphasizing online flaws, proud that I'm using my skills to educate people. I'm almost done with proofreading, giving me plenty of time to drive crosstown to attend my mother-in-law's birthday this afternoon. May is a stickler for her family getting together regularly and I can't say no, despite my complete lack of enthusiasm. An afternoon with the Parker Posse isn't my idea of fun.

Satisfied everything I've written is grammatically correct, I save the article, attach it, and hit send. I exit the newspaper's login screen and am about to shut down my computer when an email pings. I should ignore it but it could be a tip-off to another newsworthy story and I can't resist taking a peek.

That's when I see it.

The sender's name.

I freeze. A chill sweeps over me and I rub my bare arms. I blink, refocus, but it's still there. Taunting me. Haunting me.

I've only seen that name once before and it turned my life upside down.

The subject line, THE PARKERS, has my stomach clenching with nerves. Five years ago, the subject line had read GRAYSON and the accompanying picture ensured that the sorrow over my husband leaving me had turned to disgust.

My finger hovers over the delete button. Whatever is in this email may not be good, though Parker's a common enough surname in Chicago. It could be nothing.

But instinct tells me it's not and I scroll down, my gaze drawn to the startling images. Three photos, of my sisters-in-law in compromising situations, and I press my hand to my stomach to calm it.

I grew up a foster kid and don't have siblings so I'd been so hopeful when Grayson first told me about his large family. I'd envisaged fun bonding sessions with my new sisters-in-law, Ashlin, Shamira and Christine: girls' nights out, spa days, long lunches, and reciprocal childminding.

It didn't take long for reality to set in.

I'm an introvert at heart but love socializing and making new friends, probably because my job is solitary. Reaching out to the girls had seemed natural considering I'd soon be part of the family. But apart from Shamira they'd been aloof, reluctant to do anything other than swap pleasantries when in enforced proximity, and my visions for us to play happy families dissolved, alongside my self-esteem.

I'd known that hollow feeling of being second-best growing up, when at age three I'd been dumped by a father I barely knew and entered the foster system. Being shunted from home to home didn't enable the forming of close bonds and I'd craved attachment. Grayson had provided that. His family hadn't. Except my mother-in-law May, who accepted me despite knowing the truth about my upbringing. I love her for it.

Shamira is kind and welcomed me into the family, but Ashlin and Christine had been condescending, deliberately ostracizing me with talk of polo tournaments and sailing regattas and celebrity gala balls, knowing I couldn't contribute.

Ashlin had been the worst. The beautiful, thin, blonde took one look at me and I could've sworn her upper lip curled. I knew the look well. I'd seen it enough times when I first entered a foster home and the resident biological kids stared at me like I'd invaded their privacy. The older kids wanted to establish who was boss by bullying and the younger ones felt like I was taking attention away from them; I'd hated it.

My past hadn't endeared me to Ashlin, who comes from old Michigan money. She eyed me like she expected me to make off with the Parker silverware and her shoddy treatment hasn't changed since.

I never let her know it bothers me.

My gaze is drawn to the photos again. Who would want to tarnish these women and why? And why send this email to me?

Five years ago I'd tried to discover who was behind the email that devastated me. I'd used my contacts at the newspaper, experts who can usually trace anybody. But they'd had no luck and I hadn't found out who'd sent that incriminating photo of my husband.

It had bugged me for months, when I'd craved answers. Even now, a small part of me wonders where Grayson is, what he's doing, why he didn't love me enough to tell me the truth. I'm proud of my independence and the secure life I've built for our daughter Shelley, but while I hate Grayson for what he did to us, I can't help but wish I knew why.

Whoever sent that shocking photo of my husband has now sent this. I may not be as close to my sisters-in-law as I'd like but if someone is targeting them… I need to know what I'm dealing with.

Another email lands from the same sender. The subject line is ASHLIN.

I don't want to look. I shouldn't. Then I remember all the awful things she's said to me over the years and, worse, how she treats my daughter.

I'd been told by Ashlin in no uncertain terms when her girls were toddlers that she didn't want my crappy presents, so carefully chosen by me, for their birthdays or Christmases. She wanted money. Which I delivered on time—despite being outraged at her obvious insult for my poor taste in choosing gifts—with cards posted snail-mail, the old-fashioned way.

Worse, despite her demands for what I should gift her girls, she always forgets Shelley's birthday and I have to remind her. Every year. Until last week when my sweet girl turned ten and nothing arrived yet again. No money. No card. Nada.

I'm done.

So I start reading.

The first screenshot lists everything from her cosmetic procedures to her favorite personal shopper, from where she enjoys her skinny lattes to her preference for low-carb wine.

And more; the kind of information that could destroy her.

I blink and knuckle my eyes but when I open them the revelation is still there. I should feel vindicated, somehow, that she's as vile as I always suspected. Instead, I feel hollow, sorry for her girls. And Justin.

My heart gives a little twang like it always does when I think of my brother-in-law. Which is why I don't.

I may have problems with Ashlin but this could ruin her, and Justin too.

And if someone knows her secrets, they might know others.

Stifling the foreboding that this could be the start of some weird vendetta against the Parkers, I save the emails and shut down my computer. I'm desperate to discover who's behind this but if I start investigating now I'll be late for May's party.

So I'll put in a brief appearance, do my duty as a good little Parker minion, before trying to discover who knows secrets about my family and what their end game is.

CHAPTER TWO

RIA

Shelley bounds ahead of me as we enter the elaborate gardens of May's impressive Ash Park home. I follow at a sedate pace, inhaling the soothing fragrances of jasmine, daphne and freesia, admiring the riotous purple hydrangeas, the crimson roses and the vibrant fuchsia stargazer lilies. Every time I set foot in these manicured gardens I experience a little stab of envy.

I'm not jealous of May's wealth, but it's a poignant reminder of the yawning gap between us. She's never alluded to my past or condescended in any way, yet I can't help but feel inferior when I enter her twenty-million-dollar home. It's perched high in the bowl of a crescent with similar multimillion-dollar mansions flanking it. Ash Park is one of the most expensive suburbs in Chicago and is renowned for flashy cars, massive houses, and elite families who date back to when the city first settled.

I try not to ogle at the immaculate gardens, the expansive tennis courts and the Olympic-size swimming pools I glimpse when I drive into this crescent, but even now, after being part of this family for longer than a decade, I know I don't fit in.

I loathe self-pity, especially considering how far I've come from humble beginnings, and I perk up as Shelley, who's waiting for me to catch up, waves.

The gardener has water-blasted the sandstone pavers. They gleam in the late afternoon sun as I stroll toward the front door, letting the serenity of the garden wash over me. I'll need it if today's gathering is anything like the usual Parker shindigs.

The ornate double front doors swing open and Ashlin's daughters rush out. They wave at Shelley and almost tumble down the carved marble steps, skipping every second one. Shelley craves affection as much as I do and she rushes toward her cousins and hugs them both at once.

Ashlin steps out onto the front porch and my joy at witnessing the girls' effusive greeting wanes. She hasn't spotted me yet and I'm grateful for the momentary reprieve, all too aware my patience will be tested several times during the afternoon. I'm tolerant and accepting of most people, yet Ashlin pushes my limits.

Shelley releases the girls and spots Ashlin. Her genuine love for family fills me with pride as she jogs up the steps to hug her aunt, arms outstretched. Ashlin balks, her imperious glance sweeping Shelley from head to foot, before she offers a half-hearted wave, turns her back and walks inside.

Shock renders me useless. I will my feet to move but I can't, I'm rooted to the spot. Shelley glances over her shoulder, toward her cousins.

Her bewildered expression guts me.

Desperate to comfort my daughter, I finally take a step forward but thankfully she's a resilient child—she definitely gets that from me—and forgets her aunt's deliberate snub as she links arms with the girls and heads for the house.

I won't forget.

Anger is a wasted emotion, along with bitterness and regret. I should know. I dealt with all three growing up, wishing my mom hadn't died after having me, wishing my dad had stuck around, wishing I hadn't been shunted from home to home, feeling unwanted and unloved.

But in that moment when Ashlin stared at my beautiful, kind daughter like something nasty she'd stepped in, I experienced a surge of fury so strong I could've hurt her.

I need a drink and follow the paved path around the side of the mansion toward the back. I hear muted chatter, the clink of glasses and a string quartet. The music's probably recorded but with the Parkers I never know. Their wealth makes Chicago's upper echelon look like paupers.

I reach the glass-enclosed conservatory that opens onto a stone-flagged terrace, wishing I could look forward to this more. An afternoon spent with family, being plied with gourmet finger food and expensive alcohol, should be a cause for celebration. It isn't and I learned that the hard way.

As I catch sight of Christine near the makeshift bar, Shamira draped over Trent, Justin in deep conversation with his mother and Ashlin now posing on a sunlounger like a swimsuit model, I'm catapulted straight back to the first Parker party I'd attended.

Back then I'd been wide-eyed and optimistic. I'd spent a month's wages on an exquisite Vera Wang maxi-dress, rented a designer handbag and snared a pair of barely-worn Choos from a local secondhand shop. I'd had my make-up done at my nearest Estée Lauder counter and paid for a sleek blow wave at one of those cheap hairdressers that specializes in staff turnover.

My first glimpse of this house twelve years ago had daunted me, with its imposing French provincial façade and extensive gardens. It looked like something out of a magazine but I'd hidden my gaucheness and pretended like I visited mansions every day of the week. It had helped that Grayson never made me feel inferior and with his arm around my waist I'd quashed my usual insecurities as I strode into their party, determined to make my future family like me.

I'd failed miserably.

May had welcomed me unreservedly, Christine, May's only daughter, had been guarded and stiltedly polite, Shamira and Trent had been shy but sweet, Justin had been overly-effusive and his wife Ashlin had stared down her aristocratic nose and made me feel cheap and insignificant despite the effort and money I'd spent on looking good to impress.

After that, I wore whatever I wanted, intent on being me whether they liked it or not. And I'm always polite, to prove a point I'd never stoop to their level. I play nice whenever I see them but I'm saddened that out of three sisters-in-law I'm only on friendly terms with Shamira. We try to catch up for regular coffee dates and I invite Ashlin in the never-ending hope she'll accept me as one of the family, but she always has some excuse. Shamira and I are usually relieved. Christine lives too far away to be included. I think she prefers it that way.

Pasting a smile on my face, I take the final steps into the garden and manage a general wave. I'll do the rounds eventually but first I need to wish May a happy birthday.

Christine fakes a smile, Shamira and Trent wave, Ashlin ignores me. Another typical family gathering with the Parkers.

Determined not to let them get me down, I climb the steps to the terrace. Justin beams as he beckons me and for a moment my breath catches. He's incredibly handsome, with an abundance of dark wavy hair and a natural tan set off by a pale blue polo top and designer denim.

I return his smile and feel May's astute gaze on me. Unnerved by her scrutiny I quickly cross the terrace and embrace her.

"Happy birthday, May." She feels surprisingly fragile in my arms, like she's lost weight. "Shelley wants to give you your present later."

"Thanks, dear." She slips out of my hug and pats my cheek. "Your delightful daughter has already dropped a few hints."

I laugh. "But we've been here less than five minutes."

"You know kids, can't keep secrets," Justin says, stepping forward to hug me, an embrace that lasts a second too long. "How are you?"

"Good, you?"

I know what's coming as I ease away and despite turning my head slightly to the right, he still manages to home in on my lips for a kiss. It's quick and subtle so no one notices, but it makes me uncomfortable nonetheless.

"Manic workload. Long hours. You know how it is."

His warm smile is guileless and my momentary annoyance at his inappropriate greeting vanishes. I like how Justin acknowledges I work for a living and shows an interest.

"I'm getting better at managing my hours." I feign a modest shrug. "One of the perks of being freelance, I can pick and choose when I work."

May waggles her finger. "Enough shop talk, you two. Let's mingle."

Justin pulls a face behind his mother's back and I stifle a grin. We've always had a connection, this easy way of communicating. It makes life tolerable having someone who actually gives a damn about me, knowing I'm about to face the inevitable sniping and goading from his wife and sister.

Today will be harder than ever to face them, considering I unwittingly know their secrets.

I need to discover who's targeting one of the most influential families in Chicago because the startling information I was sent earlier could tear this family apart.

I accept a glass of wine from a waiter as Ashlin sidles up to me.

"Hey, Ria, haven't seen you since the last obligatory Parker party three weeks ago." She's loud, brash, the standout woman in any room. It drives me nuts because I envy her confidence. My inner introvert craves that kind of chutzpah, to be noticed and not blend into the background like I've always done. It served me well in the past to be invisible: to avoid the leers of a foster father, to slip a treat into my pocket at the shops, to elude unjust punishments at the hand of a pseudo mother pretending to care about my wellbeing.

I have worked hard to earn respect over the years, to take my rightful place in this family, yet I can't shake the stigma attached with being not quite good enough.

I don't bother forcing a smile. "I've been busy."

Because some of us work for a living. Not that I would if May had her way. My mother-in-law insists I accept financial assistance. Guilt money, for the fact her youngest son abandoned us when Shelley turned five. I accept her generous offerings and save them in a bank account for Shelley, but May also finds other ways to make life easier. Foisting her cleaner on me. Paying for Shelley's school uniforms. Ensuring her caterers drop off a weekly delivery after they've been to her place.

I don't have it in my heart to refuse her all the time. May is the matriarch of the Parker family and she actually likes me, so I don't want to offend. I need someone onside.

Though technically that isn't true. Justin likes me too. A bit too much for a brother-in-law, the thought eroding my meager confidence even more considering I'm making small talk with his wife.

"Don't you get bored sitting at a computer all day?" Ashlin wrinkles her nose, no mean feat considering the amount of fillers she has injected into her face on a regular basis. "It would drive me mad."

"I love my job." I down a gulp of Chardonnay and eye the bar nearby. As usual, Ashlin will test my vow to stop at two. "And I do some of my investigative work on the road so I'm not on a screen all day."

I sound stuffy and pompous and don't give a damn. The airhead isn't interested in hearing about the intricacies of journalism. She's never once asked me about my work beyond inferring I must be a corrupt, unscrupulous lunatic who spends all day online exposing secondhand news stories.

"Investigative work." She sniggers and eyes me with faux curiosity. "Is that why Grayson left you? Too much poking your nose where you shouldn't?"

She's baiting me as she always does when she's had a few drinks. Hoping I'll lose it in front of the family. Deliberately being a jerk so if I retaliate I'll end up embarrassing myself. Her callous treatment is always worse after she's had a few wines and by the contemptuous gleam in her eye, she's on a particularly vicious roll today.

I can do what I always do in this situation: feign indifference. Or I can cut her down to size like I've yearned to do so many times before.

I don't like taunting, having endured my fair share as a kid. I usually ignore Ashlin when she does it but after witnessing her appalling treatment of Shelley earlier, I can't help but retaliate.

"From what I've recently learned, I'm not the one being investigated." I lean in close, not wanting everyone to hear the truth. I don't want to reveal anything until I know what I'm dealing with regarding those incriminating emails.

But she's pushed me too far today and I can't resist demeaning her so she knows how she makes me feel. "One of the dangers of living in the digital age, Ash. You never know where those footprints will lead."

She flushes a nasty puce and stares at me in open-mouthed disbelief, whether because of my unsavory insinuation or the fact I've verbally retaliated for the first time, I don't know.

She starts to bluster, to clear her throat, like she's swallowed one of the bees May keeps at the back of her property.

I allow a slow victory smile. I don't have to say anything else. Her reaction confirms what I already know.

Ashlin is cheating on Justin.

She's having a seedy affair with a major business rival.

And it isn't her first.

I'm disappointed. I want so much to believe this family is special, that they deserve the pedestal society places them on. The Parkers are invited to every major event in Chicago and beyond, from the opening nights of exclusive boutiques to select sailing regattas on Lake Michigan, from courtside seats at the US Open to private screenings on Broadway. More often than not they're oblivious to how revered they are in the elite of this city's wealthy.

So what I discovered earlier today could have far-reaching consequences.

For everyone.

Maybe I've said too much and I walk away, as she mutters, "I don't know what you're talking about."

I pause and glance over my shoulder, one eyebrow raised in provocation. "Don't you?"

CHAPTER THREE

ASHLIN

"What the hell does she know? Busybody cow."

I want to scream it across the garden so everyone can hear. Instead, I settle for venting with Christine, my eldest sister-in-law, who's never fully trusted Ria either.

"That's a tad harsh." Christine tops up my champagne and pops a strawberry into the flute.

"Yeah, you're right." I clamp down on my fury a second before I say too much, like how the hell does Ria know I'm ruining my marriage. I settle for a more sedate, "I'm the cow but there's something about her that never fails to rile me. She always acts so damn superior."

"Don't let her get to you." Christine clinks her champagne glass against mine. "If Mom wasn't such a soft touch, we wouldn't see her."

"Yeah, your mother is too sweet."

Utter BS, because I happen to think May Parker is an overbearing, interfering old bat and I hate my mother-in-law almost as much as I despise Ria. But Justin worships his ma, does everything the battleaxe says, and as long as she lives and controls the Parker fortune I play nice.

"I don't get it." Christine sips at her champagne. "Grayson abandoned her five years ago, so why does Mom still feel guilty? It's got nothing to do with her."

"Because Ria's taking advantage." I widen my eyes in a fair imitation of Ria. "She acts all innocent to fool people, while laughing at us for our gullibility behind our backs."

"You really think she's like that?" Christine's gaze travels to where Ria is chatting with Justin, smiling up at him like he's the funniest guy in the world.

That's another thing I hate, the way my husband looks at her. He doesn't think I notice but I do, since way back when Grayson first introduced her to the family.

Justin had a gleam in his eye… like he'd seen something better than me. It's why I keep my distance from Ria. It's not her fault my marriage is falling apart but I don't need to see the evidence of my husband appreciating another woman when he can barely look at me.

If he ever finds out what I've been doing to get back at him… what Ria said a few moments ago is too close to home.

And I'll do whatever it takes to ensure she doesn't learn the truth.

"I think she's cunning. And capable of anything."

I could've been describing myself and we both know it, as Christine casts me a curious glance but says nothing.

I like Christine but rarely see her beyond May's family get-togethers once a month. She lives in New York City, we chat on the phone occasionally, but don't have a lot in common. She's a true Parker, I'm just a ring-in, like Ria and Shamira.

Not that Shamira and I are close. She's too busy mixing up essential oil concoctions, twisting herself into unnatural yoga poses or fawning over Trent to care about anyone else. Besides, she's too wheatgrass-mung-bean-free-love-inner-peace for me.

"How's my big brother treating you?"

I dart a glance at Christine, wondering if Ria has said anything to her, but her stare remains ingenuous.

"Justin is great. Putting in long hours at the firm but what's new? He was a workaholic when I met him and I admire how driven he is."

More BS but Christine is like her brother: too narcissistic to see through my lies. All the Parkers are self-absorbed, something I gladly overlooked when I married the moneyman. Justin runs the family's financial company, long established by his father and his grandfather. Old money. At forty-five, Justin is one of the richest men in Chicago and I enjoy the spoils. My girls attend the best private school, we live in upmarket Rockland Grove in a sprawling modern monolith designed by Illinois's most in-demand architect and I don't have to work. Which is why I have too much time on my hands to dwell on my empty, faux-shiny life and mull ways to fill it. Foolish ways that can come back to bite me if I'm not careful and by Ria's taunt earlier, that could be sooner rather than later.

I only see Ria every few weeks at May's insistence that the family assemble regularly, and today is the first time she's fired back when I goad her. It's petty, I know, but I do it because I secretly admire her. It's impressive that someone raised penniless in the foster system has a degree in journalism and works as a freelancer with a recognizable byline. She's intelligent and I can see why Justin practically gushes when he talks about her. That's the real reason I don't like her. I'm jealous. Not because of Justin's laughable crush on her but because I see her pitying glances, like she can't comprehend how I don't work for my money, like I'm vacuous and vain.

"Justin always puts family first," Christine says, raising her glass in a toast. "But I'd be careful if I were you, Ash. Because Ria is family too and the way he acts around her, like a puppy dog waiting for scraps of affection…" She trails off with a smug smile, knowing she's made her point when I feign indifference but end up tipping some of my champagne down the front of my chartreuse strapless sundress.

"What are you saying?"

I'd prefer to walk away from her usual passive-aggressive games but maybe she knows something I don't? I'm already rattled by Ria's earlier jibe and can't afford to ignore Christine's casual inference there could be something going on between Justin and that woman.

"Men are idiots and they're suckers for a damsel in distress." She swirls her champagne, a slight frown marring her brow. "Ria insinuated her way into this family by fooling Grayson and now that he's gone and she's back on her feet…" She gestures toward Justin. "Maybe she's set her sights higher?"

A sliver of fear lodges in my heart. Maybe I've played this all wrong, taking Justin for a fool. If he ever finds out what I've done… What if Ria does know something? She'd have contacts everywhere and I can't believe the thought only crosses my mind now. I really need to stay off the booze.

"She doesn't need the money," I scoff, acting like nothing Christine has said bothers me, when in fact I'm worried. "She got a good pay-out from the divorce and earns a squillion according to Justin."

A sly grin lights Christine's face. "So he talks about her?"

My patience snaps. "She's part of this family. Of course he mentions her." I pause for dramatic effect. "We talk about all of you."

Something akin to fear flickers in her eyes before she blinks and I wonder if I imagined it. "Considering what you say about Ria, I'd hate to think what you say about the rest of us."

I tap my bottom lip, pretending to think. "Let's see. Trent is a eunuch because Shamira carries his balls around in her macramé handbag. She's a try-hard hippy wannabe who inhales too many fumes from those remedies she mixes. And you…" I trail off deliberately, making her squirm.

A fine sweat breaks out over her forehead and a bead trickles down her temple.

"What about me?"

I draw out the moment, before laughing so loud she jumps. "You're an open book, Chrissie dearest. You have the most boring job in the world, you're too smart to get married and you live eight hundred miles away from this rabble." I pat her arm in pure condescension. "I almost envy you."

Her confusion is palpable. She doesn't know whether I'm joking or having a dig, like I usually do.

"There's nothing boring about being a property manager." She squares her shoulders. "Especially when I own all the buildings I manage."

I snicker. "You know you can pay someone to do that for you, right?"

"I'm not a lazy trophy wife."

It's a direct jibe and for a moment I consider escalating this game by retaliating. But it's not worth it. I have more important battles to fight, namely discovering exactly what Ria knows.

"You're so right." I fake yawn and stretch. "Not everyone can lie around all day doing nothing and looking this good. It's a skill born of years of practice."

She laughs as I intend and the tension between us dissolves. It's always like this, a game of one-upmanship that one of us eventually backs down from. I hate giving in because I always have to win. It's my thing.

I never let anyone get the better of me.

Ever.

CHAPTER FOUR

MAY

"Gran, what do you call a mushroom at a party?"

I tap my bottom lip, pretending to think. "What, Jessie?"

"A fungi. Get it? A fun-guy," Ellen pipes up, beaming at besting her sister, who proceeds to stick out her tongue while pinching Ellen under the table.

"Ow!" Ellen yells, and punches Jessie in the arm, who immediately tears up. I can tell they're crocodile tears as her furtive glance sweeps the nearby garden to see if anyone is watching.

Just like their mother Ashlin, they're great actresses.

"Girls, I'm sure there are plenty of other jokes you can tell me." I frown at them and it has about as much effect as it did on my kids many years ago: absolutely none.

I had my four close together in the hope they'd learn from each other. Instead, they'd been individuals from the start, as different as siblings could be. Even now, their differences are startling. Justin puts as much distance between him and Ashlin as possible, whilst Trent dotes on his wife like a lapdog grateful for scraps of affection. Christine hovers near the bar, topping up her glass frequently, enjoying the lavish lifestyle she's become accustomed to, and I have no idea where Grayson currently resides since he abandoned his family five years ago.

I don't like my children being so disjointed. I always wanted my family to be close, but my daughter moved interstate to get away. And out of my three daughters-in-law only Ria is worth a damn.

Shamira can be sweet but she's making Trent softer every day. He should've followed Justin into the family business; he chose to teach music instead.

As for Ashlin, the only reason I agreed to let Justin marry her was her family connections. The Garners are as well respected in financial circles as the Parkers and it had been a mutually beneficial alliance. But Ashlin's carefully constructed veneer hides a nasty, shallow woman and I don't have much time for her.

Which leaves Ria. Poor, slighted Ria, abandoned by my flaky youngest son but standing proud regardless. Despite her upbringing Ria exudes pure class, with an inherent grace money can't buy. I like her and the feeling's mutual. Ria works hard, raises Shelley right and is still part of the Parker family despite the attempts of some to ostracize her.

Which makes what I have to do all the harder.

"What about you, Shelley?" Ellen elbows her cousin. "Do you have a joke to tell Gran?"

Shelley, as reserved as her mother, shakes her head. "The only jokes I know are dumb."

"Why don't you tell me one anyway?" I place my hand on Shelley's shoulder, startled to feel the bones beneath her cotton sundress. At ten, Shelley's in that prime tween age where girls can be introduced to eating disorders via peer pressure. I'll have a word with Ria later.

Shelley screws up her face, reminding me so much of Grayson at the same age that my chest gives an uncharacteristic pang, while the other girls egg her on.

"Come on, Shelley. You must know some jokes." Ellen pokes her in the ribs and Shelley swats her hand away.

"Okay. Here's a good one." Shelley glances around the table, ensuring she has our attention, before continuing. "Knock, knock."

"Who's there?" Ellen leans forward, her eyes gleaming. She loves knock, knock jokes, the cornier the better.

"Cows go," Shelley says.

"Cows go who?" Ellen's eyes crinkle slightly, as if she's trying to figure out the punchline.

"No. Cows go moo," Shelley deadpans, before breaking into a giggle that warms my heart. My darling granddaughter doesn't laugh often but when she does it dissolves the residual tension in my ageing muscles.

I despise my youngest son for abandoning his family and shirking his duties. He'd always been a wanderer, even as a child: walking in his sleep, exploring the neighborhood on his own, getting lost at shopping malls. I'd hoped Ria would be a good influence on him and that he'd settle down when they married. And when Shelley arrived I'd watched him grow into a devoted father. That had lasted five years before he'd taken off. I could've hired a PI to discover his whereabouts but the day he'd abandoned his family was the day he was dead to me. Family is everything and I can't abide a child of mine shirking his responsibilities.

Since then, I've made it my mission to ensure Ria and Shelley don't want for anything. Not that Ria lets me help much. She has her pride and I respect that. I admire her independence. But I'll be damned if I'll abandon them like Grayson did.

"That's not bad, Shell." Jessie, a year older than her cousin, can be snide like her mother one second, yet sweet the next. "I've got one for you. Knock, knock."

Shelley idolizes her older cousin and leans forward. "Who's there?"

"A little old lady."

Ellen, who's obviously heard it before, rolls her eyes and Jessie shoots her a scathing stare that channels Ashlin perfectly.

"A little old lady who?" Shelley asks.

"I didn't know you could yodel." Jessie grins and it takes me a moment to understand the punchline.

The girls fall about laughing and in that brief snapshot of time I'm happier than I've felt in ages. I need this. Not a party to celebrate my ever-increasing age, not a reminder of how dysfunctional my family is, not another gathering fraught with undercurrents and faux cheer, but this: my grandchildren and their innocence, untouched by the lies and secrets that drive the rest of them.

I blame Percy for this family's failings. My husband died five years ago but he'd taught our children to be as manipulative and conniving and reticent as him. We may have secured the family's financial fortunes for years to come when we married, but a day doesn't pass that I ponder if I'd done the right thing in agreeing to be his wife all those years ago.

Ellen snuggles up to me. "What about you, Gran? Don't you have any jokes to tell us?"

"Okay, I'll tell you one, then it's time to wash up before cake."

The girls clap their hands and I continue. "What did one wall say to the other wall?"

They stare at me with wide eyes.

"I'll meet you at the corner." I bite back a smile.

The girls groan and I chuckle, accepting their embraces as they clamber over me, tickling and poking.

This makes it all worthwhile.

Every furtive move I make to control my family, this is why I do it, for my beloved granddaughters.

For their futures.

CHAPTER FIVE

RIA

Justin finds me hiding near the conservatory. "Want to help me with the cake?"

Usually, this is the point I take my leave from Justin at a family gathering. His subtle flirting makes me uncomfortable. He'll stand a tad too close. He'll lock gazes with me a tad too long. And he'll deliberately seek me out when no one else is around.

But today, residual bitterness against what Ashlin's doing behind his back makes me return his broad smile and nod. "Sure, let's get the cake ready and bring it out."

His right eyebrow raises a fraction in surprise because I haven't fled as usual, before he masks it with a wink. "I wouldn't mind seeing you jump out of it."

I roll my eyes. "That's lame, even for you."

He laughs, the crinkles at the corners of his eyes adding to his appeal. Justin Parker has the looks to back up his confidence. He's six-two, with a ripped body from hours at the company gym—according to Grayson who'd worked out there too—a strong jaw, hazel eyes and a smile that can make women weak-kneed if they're prone to that kind of thing.

I'm not but today I'm filled with righteous indignation that Ashlin cuckolds this man without compunction. He doesn't deserve it. From what I've observed over the years he's a loving, attentive father whose girls adore him. He attends every school event from sports days to ballet recitals, he ferries them around to weekend activities and he organizes special daddy-daughter dates that often make me feel inadequate for not doing more with Shelley. He also never says a bad word about Ashlin and stays by her side at functions, which I like, because it means his light-hearted flirtation with me is innocent.

Though I haven't seen as much of that lately. In fact, I can't remember the last time I saw the two of them standing together at a family gathering. Maybe Justin suspects his wife's infidelity? Maybe he accepts it? I have no clue what goes on in people's marriages, considering mine had imploded and I'd been clueless then too.

"Are you okay?" He touches my arm, the barest skim of his fingertips against my skin. It pebbles, the tiny goosebumps sending a message to my brain I should ignore: I like his touch way too much.

I've never acknowledged the subtle flare of attraction between us because I have too much respect for the Parker family. Justin is a married man, who happens to be my brother-in-law, and I'll never mess with that.

"Just tired." I don't shrug him off like I usually would, allowing his fingertips to linger. I miss the touch of a man. "Pulling long hours."

"What are you working on at the moment?"

I glance up and catch Christine and Ashlin staring at us from across the garden, and step away from Justin out of habit. His hand falls away and I immediately feel cold. "An article on security breaches for small businesses."

And discovering way more than I should, via emails some lunatic targeting this family is sending me.

"Sounds interesting." He leans in, too close, yet I can't help but inhale, savoring the bite of his expensive citrus aftershave. It's crisp and understated, inherently Justin. He doesn't flaunt his wealth; he wears it like the finest cashmere. It makes him even more appealing. "But when are you going to interview me?"

That's all I need, to be confined in an office space with a tempting man distinctly out of bounds. Not that I'd officially turn down the Parker Partnership if they asked me to do a feature on them. They handle billions and are a prominent company in this city but they've never asked me to write an article and I'm secretly relieved. Seeing Justin and dealing with this subtle attraction between us is hard enough when I see him once or twice a month surrounded by family. I have no idea how I'd react if we were in an office together, isolated, away from the safety net of our family.

"When you can afford me," I quip, pointing at the kitchen. "Now what about that cake?"

I don't need the guidance but when he places his hand in the small of my back, I savor the illicit thrill of heat—knowing it's wrong to yearn for things I shouldn't but beyond caring. I'm in a weird mood today, aware of Justin in a way I haven't dared acknowledge in the past. He's incredibly sexy and dynamic, the type of man who commands attention and I struggle not to give it to him. It's like a fissure has cracked my resistance and I'm not entirely sorry. I blame Ashlin. Discovering evidence of her betrayal, then seeing her callous indifference to my warm-hearted girl… if Justin wants to flirt with me today, too damn bad for her.

We enter the spacious kitchen and rather than drop his hand Justin splays his fingers across my lower back, branding me as his when he shouldn't. The pressure of his fingers is firm and I'm aware of each and every pad, which is crazy considering there's a layer of cotton between us.

I should move. Step away. Establish distance between us. I don't. I lose all sense of time as we stand together, a good few inches between us but his palm connecting us in a way that's unobtrusive to others yet has the potential to mean more.

I dare not look at him because I'm not ready to face whatever I might see in his eyes; and I never will be.

I hear the girls squeal from somewhere behind me in the garden and it breaks the spell. What the hell am I doing, lusting after another woman's husband? This isn't me. I must be feeling particularly vulnerable to let his ingenuous flirting get to me.

"I'll get the candles." I try to sidestep and for a second I think he won't let me past. But he shrugs and his hand falls away, leaving me wondering if I imagined the whole thing. The cake is on the island bench, already set out on an exquisite porcelain stand. I carefully place a matching server alongside it and pick up the lighter when I sense Justin behind me.

The nape of my neck prickles and I resist the urge to rub it. He's close and I grit my teeth against the urge to lean back a little.

"Are you seeing anyone?"

The question comes so far out of left field that I drop the lighter and it clatters to the bench. I can feel his heat again, like he's radiating some kind of force field only I'm aware of, and I wish he'd move away. I don't like feeling this befuddled. I'm a logical person who weighs decisions and values facts. I don't feel flustered or acknowledge irrational attractions. What's the point? I have an impressionable daughter to raise and Shelley is my priority. I haven't had a relationship since Grayson. Which might explain why I'm standing in my mother-in-law's kitchen, secretly enjoying the forbidden thrill of having this attractive man flirt with me. Sick.

"No, I don't have time to date." I inject flippancy into my voice in the hope he won't hear the inevitable yearning that question elicits whenever anyone asks.

The truth is, I wouldn't mind dating, to feel the rush of attraction again, to go through the ritualistic fun of flirting before getting physical. But between work and Shelley I don't have the time or the inclination. I've had sex a grand total of twice since Grayson left me five years ago. Both had been at work Christmas parties, quickies in the nearest empty office that had barely scratched an itch.

I crave intimacy, the kind of closeness that evolves into a relationship. But I've become discerning since Grayson and shield my heart well. I need a strong, caring, funny guy.

Justin clears his throat at that moment, as if reinforcing what I need.

Someone like him.

"You're a vibrant, intelligent, beautiful woman, Ria. You shouldn't be alone."

He moves alongside me, standing close enough that our shoulders touch, his low voice rippling over me, making me crave. I hate him for it. This can be nothing more than a game to him, seeing how far he can push the poor, pathetic, single sister-in-law. What does he think, that I'll be seduced?

Screw him.

Unfortunately, deep down, I know that's exactly what I'd like to do.

"It's none of your business," I say, managing to sound aloof and uninterested as I snatch up the lighter off the bench. "Why don't you go outside and be with your wife and I'll take care of the cake."

"I haven't been with my wife for a long time." He sounds resigned, resentful, and I hate the tiny flare of hope his admission elicits. "Six months, to be precise."

While I absorb the implication behind his words, he continues. "You're lucky. At least you're free of Grayson. I'm stuck in a dead-end sham of a marriage, for what? For the sake of appearances? For the precious company? For the family? We've turned into one of those cliché marriages, sticking together for the kids and not much else." He drags a hand through his hair, his expression tortured, while I resist the urge to embrace him and offer whatever comfort I can.

I have to admit a small part of me feels relieved, because his flirting has picked up momentum the last six months, corresponding with his lack of intimacy with Ashlin. So he isn't a sleaze as much as a guy desperate for a little female attention.

Which his wife is freely dispensing elsewhere, according to those incriminating emails.

I wonder why he's confessing all this to me now, while part of me is sad that this great guy is tied to a woman who doesn't deserve him.

"Have you talked to her?"

His snort borders on a snigger as he gestures to where his wife is topping up her champagne glass for the third time since I arrived. "Try talking to her…" He trails off, embarrassment flushing his cheeks. "I guess you know what she's like."

I want to ask, "Why do you put up with it?"

Instead, I settle for, "Why does she hate me so much?"

He takes a long time to answer, the silence becoming awkward, when he finally says softly, "Probably because I don't."

His honesty surprises me. We've never broached the taboo subject of the attraction between us. His light-hearted flirting and my witty comebacks are the only sign there is something more than familial obligation between us and even then it's so sporadic I wonder if it's real.

But Justin has just articulated the number one reason I assume Ashlin dislikes me and I can't do a damn thing about it.

He has also admitted he likes me.

I'm momentarily buoyed—there *is* something between us—before reality sets in and my senseless hope deflates. Justin and Ashlin having marital problems has nothing to do with me. He's still off-limits and will remain so forever. I know this. I've always known this. But it's easier to deal with delusions when the object of my fantasies doesn't admit how much he likes me too.

"We can't do this." I move away, putting some much-needed distance between us, voicing what one of us has to. "It's wrong."

"Yeah, I know." His gaze locks with mine across the kitchen and something inexplicable, something addictive, arcs between us.

My body buzzes with it, hyper-alert and attuned. "But you have no idea how I wish it was right."

With my heart pounding in my ears and my body alight, I stalk out of the kitchen. Let him sort out the cake, and his life.

I can't be a part of it, no matter how much I might secretly crave otherwise. I've worked too hard to lose everything now.

CHAPTER SIX

ASHLIN

The Hippy rarely seeks me out so when Shamira ambushes me by the fountain I can't hide my surprise.

"What do you want?" I sound snappish courtesy of the champagne buzz making my head ache. I'm not a lush but alcohol, and a lot of it, is the only way I can cope being around Justin's family for more than five minutes.

"Hello to you too," she says, her soft voice annoyingly melodic. "How are you, Ashlin?"

"Getting better by the minute." I raise my champagne flute, biting back the rest, that a few more drinks might actually help me tolerate being stuck here with all of them.

Shamira laughs, a gentle tinkle that grates on my nerves as much as the patchouli fragrance wafting over me, and the tie-dyed purple kaftan mini-dress she wears with aplomb.

I hate the lengths she goes to in perpetuating this hippy lifestyle, every clichéd inch of her, and wonder how Trent hooked up with this bogus aromatherapist. Women like her will do anything to claw their way out of their pasts and I assume this peace-loving phony targeted Trent. He's one of those harmless guys who are oblivious to everything but his adoring wife. Their mutual doting makes me sick and more than a little jealous.

When was the last time Justin looked at me with admiration, if ever? It's silly, really, to expect that whole lovey-dovey thing when we're matched so well in other ways. But I'm not a complete fool. I know Justin initially dated me because of my family name. We were the wonder couple of Chicago's elite and everyone gushed. I'd basked in the attention but while Justin had been attentive and eager, he'd never looked at me the way Trent looks at Shamira.

I sip my champagne to dislodge the uncharacteristic lump of emotion in my throat. I'm annoyed that I'm jealous of this woman. I could confront her with what I know, meaning she'd back off and not come near me again, so the next time I get maudlin over the lack of romance in my marriage I'll remember that.

"We need to talk." Shamira touches my arm in a way that makes my skin crawl, a claw-like grip bordering on demanding, almost possessive. Like she has any right to be that way with me.

I snatch my arm away. "About what?"

Shamira darts a nervous glance around. "Not here."

"Whatever," I mutter, sounding like Jessie at her recalcitrant best. It surprises me how my eldest regresses around the Parkers, morphing from a smart-mouthed pre-teen to a young girl happy to play. That's one of the reasons I make an effort to come to May's soirees. Being around family makes my daughters happy and they are the one bright light in my sham of a life. I glance across to where they're currently enraptured by their grandmother, horsing around with her and Shelley. Seeing their smiles, hearing their giggles, definitely makes being here worthwhile.

We move toward the far end of the Olympic-size horizon pool and stand in the shade of the pool-house. She's fidgety, plucking at the frayed ends of her kaftan sleeves, unable to meet my eyes. I have little interest in what Shamira has to say. She probably wants to organize some lame surprise for my brother-in-law but her nervousness is odd.

"What's so important that you had to drag me down here to discuss it—"

"I saw you." She blows out a long breath, like she's worked up to the mystifying declaration. She tucks her hands under her arms to stop fidgeting and when she finally eyeballs me, her disdain makes my hackles rise. "Last week, near the Palais in Beale Hill."

I freeze as the implication sinks in and resist the urge to rub the chill making my skin pebble. Not that she could've seen anything too nefarious. I'm usually very careful. But the fact she's bringing this up means I could be in trouble. First Ria, now her. Don't they have anything better to do than interfere in my life?

They don't know the first thing about me. How I strive to appear flawless on the outside while doubts erode me on the inside. How perfection has its price and I pay for it every day. Not in monetary value but in the high expectations I place on myself, and those around me. I want to have the best. I want to be the best. But that kind of pressure is wearing and when it gets too much I do stupid things.

Like seek out inappropriate men as soulless as me.

It's self-sabotaging, I know. I'm trying to fill an emptiness deep within by inadvertently lashing out at the one person who should be more attuned to me.

Justin never *sees* me, but other men do. It's why I repeatedly take stupid risks. I wasn't so dumb at the start. Back when we first married I'd been filled with optimism and hope for the future. When Justin wasn't parading me in front of his business cronies, he'd whisk me to theatre premieres and restaurant openings.

We were regular fixtures in the society pages, snapped at The Music Theater or the Athenaeum, at Vue Mode for the launch of their latest exquisite creation, or front row at Fashion Week. In each of those photos, Justin would be staring at me with stars in his eyes. Posed? Probably, but while the attention he paid me became increasingly rote, the last six months have been particularly bad. He works long hours and is rarely home before midnight. The weekends are filled with the girls' extracurricular activities, which he happily volunteers for; probably to avoid spending time with me. Gone are the date nights and the weekends away, where he'd whisk me to an undisclosed destination on a whim.

I've been forced to face facts. I have become invisible to my husband.

So I source attention elsewhere.

It doesn't help my plummeting self-esteem, seeking solace with other men. But for the all-too-brief moments when we hook up, I feel more special, more alive, than I have in a long time.

I have a husband who doesn't care if we sleep together or not and an inherent hollowness that no amount of designer clothes or expensive jewelry or spa dates can fill. And the last thing I need is this woman judging me.

"What did you see?" I feign nonchalance and take another sip of champagne. It burns like acid down my throat.

"You. And the family's nemesis."

Relief floods me. I can easily explain this away and she won't be any wiser.

"So? We were discussing a mutual business interest—"

"I'm not an idiot," she says, hesitant, an embarrassed blush staining her cheeks, before she adds, "He had his hand on your butt so it didn't seem like business to me."

Shit. I've been so careful this time around. Ensuring discretion. Keeping my carefully built façade of a life isolated from my needs. I got away with an affair before, it has almost been too easy when I targeted the arrogant, self-assured charmer who'd bang anything in a skirt. Especially as he competed with Justin for every single dollar in the financial world, so screwing me would be the ultimate revenge.

It hasn't been about the sex for me. It never is. For someone who's been ignored most of my life growing up, and now suffers the same fate from my husband, I need the validation. I crave it like Christine craves her next cocktail.

I wonder if May knows that her daughter is borderline alcoholic. Probably not. The harridan is too busy hovering over Justin, ensuring the family fortune continues to accumulate. A fortune I intend on enjoying for a long time to come, which means I have to shut Shamira up once and for all.

"Every woman in Chicago knows he's a flirt. If you'd stuck around to snoop further, you'd have seen me shove him away—"

"Don't patronize me." She has the audacity to jab a finger into my shoulder and I stagger, a tad off-balance. "You came out of a hotel and walked down Fitzroy Street, where he touched you four times before you reached your car and then he palmed your butt."

Her smugness riles as she folds her arms, disapproval radiating off her. Like she has the right. What she's done in her past is far worse.

I have to play this cool. Deny, make her doubt what she saw; and if she doesn't back off, go for the jugular.

I shrug, faking indifference, as my heart pounds so hard it feels like it's about to leap out of my chest. "Think what you like. We had a meeting in the hotel's restaurant, which is the best in Chicago and you'd know it if you ever ate real food rather than ingest wheatgrass shots morning, noon and night. Then he walked me to my car—"

"Perhaps I should get Justin's take on the situation?"

She speaks so softly I barely hear the threat. But I see her goddamn superiority, lording it over me that I've screwed up and she knows it. "How you choose to live your life is none of my business but the identity of the guy you're screwing can potentially tear this family apart. Have you thought about that?"

Fury surges through me at the thought of this upstart ruining the precious life I've worked so hard to build and I lunge toward her, unable to contain my rage. She startles and stumbles, her back hitting a marble column of the pool-house while I lean forward to leer in her face. "Keep your mouth shut or I'll tell everyone about your past."

She blinks, but not before I glimpse a flicker of fear. "Everyone knows I grew up poor."

"But not the rest."

She blanches and I drive the stake in harder, determined to skewer her like she's done to me a few moments ago. I need to make her understand I won't tolerate her threats, not when my entire life is wrapped up in appearances.

"I know all about what you've done and I don't think your husband would approve. And neither would May."

Shamira's pallor matches the wall behind her, a sickly off-white, making her eyes pop like fathomless dark orbs. Her gaze darts around, as if seeking out potential eavesdroppers, and a nervous tick makes an eyebrow twitch.

Oh yeah, I have regained the upper hand. She won't say a word about my indiscretion.

I wait, and after several long moments she pulls herself together and carefully blanks her expression. "You don't know what you're talking about—"

"Shut up." I invade her personal space, our faces almost touching, close enough to smell the garlic on her breath from the hummus dip she devoured earlier. "We've all got our secrets, every single one of us. So let me make this clear. You don't tell anyone what you think you saw and I'll do you the same courtesy regarding your past. Got it?"

I can't believe her audacity in confronting me. What did she hope to achieve? She's usually meek, so the fact she's chastising me for my bad behavior means the woman actually has a backbone. I just wish she hadn't discovered it now.

After a long pause, she nods. "I won't say anything."

"Good." I step away, the stench of her patchouli perfume overpowering. She's such a hippy cliché. "Remember, dearest sis-in-law, that what you have on me is circumstantial but I've got proof of your past and if you ever threaten me again… it won't end well for you."

I turn away but not before I glimpse fear in her eyes, mixed with something far scarier.

Defiance.

CHAPTER SEVEN

MAY

I watch Ria as she stalks from the kitchen like she has every devil in Hades after her. Something's bothering my favorite daughter-in-law. When Ria first arrived I noted the slight frown, the shadows under her eyes, the tension pinching her mouth. It hasn't eased. If anything, Ria appears more harried now.

An afternoon with my family can do that to a person. I know the feeling.

Ria forces a smile as I approach but it doesn't reach her eyes.

"How's the birthday girl?" Ria touches my arm, her affection genuine. None of the phoniness Ashlin and Shamira pull whenever they're around me.

"Feeling every one of my sixty-five years." I grimace and roll my shoulders. "Remind me to never have one of these shindigs again."

Ria wants to call me out on my whining; I see it in her eyes, the judgment that I haven't lifted a finger today. The caterers cooked all the food, the wait staff served and the cleaners made everything spotless and they'll return after everyone leaves to clear away. But Ria doesn't say a word. Another thing I admire about her. She knows when to hold her tongue.

"The kids are having a good time." Ria gestures to where Jessie, Ellen and Shelley are engaged in a game of princesses and dragons, an invented game they've played since they were toddlers.

"They'd be the only ones."

Ria chuckles at my dry response. "You can't fool me. You love having your family together."

"Guilty as charged." I hold up my hands in agreement while silently contemplating what Ria would think if she knew the truth.

I don't like many members of my family, let alone having them all in the same place. But I do it to foster harmony. I'm not a fool. I know why most of them pretend to care. Money is a great incentive to play nice. It's why I intend to test them.

"Do you have secrets, Ria?"

My question surprises her. I mean to catch her off-guard and I've succeeded by the way she flinches before quickly masking her reaction with a nonchalant shrug.

"Don't we all?"

She sounds flippant, like she hides nothing. I want to believe that. I tried to dig into Ria's past to discover something I can use if needed. Everyone has a flaw. I want to know what Ria's is. Interestingly, my question has made her nervous as a tiny vein pulses at the outside corner of her left eye. But I let it go for now. Because what I'm about to say to the family will make them all anxious.

"Could you do me a favor and round up the troops? I have an announcement."

Ria stares at me with open curiosity before nodding. "Sure. I'll gather them to cut the cake."

"Cake before revelations, how fitting."

Ria hesitates, as if she wants to say more, before moving toward Christine. My daughter is currently intent on consuming her body weight in expensive French champagne. That's my girl; always about excess. It makes me worry even more.

I never over-indulge in anything. I eat freshly prepared and carefully proportioned meals. I avoid alcohol. I don't squander money on frivolous treats or the latest fashions. I learned from a young age, moderation in everything. My mother's harsh lessons had served me well. Going without dessert to fit into a dress.

Jogging alongside Lake Michigan until sweat poured off me as a way to learn self-discipline. Withholding sexual favors until every rich boy in the district wanted me.

My mother's teachings enabled me to land Percival and marry into the Parker family. *A match made in heaven*' the social columns had decreed in every Illinois newspaper. *'The lakeside princess and the city prince.' 'The heiress to the fortune of Lake Michigan's wealthiest landowners and the sole heir in the richest Chicago family of financial wizards.'*

If they only knew that their version of heaven had been my private hell.

No longer. Percy left me the richest widow in Chicago and I have no intention of allowing any of that fortune to be dissipated at the hands of people with no self-control.

I watch as diligent Ria gathers everyone. She doesn't see the venomous glares directed at her back when she walks away from Christine and Ashlin; only Shamira falls into step beside her, happy to chat. Though that girl harbors sadness too, like she hides something too big to bear.

Ria heads for the children last, pretending she can't find them, enabling them to leap out at her from behind the manicured hedges. She pretends to stagger in shock, one hand clasped over her chest, before Shelley flings her arms around her mom.

Some of the ice surrounding my heart melts. Ria's a good mom, a good person. I'm right to trust her when I don't trust many people in my family.

Jessie and Ellen hover, unsure what to do. Ellen's expression is yearning, wistful, while Jessie's, confused initially, quickly morphs into resentment. Those poor mites probably aren't embraced that often, what with Ashlin running around perfecting her socialite image and Justin avoiding her by working long hours at the office. I hate the thought of my granddaughters suffering.

It's part of the motivation behind what I'm about to do.

A lump forms in my throat and I clap loudly, eager to proceed with my announcement.

I clamp down on my outrage at what this family has become and feign enjoyment as they gather around me, fussing over lighting the candles on the exquisite choc-marble cake I provided, singing a rousing rendition of 'Happy Birthday' and the inevitable loud 'hip-hip-hoorays'.

I wait until one of the wait staff whisks the cake away to the kitchen to be dished up, then pick up the nearest knife and tap it against my untouched wine glass.

"May I have your attention?"

Trent and the kids look bored, Christine glassy-eyed, Ashlin sways a little like she's consumed one too many champagnes, Shamira's politely interested. Ria offers a genuine smile and Justin does the same.

"As you all know, the financial climate is unstable at the moment. Many companies have sustained heavy losses with market plunges all around the world. So with that in mind, I'm instigating some changes."

Now I have their attention. Even the kids seem to sense the importance of what I have to impart and stop shuffling their feet.

"I'm closing the family account."

I hear a stifled gasp but don't know who it comes from. Until now, I allowed family members to withdraw money from a joint family account as needed. None of them take advantage but they have free access to a sizable chunk of money I oversee. It's my way of maintaining control. But there are changes on the horizon and I want to prepare them.

"Moving forward, there will be a trust for each of your families and you'll be paid a minimal wage from that account and not a penny more. So I recommend you invest what you have wisely. Preserve your money."

I wait, the pause dramatic. "Because the Parker fortune won't be around to sustain you forever."

A scare tactic designed to test and I see the mirrored expressions of shock, their mouths perfect round Os, all except Ria. She stares in blatant admiration, as if she wants to applaud. I knew this is how she'd react. Ria's proud of her independence and so she should be, not hanging off me like a goddamn leech, usurping whatever she can get like the rest.

"Does that mean we're poor now, Gran?" Jessie's eyes are round, as worried as her mother's.

"No, sweetheart, but I want us all to understand the value of money and how to look after it so it doesn't dwindle away."

I glance at my daughter first, then Ashlin, finally Trent and Shamira. I avoid looking at Justin. He'll be furious I hadn't mentioned this to him.

"Now, let's get back to enjoying ourselves." I clap my hands with false gaiety and beckon the wait staff in the kitchen, who immediately come out to hand around pieces of cake.

I notice no one eats it, apart from Ria and the kids. Maybe the others have already had their cake for too long and gorged on it.

Times are changing in the Parker family.

I'll make sure of it.

CHAPTER EIGHT

SHAMIRA

I'm trembling by the time we reach home. Exhaustion from faking a happy-disposition mingles with something far more sinister.

Fear.

A bone-deep, petrifying, confidence-destroying panic that rendered me mute on the thirty-minute drive from Ash Park to Donvale Heights. I'm terrified that my carefully constructed lies are on the verge of unraveling. I have spent years—and a small fortune—on creating the perfect life. No one, especially not some uppity cheater like Ashlin, is going to ruin it.

I've taken care of problems in the past. It has been a constant burr, the fear of being found out. More recently, I think I'm finally safe. Considering how Ashlin threatened me at the party, maybe not.

"Hey, you." Trent slides his arms around me from behind and I melt into his embrace. It isn't difficult. I love this man, every soft-hearted, gentle inch of him.

"Want to take a bath?" He nuzzles my neck, leaving me under no illusions why he wants to get clean together.

"I'd love to, but I promised a sick client I'd have her batch of oils ready for her to pick up tonight."

A glib lie but then, I'm good at it; an expert, born of many years of practice. Nobody knows the real me and I want to keep it that way.

"You work too hard." He releases me and whacks me on the butt. "Don't be long, okay?"

I spin around and kiss his mouth. "I won't be."

He tweaks my nose like I'm a kid, before padding into the kitchen, his bare feet leaving imprints in the dust on the floorboards. Cleaning isn't our strong suit. We prefer chilling in our downtime. Taking walks lakeside. Strolling up Auckland Street. Dining street-side, people-watching.

I love living in this hip lakeside suburb where tourists mingle with locals, sampling exotic food or listening to the latest grunge band at a dingy pub. Where a chilly breeze off Lake Michigan brings a welcome cool in the depths of summer. Where I can appreciate my new lifestyle and how far I've come.

Right now, I'd like nothing better than to grab Trent's hand and head downstairs to follow the indie music drifting in our window from one of the many trendy bars. To indulge my passion for raw vegan fare. To browse through one of the bohemian boutiques in search of that elusive knitted, knee-length olive-green cardigan I'd glimpsed once and never again.

Instead, I glance around our spacious apartment as an affirmation. I can't lose this. The honey-oak floorboards, the quirky art-covered walls, the monstrous wide-screen TV at odds with the funky purple suede sofas, all of it signifies a life I built with Trent. With his money.

I hear him rummaging in the kitchen, humming a recent pop hit and know I have to make my escape before he comes back and insists I take that bath. I can't, not right now, I'm too wound up.

I slip on a crocheted poncho and head downstairs, punch in the code for the alarm and open the back door to Makes Scents, my aromatherapy shop, that also houses a large room where Trent teaches music. We're living the dream. A dream built on his bank account.

I have no intention of allowing it to turn into a nightmare.

The aromas hit me first. Lavender. Geranium. Marjoram. Rose. Pungent and intoxicating, familiar and comforting, I inhale deeply, waiting for the usual calm to infuse me.

It doesn't and I know why. I hate how May made that big announcement at the party, like we're wasteful kids who need to be taught a lesson in reality. We all know she controls the family fortune and she can take it away as fast as she bestows it. But to have our noses rubbed in it…

I can't go back to being poor. My fears are silly, really, considering I have the shop now and a steady clientele who pay way more than the overheads for my concoctions. But the lease is in the Parker company name, as is the apartment.

Trent and I will be screwed if May cuts us off. Sure, we have an investment portfolio carefully managed by Justin, but how far will that get us if May only doles out a small wage from a trust fund?

The average house price in inner Chicago currently sits in the high six figures and there aren't many steady jobs for aromatherapists and part-time guitar teachers.

I'd been rattled enough after my confrontation with Ashlin and May's surprising announcement intensified my unease.

I've paid my dues.

And paid a small fortune online to create a history far removed from my actual past, knowing a woman like May would have me investigated once I started dating Trent. Money well spent the day a Parker asked me to marry him.

I'd targeted him initially. He'd been playing in a talentless band at the same pub for a year, a rich kid flaunting the fact he didn't need to work. I recognized him from a newspaper article on Chicago's richest families and known right then he could be my way out.

I'd insinuated my way into his life. He loved my carefree spontaneity; I loved his sizeable apartment and bank account. But once I got to know him, I knew how lucky I was. Trent was one of the good guys and I hadn't had many of those in my life. I fell in love for the first time, heady and surreal for a girl like me. We shared our hopes and dreams and he asked me to move in.

May didn't approve at first but I won her over. People like me. It's a skill. I'm genuine and sweet and guileless; when I want to be. We married six months later and opened our business three months after that.

That had been thirteen years ago and I've grown complacent, secure that the lies I've concocted will never be discovered. The thing is, while having money is nice and I've grown accustomed to it, it's the thought of losing Trent that has me in a spin. I can't bear the thought of him not loving me. He's my world.

Because for that terrifying second when Ashlin confronted me at the party I thought she knew my other secret, the one I don't think Trent would be able to forgive.

Panic fills my chest, squeezing it in a vise, and I force breaths deep into my lungs to calm down. Everyone thinks I do yoga because I love it; little do they know. It's a necessity, a way for me to keep the ever-present apprehension at bay, the fear that at any moment my carefully constructed life will come tumbling down around me.

That's what has me worried. If Ashlin has somehow discovered the truth about my past, what else does she know?

My fingers tremble as I mix up a concoction of frankincense, sandalwood and ylang-ylang, perfect for anxiety. I pour the mixture into a burner and light the candle beneath. In another beaker I mix bergamot, geranium and frankincense for calming and add it to an electric burner. Overkill, maybe, but I need all the help I can get right now.

I'll need to call that client to come by later to pick up a batch of my famous arthritic remedy so Trent doesn't discover my lie. I need a few hours to clear my head, to calm down, so he doesn't pick up on the fact that Ashlin freaked me out. So I set to work.

Lining up the bottles of essential oils: chamomile, cypress, lavender, lime. Measuring out the base oil. Adding the right amount of drops. Mixing.

Yeah, this is exactly what I need. The soothing repetition of a familiar activity, far removed from vindictive Ashlin and her too-close-to-home accusations.

CHAPTER NINE

RIA

I don't have to wait long until Shelley is in bed and I can fire up my computer. She's exhausted after the party and talked non-stop on the way home about the cool stuff Jessie is doing: ballet, horse riding, piano, golf, polo. I refrained from saying that the poor girl doesn't have time for a childhood with that extensive list of after-school activities. And when does she find time for homework?

Then again, the Parker women don't have to study because when they finish school they get unlimited access to a seven-figure bank account to live off.

Though that's changing, considering May's surprising announcement earlier this afternoon. I'd almost applauded when she'd divulged changes that would encourage her children to stand on their own feet. It would have no effect on me but as I'd looked around that table I'd seen shock and horror. And anger from Justin, who'd obviously been blindsided like the rest.

For as long as I've known May she's never played games. She doesn't pit her children against each other or lord it over them that she's still the matriarch of a powerful financial family. She's caring and down-to-earth, to the point of stoical. I admire that about her. So I have no idea what her motivation is for the announcement today that has her family so rattled. I'd contemplated telling her about the emails I'd received this morning but, after her announcement, the party had quickly dispersed and Justin hadn't left her side.

Besides, I want to delve deeper, to discover who is behind those emails. Are they a first step in blackmailing the Parkers? If so, why send them to me and not May? Unless… I haven't thought about it until now but maybe other family members have received those revealing emails too and they're too embarrassed to say anything?

There's only one person I can ask and I pull up Shamira from the contacts list on my cell and hit the call button. She answers on the third ring.

"Hey, Ria, everything okay?"

Her greeting isn't surprising considering I wouldn't usually call her after we saw each other only a few hours earlier.

"Yeah. We didn't have much of a chance to chat at the party so I thought I'd touch base."

"That's sweet of you." I hear an odd bubbling sound that's muffled. "I'm down in the shop mixing up a batch of arthritis remedy."

"You're working late."

"The joys of being self-employed, you know how it is."

I join in her chuckles, not wanting to point out Trent and Shamira freely access the family account May mentioned earlier and haven't had to worry about money a day in their marriage.

I'm the only one who withdraws a sedate one thousand dollars a month, and that's only because May forced me into it, saying she'd open up an account in my name and deposit ten times that every four weeks.

As if sensing the direction of my thoughts, she says, "What did you think of May's slap on the wrist earlier?"

"It's surprising, considering she's given the family financial carte blanche for so many years. Maybe the company's in trouble?"

"Yeah, maybe." I hear glass clinking. "I'd love to chat, Ria, but I've got to get this mixture into sterilized bottles before it cools. Can we catch up for a coffee soon?"

"That sounds lovely." There's no easy way to skirt around the issue and I can't think up a logical excuse, so I blurt out, "Hey, have you received any weird emails lately?"

"Apart from the usual spam for penile enlargements and hooking up with hot Russians online, no."

I laugh and she continues, "Why?"

"I'm writing an article about phishing scams at the moment so I'm just checking with family first to see if they receive that kind of thing regularly."

The lie slides from my lips, perfectly plausible.

"Nope, nothing here." I hear a muffled curse and clinking of more glass. "I really have to go, Ria. See you soon?"

"Absolutely. Take care."

She ends the call quickly and I sigh, placing my cell next to my laptop.

Shamira hasn't received the revealing emails and I don't want to ask May, Justin or Christine. Which means I'll have to delve deeper. Lars is my go-to-guy for researching the cyber world and has helped me with so many articles I've written I've lost count.

He's online, which isn't surprising. I often joke that he never sleeps and when he does his brain is hardwired to his PC.

I send a message.

I need help tracing an IP address.

I forward him the sender's details. However, his response a few minutes later says that tracing the IP address proves as frustrating as my contacts who'd tried five years ago. Lars is one of the best in cyber mysteries but whoever sent these emails is better.

He loves a challenge and if he hasn't found anything I know he'll be willing to go where he's not supposed to, like accessing the police database.

I fire off another instant message to him.

You're not giving up, surely?

Don't you journalists know when to quit?

I smile and answer, pandering to his ego.

You know me, I never give up. Besides, I need a cunning, street-smart expert and isn't that you?

Cut the sweet talk. You really need this IP address?

Yes. Please. It's important.

I wait as the dots appear on the screen, before his response pops up.

Give me a few minutes to hack into the police database.

With a sigh of relief, I wait. Lars has a degree in computer science and knows how to get a job done, legally or otherwise. He's helped me get the scoop many times since I've gone freelance and I trust him completely. We'd met during my last year at college through another journalism major and stayed in touch because I'd been suitably impressed when he showed me how he could reroute an IP address around the world many times to make it unidentifiable, then enter the dark web where anything and everything is for sale.

I don't usually ask questions about where he finds his information but it's usually accurate and, when I'm chasing a story, that's all that matters.

The dots appear on my screen again and I hold my breath, hoping he's come through for me yet again.

Sorry, still nada. Whoever's behind this is a virtual ghost. You know me. I can find anything and anyone online. Not this time.

*But I love a challenge so leave it with me, I'll keep digging and
if I discover anything I'll get back to you.*

Disappointed, I fire back: *Thanks.*

This is crazy. Lars is good at his job and he's stumped.

There's one other option I hate to contemplate. I know another
computer genius who is smarter than Lars.

But I can't reach out.

I don't want to.

My heart pounds and my palms are clammy as I contemplate
contacting the last man on earth I'd ever approach for help.

And that's even if I can get in touch with my ex-husband.

CHAPTER TEN

ASHLIN

I'm spoiling for a fight by the time we make it home.

I can feel my anger simmering, a slow burn that needs an outlet before I explode. But I say nothing in the car because I don't like my daughters witnessing the friction between Justin and me. The girls are prattling in the back seat, their usual exuberant selves after they've spent time with their cousin. They're close to Shelley thanks to the regular Parker catch-ups. It makes me feel guilty for not organizing more play dates and accepting Ria's occasional invitations but then I'd be indebted to her and I don't want that.

Shelley is sweet but also incredibly naïve for a ten-year-old. At eleven, my Jessie is far worldlier. She's on every social media app and is proud of who she is, flaunting herself in a way that screams confidence. I initially balked at giving my approval, considering the legal age for a child to sign up to those apps is thirteen, but Jessie provided logical, well-thought-out arguments as to why she should be on them and I caved. Besides, it's healthy for my girls to be self-assured and I want them to own who they are and use common sense to traverse the online minefield. It will teach them independence.

I want my girls to develop their personalities, their likes and dislikes. No point skulking in the shadows. That kind of recalcitrant behavior never helps a woman, especially in the cutthroat world of Chicago's elite. Shelley is the antithesis of my confident children. She's reserved, though playing with my girls brings out her boisterous side. She's pretty too, with her mother's big brown eyes and long dark hair and lips I can only obtain by regular visits to my cosmetic surgeon for fillers.

But I find her craving for affection irritating. She's always been a hugger and I don't like kids other than my own embracing me. I'd seen her crestfallen expression when I greeted her with only a wave at May's party and wished I could be a better aunt, a better person, but it's too late for that.

"Wasn't it a great party, Mom?" Ellen pipes up from the back seat.

"Just swell," I mutter, shooting Justin a venomous glare, likes it's his fault I'm in this mood, when in fact he's only partially responsible.

He ignores me, his stare focused on the car's camera screen as he reverses into our garage.

"We had fun playing with Shelley," Jessie adds, sounding less like the poised, mature girl I'm raising and more like her younger cousin, all bright-eyed enthusiasm.

"That's great, but haven't you both got to do prep for pony class in the morning?"

The girls groan in unison and tumble from the car as soon as Justin kills the engine. The ensuing silence is taut with unspoken accusations.

I know what's coming.

He'll say I always behave badly around his family, I'll say he's sniveling and weak-livered for pandering to them.

When was the last time we spoke a civil word to each other? I can't remember. I hate being in a marriage that gives me everything I could want but not the one thing I crave: love.

I hate myself more for being this superficial, brittle woman who'll tolerate it for the sake of appearances when I want so much more from my husband.

Back when we'd first met fourteen years ago he'd labeled me elegant and classy, and wooed me with first-class trips to Europe on a whim and four-carat diamond studs. It helped that I found him incredibly attractive, along with his massive fortune.

We've been a power couple in Chicago ever since; we both get off on attention and when I produced the requisite two kids not long after we married, I could do no wrong. Even May thawed toward me when I gave her grandchildren.

But over the years the family's tolerance of me has waned. Most of them are polite to me because they have to be; I'm family. May is civil but I see the judgment in her steely gaze, like she knows what I'm doing in cuckolding her workaholic son who barely acknowledges I exist these days.

I can't pinpoint when Justin's attitude toward me changed. Not that I expected the heady days of our early courtship to continue indefinitely but I married a charismatic man who makes me feel good just by being next to him. So when he started distancing himself, physically and emotionally, I predictably shut down too.

His continuing silence unnerves me. It's a game we play, to see who'll crack first. We do this all the time, a stupid, childish one-upmanship that results in neither of us winning. We're both stubborn but today I won't be able to hold out. I'll cave first. I'm too pissed off. I don't like firing the first barb but the six champagnes I consumed earlier are making my head pound and I want to go inside.

I half swivel to face him, irritated that his profile is still so goddamn attractive. Strong jaw. Straight nose. Defined cheekbones. Smooth skin. His perfection annoys me today; as if I'm not feeling insecure enough after Ria's hint at my impropriety. It makes me want to lash out.

"What's going on between you and Ria?"

He has the audacity to laugh, a harsh sound devoid of amusement, as he stares straight ahead like a motionless robot. "You've got to be kidding me."

"Actually, I'm deadly serious." My drawl hides my growing fear that I've broached a subject I would've been smarter avoiding, but I want to rattle him as much as his immobile posture is rattling me. If Ria's implication she knows what I'm up to and Shamira's accusation aren't bad enough, May's announcement has thrown me completely.

Everyone assumes I'm rich in my own right; that the Garner fortune would tide me over if anything happened to my marriage. They're wrong. My narcissistic parents, in their infinite wisdom, decided that when I married into the Parkers I'd be set for life so left everything to my sister. We don't talk for this very reason. And with my parents gone, she's my only family and there's no way in hell she'd give me a cent if I needed it.

Which means I shouldn't be riling my husband, no matter how much I want him to admit he has a thing for Ria so I can blame him for the farce that is our marriage rather than the other way round.

When we usually argue, he eyes me with obvious pity or warns me to calm down. But today he's not even glancing my way and the change in our usual push-pull is disarming.

So I continue to prod, hoping to get a reaction out of him, because his bizarre frostiness is freaking me out. "Even Chrissie noticed. It's beneath you to flaunt your pathetic crush in front of your own family—"

"Shut up."

He doesn't yell and the chill in his low voice, barely above a growl, scares me more.

I'm a fool for picking this fight, well aware that any jibe directed at saintly Ria will be met with hostility.

Those six champers definitely haven't helped either.

When he continues to ignore me, I study my manicured nails at arm's length, like I don't give a damn one way or the other. "You'll soon tire of her, like Grayson did. Don't sacrifice everything we've built for a quick tryst with some eye candy you think you can have. She'll use you just like she did him. And you have a lot to lose."

A vein pulses at his temple but he doesn't explode and I'm almost disappointed. I'm about to goad him again when he finally responds.

"You know something? I don't give a shit what you say about me but don't you dare malign Ria. She doesn't deserve your vitriol."

He sounds way too calm and when he finally turns to face me, his jaw juts with tension. Only then do I see I've gone too far. His eyes glitter with malice, like he could wrap his hands around my neck and squeeze the life out of me without breaking a sweat. "Just like you don't deserve any of this."

A chill ripples over me but I resist the urge to rub my bare arms. "What do you mean?"

"This." He gestures at the house, his upper lip curled in a sneer. "This life. The kids. The lifestyle. You don't deserve any of it."

He leans toward me and I instinctively recoil. Justin isn't a violent man; he rarely loses his temper, even during all the fights I've picked over his unswerving loyalty to his stupid family. But there's something about the way he's staring at me now that makes me wish I hadn't pushed so far.

"And all of this can be taken away, just like that." He snaps his fingers in my face and I flinch. I hate showing weakness but now I'm seriously panicky that I could lose everything. I can't live on alimony. And with the Parker fortune backing him, Justin will make sure to screw me over, ensuring I get nothing. I have no doubt May will help him in that department.

That's when it hits me. Do they know about my indiscretions? Is that what May's announcement had been about? Cutting off my access to the family fortune, doling out a meager wage and when we divorce, removing that too?

I'm terrified I've gone too far this time but before I can apologize for my melodramatics, he starts the car again.

"Get out," he says, in a soft lethal tone that brooks no argument.

I want to applaud him for finally having the balls to stand up to me. I don't, because I see the way his hands grip the steering wheel, his knuckles standing out white and stark, like they're about to break through skin. He's on edge in a way I've never seen before. Who knew my placid husband has a fiery side?

I should apologize for being a bitch, I really should. But then the memory of Ria taunting me with her suspicions of my affair comes back and I'm mad all over again. Mad at her. Mad at Justin for acting like a lapdog around her. Mad at myself most of all for getting myself into a situation where someone like Ria can lord my faults over me.

I made a bad decision having an affair with a business rival. I know that. And blaming my husband for his lack of attention only serves to make me feel worse. I take it out on him, as always.

"You're an asshole," I say, opening the car door and getting out.

He barely waits for me to slam it before revving the engine and peeling out of the garage in a loud skid.

Arguments usually invigorate me because I take them as a sign that deep down he still cares. Ultimately that's why I pick fights with Justin. By goading him into some kind of reaction, even a negative one, means he might still love me. It's warped logic, I know, but I'm so desperate for affection I'll do anything to get him to notice me. However, this time I don't value his snapped responses. Instead, I feel a deep-seated insidious fear as I recall his threat.

"All of this can be taken away, just like that."

No one messes with my life.

Not Ria. Not Shamira. Not May. Not my husband.

I protect what's mine and if they don't know that by now, they soon will.

CHAPTER ELEVEN

MAY

I breathe a sigh of relief when everyone has left. I never experienced empty nest syndrome. When my children deigned to move on, usually as soon as they finished school, I hadn't wept. I'd rejoiced in the freedom of having the house to myself; as alone as one can be with an absentee husband who preferred to entertain his latest mistress at his plush apartment in the city and a plethora of staff. But Percy is gone, a fact I'm eternally grateful for every day, and no staff live in anymore, so once the housekeeper leaves at five I revel in the peace.

I don't need to be surrounded by people to feel good. In fact, the opposite is true. As I get older, people annoy me more: their frailties, their whining, their self-centeredness that only increases with age. I don't have the patience I once had and having to spend an afternoon in the company of my tension-fraught family only adds to my uneasiness.

Because I've done something foolish, something so out of character that even now I can't quite fathom what possessed me.

I asked Christine to stay after everyone left so we can talk.

When it comes to my daughter, I've kept up the art of pretense for years. We live far enough away that I can plead indifference to our cool relationship. But today, witnessing Christine's antics after she'd imbibed too much alcohol, had pierced my apathy. It jolted my conscience into asking her to stay after the party so we can chat. I don't know what's going on with her and I'm worried.

I'd attributed her erratic behavior to one too many glasses of French champagne, but watching her screech and chase Shelley, Jess and Ellen around the back garden, stumbling and falling several times, had me wondering if there was something else going on.

My granddaughters had been highly amused. I hadn't been. I dare not mention anything unsavory, but I need Christine to understand how her behavior can be misconstrued and taint the family if it becomes public, especially at this critical time for the business.

I hadn't been lying about cutting off their access to the family fortune. I announced it today to scare the family, to give them the reality check most of them need. I haven't told them the rest, about a highly lucrative sale worth hundreds of millions that will ensure my grandchildren are taken care of despite the excesses of their parents.

Money equals security; I learned that from a young age and I'll make sure my granddaughters are protected.

But I have a daughter too and seeing Christine's bizarre behavior, unsure whether it's normal or not these days, makes me feel guilty. If my daughter is struggling, I should know, I should be there for her, and I'm going to be. Better late than never.

Christine's lilting off-tune voice drifts toward me from the conservatory and I follow it, not recognizing the weird folksong but hating how melancholic it makes me feel. I usually love walking the wide hallways of this magnificent mid-nineteenth century mansion, my loafers barely making a sound on the polished parquetry. Today, my feet drag as I brace for a confrontation Christine won't want but I'll demand nonetheless.

I never prioritized fostering a closer relationship with her. My maternal instincts have taken a back seat to the company for many years but I hadn't thought the children had suffered. Maybe I've been naïve in my assumption. Even when the kids were growing up, I'd favored the boys because they were simple creatures, less complicated than my girl who would stare at me with those all-seeing eyes, like she could penetrate beneath my carefully polished exterior. She'd always made me uncomfortable and I'd ended up avoiding her, focusing my attention on the boys: sitting courtside at basketball games, waiting patiently on the bleachers at baseball innings, driving them wherever they needed to go. Christine had been self-sufficient before she'd hit her teens, preferring to hide away in her room and read rather than socialize, shunning after-school activities in favor of taking long rides on her beloved pony. I had neglected her…

When I reach the conservatory I pause in the doorway, stunned to see Christine dancing in complete unrestraint. Arms flung high, legs kicking, in some odd imitation of the can-can. Her long blonde hair tumbles in a tangled mass down her back, like she'd twisted it up and let it fall once too often. Her designer black T-shirt has a stain down the front, probably frosting from the cake she'd toyed with but didn't eat, and her bare feet poke out from the flowing floral skirt that skims her ankles.

The sheer abandon with which Christine dances catapults me back to simpler times when my tween daughter would do this very thing, presuming she'd be unobserved because I was never around for her.

Regret clogs my throat and I make a subtle noise to clear it. Christine's head snaps up, her gaze defiant as it meets mine, as if expecting judgment.

I sigh and drag my weary bones into the room. Darkness has descended quickly and the automatic garden lights bathe the lawn in a becoming glow. I love sitting in this glass-enclosed conservatory of an evening, sipping on a honeyed chamomile tea, surveying the rewards of my labor.

Tonight, I know the calmness that floods me whenever I enter this room will elude me.

"Don't let me stop you." I wave at Christine to continue her odd ritualistic dancing before taking a seat on a wide royal blue pinstriped sofa big enough for three. "I used to love watching you dance, even if you didn't know it."

Christine stumbles and would've fallen if she didn't grab onto the nearest thing, which happens to be a tall corner table, housing a favorite vase. The vase wobbles, teetering on the edge for a moment before plummeting to the floor. It smashes into eight neat pieces and Christine leaps back, her hand covering her mouth.

I want to scream at my clumsy, drunk daughter but I don't. Because when Christine's tear-filled, guilty gaze meets mine, I know that how I handle this and what I say in the next few moments will affect my daughter profoundly. I want Christine onside, not grabbing at the flimsiest excuse to flee, which is what she looks like doing.

"Leave that and come sit here." I pat the empty spot beside me. "Be careful any stray shards don't cut your feet."

Christine stares at me in confusion for a second, as if she can't quite believe she's escaped a tongue-lashing, before skirting the broken pieces and perching on the sofa like she expects to make a run for it any moment.

I smell alcohol, a potent cocktail of sour champagne and acid bourbon, so strong I wonder if it's oozing from her pores.

"I'm sorry, Mom." Christine stares at her hands, a slight tremor making her fingers tremble as she plucks at non-existent lint on her skirt.

I know Christine's referring to the vase but vainly wish it's for everything else. Though our lack of closeness isn't her fault. As she withdrew from me as a teen, I let her. When she left straight after school, I let her. The boys were always easier to understand but I'd never felt close to my daughter, whose deliberate aloofness often reminds me of me.

I'm older now. I should know better than to squander a relationship because I'm too damn stubborn, and more than a tad embarrassed, to admit I barely know my own daughter.

"The vase is replaceable." *But you aren't*, I want to say, settling for, "I'm glad you're home."

Christine stiffens and stills her fiddling fingers by interlocking them. "It's your birthday, I couldn't not come."

"I'd understand if you had other commitments." I keep my tone low and soothing, knowing it won't take much for Christine to bolt.

She finally looks at me, her glare accusatory. "Would you?"

"Of course—"

"Because it always feels like a summons when you invite the family over."

That's because my self-absorbed children would rarely visit if they weren't formally invited, but I swallow that particular retort.

"My invitations can be a little heavy-handed, I'll give you that."

Christine deflates, some of her animosity draining way. "Living in New York doesn't build close family bonds. It always feels odd when I'm back."

"Is that why you felt the need to drink too much at the party?"

I struggle to keep my tone nonjudgmental, hoping this won't end like the last time we'd had a 'big' conversation, when Christine had turned eighteen and left home for three days on the back of a stranger's motorcycle. Back then, when I confronted her on her return, Christine had moved interstate and hadn't spoken to me for four months.

I blamed Percy for that too. If my pig-headed husband hadn't insisted on gifting our kids two million dollars at eighteen rather than setting up trust funds to dole out controlled wages as suggested by our attorney, I could've maintained some semblance of control over Christine. I could've cut her off financially and demanded she come home. Because ultimately, having my family close is what I want. They think money protects them but it's more than that. It's me. I hold this family together. I look out for them in ways they don't realize. I want to keep them safe because I know the dangers out there.

That's why I set up a joint family account they could all access, as a means of keeping control over the money and the kids. That's why I'm particularly worried about Christine because she's making regular withdrawals of the same amount that are increasing in frequency, and I'm wondering if those withdrawals signal a greater problem than alcohol.

"Christine, why did you feel the need to get drunk at a small family gathering?"

I hold my breath, waiting for her to speak, hoping this won't end in an explosive argument like in her teens.

To my horror, Christine's eyes fill with tears as she slumps back into the sofa like she's boneless.

"I like drinking," Christine finally says after an eternity. "It's a way to blow off steam, have a little fun."

"It can turn into an addiction." I don't want to lecture but it comes out sounding like one.

"Maybe it already has." Christine's listless shrug reveals bony shoulders I hadn't noticed until now. I thought Christine had lost weight in her face, now I wonder exactly how thin my daughter is beneath the loose T-shirt and ankle-length skirt.

Relieved she's admitted she has a problem, I ask, "How bad is it?"

I yearn to reach out and lay a comforting hand on her but know that won't go down well. We've never been touchy-feely and I blame myself. A life spent recoiling from my husband's touch does that to a woman. I blame Percy for so much and my inability to express emotion through a simple hug is something I hate him for. Yet another thing to add to a long list.

"Bad enough." Christine closes her eyes and rests her head on the back of the sofa. "I'm tired, Mom. I have been for a long while."

Aren't we all? hovers on my lips but I bite back the response.

"Then stay here for a while. A few days, a week, whatever you like."

The offer comes out of nowhere, leaving us both a little stunned. I don't want to deal with my alcoholic daughter infringing on my well-maintained peace. I have no tolerance for drama these days and have a feeling any time spent in Christine's company will bring plenty. But I can't abandon my daughter, not when she obviously needs guidance or help or something. Besides, I can't take back the offer now.

"You don't want me around." Christine sounds so much like the recalcitrant teen she'd once been that my heart twangs.

"I wouldn't have asked if I didn't."

I sound so cold, so distant. Is that what my daughter and family hear every time I speak? I hope not. I may not be demonstrative but I value each and every one of them.

Christine drags in a few deep breaths, as if steadying herself for a confrontation, before opening her eyes and staring at me like she's seeing me for the first time.

"Okay, I'll stay for a week."

I exhale, unaware I've been holding my breath. "I'm glad—"

"But I'm not making any promises and I won't tolerate any lectures, okay?"

I hold up my hands. "You'll get no lectures from me, but do us both a favor and go see Doc Limstone while you're here."

Christine wrinkles her nose. "I'm not an alcoholic—"

"You sure?"

She glares at me, defiant. "You don't know the first thing about me, Mom, so please don't sit there and pretend like you do."

I want to say many things, like how she stopped needing me years ago, like how she never visits unless invited, like how she never seems to care even when she is around, but I don't. I settle for honesty because I know, out of all the things I can say, the truth has the best chance of getting through to her.

"You're right, Christine, I don't know what's going on in your life because we're not close and that's my fault." I pat my chest. "I admit I wouldn't win any mother of the year contests, but seeing you so drunk today has me worried."

I stare into her eyes, beseeching her to understand what I'm saying comes from a good place in my heart and I'm not interfering for the sake of it. "There's something more going on that you're not telling me, and that's fine, but I hope that while you're here you'll trust me enough to open up."

Her lips remain mutinously shut and I want to ask about the money withdrawals, but I don't. I can't afford to push her away. Not after we've made significant progress. "Anyway, if you don't want to talk to me, please go chat to Doctor Limstone."

After a long pause, she shrugs. "Can't hurt."

It won't, I'll make sure of it. I'll encourage the doc to give Christine a none-too-gentle nudge toward a private rehab facility on the city's fringes that has hosted many celebrities in need of help without the publicity.

"Why don't you go up to your room and rest?" I finally risk a touch, patting Christine's hand briefly.

She nods, hauling herself up from the sofa like she's a hundred. She scuffles toward the door, pausing to glance over her shoulder.

"Thanks, Mom."

"You're welcome."

Relieved I've made some inroads with my daughter, I need to move on to the greater challenge: ensuring the rest of the family fall into line with my plan.

CHAPTER TWELVE

RIA

Eight thirty every evening is my favorite time of the day when I get into bed next to Shelley and we read. No matter how bad my day has been, no matter how demanding or challenging, the peace that envelops me the moment I slip beneath her butterfly-covered quilt is overwhelming.

I glance at my daughter and resist the urge to squish her tight. Her gaze is glued to the page of her favorite author's latest pony book release, the tip of her tongue poking out and resting on her bottom lip, her head tilted at an odd angle as if she can't fathom the story. She's adorable and I never get tired of looking at her.

As if sensing my stare, she glances up and rolls her eyes.

"Mom, this is a really good bit. Stop disturbing me."

"I didn't say a word." I duck down to plant a kiss on her forehead and she shoves me away, but it's half-hearted. She loves my kisses and cuddles as much as I love bestowing them.

"Read, Mom." She elbows me away and points to my e-reader. "You'll never know if that lady doctor falls in love with the cowboy unless you keep reading."

Surprised, I stare at the print on my backlit page. "How do you know that?"

"Because I always peek at the page you're reading before you turn out the light. Duh."

"You little—" I tickle her and she squeals, trying to push me away while tickling me back.

God, I love this kid. My heart fills to bursting with it every single day. That's what I've never been able to fathom about Grayson. How he could leave this wonderful girl behind and not care if he ever saw her again?

I can pinpoint the exact moment I knew he'd been hiding something, about a month before he left us. Shelley had been almost five, a bright, precocious girl who never stopped chattering. She'd wanted to go to the zoo forever and we'd agreed to take her the following weekend. But after building up his daughter's hopes for a week, Grayson pulled out at the last minute, citing a major work project.

I'd watched him squat down to tell Shelley, trying to buy her off by presenting her with a ridiculously expensive jewelry box for a four-year-old. She'd accepted the gift and hugged her dad, but I'd seen the sadness in her eyes and the secrets in his, and in that moment I knew Grayson wasn't the man I thought he was. Our daughter didn't want gifts, she wanted to spend time with her father, something I knew only too well from my own childhood.

He'd continually withdrawn in the four weeks following that incident, spending more and more time at work, ignoring us. The day after he'd left, I took one glimpse at that emailed photo and wanted to vomit. Turns out, I was right: I didn't know the man I married at all.

"Truce," Shelley yells, her giggles piercingly loud, and I stop tickling.

"How about I get back to my cowboy and you get back to your ponies?" I point at her book. "Though it's been a long day, so another five minutes then it's lights out."

True to form, my angelic daughter doesn't argue. "Okay."

She's quickly absorbed into the world of gymkhanas again and I try to read but my attention wanders. I can't stop thinking about those emails and how I'll deal with them.

When I realize I've read the same sentence eight times and Shelley yawns, I close my e-reader and gently shut her book.

"Goodnight, Shell-Bell." I hug my daughter, grateful that she still wraps her arms around me in return. This will change all too soon over the next few years, I know that, which makes me cherish every single one of these hugs before the fraught teen years.

"'Night, Mom, love you."

"Love you, too." I kiss her forehead and ease out of the bed, immediately missing her warmth and the fruity apple smell that clings to her pillow from her shampoo.

I turn off the lamp and barely make it to the door before I hear her breathing deeply and I know she's asleep. I envy her. I wish I could put my head down and fall asleep instantly but it's been years since I've had a restful sleep. When I go to bed I mentally rehash my day, make a to-do list for tomorrow and when I drift off eventually, I can't help but remember the past and hope the future will be different.

I shut her door with a soft click and pad to the front of the house, knowing it'll take more than the usual hour to fall asleep tonight. Ever since the idea of contacting Grayson for help popped into my head I can't ignore it. He's the only person I know who's better than Lars at anything to do with computers.

He'd helped me countless times when I'd initially started my freelance career, desperate for a hint of a story, delving behind the scenes online so I could write the best damn articles to get ahead. I'd reveled in the closeness it created between us. He'd been content to work for his family's company's IT department when he could've been so much more but I admired his loyalty. Pity it didn't extend to his daughter and me.

Maybe I should wait, see if any more emails land in my inbox. Then again, considering what those explosive emails contain, waiting could be foolhardy. I'll do a little more digging online tonight and if I still can't find anything, I'll instigate steps to reach out to Grayson, wherever he may be. I can't help but hope he might know who's behind this, considering the same person sent that email and photo of him.

There's a soft knock on the door as I'm about to enter the den. No one visits us at this hour. I don't have many close friends, just a few reporters I keep in touch with, and they wouldn't drop by without a text or call first. There's been a spate of home invasions in Chicago lately, reported on the news daily, and I'm nervous.

I peek through the peephole and slump against the door in relief. It's Justin. Though that relief is short-lived as I wonder what my brother-in-law is doing on my doorstep at eight forty-five on a Saturday night after we've seen each other only a few hours earlier.

I open the door as he's about to knock again. "Hey, what are you doing here?"

"Can I come in?"

He sounds calm enough but his hair is spiked, like he's run his hand through it a million times, and his skin is pasty beneath its usual tan. But it's his eyes that have me wondering what's happened, clouded with worry that lends him a dazed, disoriented look.

"Sure." I clamp down on my initial urge to send him away and open the door wider, waiting until he's inside before closing it. "Shelley's asleep so we can talk through here."

He hasn't been here all that often over the years but he strides toward the lounge room and I follow, biting on my bottom lip to prevent myself from inhaling his intoxicating citrus aftershave.

I hover in the doorway when he starts to pace, staring at his feet like they hold the answer to some complex unsolved problem.

"Can I get you anything?" I offer out of politeness, when in fact I hope he won't stay long.

I have no idea what has him so agitated and I don't want to find out. I can't be this man's confidante, family or not, because after this afternoon and the strange frisson of something between us, I don't trust him. Or myself. Besides, he's never visited my place alone, and the fact he doesn't have the girls or Ashlin with him has me on edge.

"Wine. Beer. Anything alcoholic," he says, dragging his gaze away from his feet to stare at me, a little wild-eyed.

I should make coffee but wine's quicker and the sooner he drinks it the faster he'll be out of here. I pad into the kitchen, belatedly realizing I'm in my cotton PJs. They are pale blue, loose elastic-waist pants and a singlet top, more like workout gear really, but I'm still uncomfortable.

But making a big deal of changing would signal that discomfort and I want him out of here ASAP. So I pour two glasses of Shiraz, half-glasses for speedier drinking and a faster exit on his part, and head back to the lounge room. He's sitting on the sofa, his head resting against the back of it, eyes closed. Worry lines fan from the corners of his eyes and tension brackets his mouth but even in obvious distress he's strikingly handsome. I must make some kind of embarrassing sound because his eyes snap open and fix on me with unerring accuracy as I cross the room, my heart sinking as I realize where I'll have to sit.

One chair is covered in a stack of Shelley's artwork; the other has a pile of folded laundry yet to be put away. Leaving me no option but to sit next to him on the sofa. It's silly, this awareness on my part. He's my brother-in-law. He can visit any time he likes. But he doesn't and the fact he's arrived alone at this time of night and is wound tighter than a spring indicates that what's about to transpire may not be good.

I hand him the glass in silence, hating how uncomfortable I feel in my own house. It's crazy. I should be welcoming him, especially if he needs help, considering he wouldn't have arrived on my doorstep otherwise. But I can't forget this afternoon and how for the first time we skirted around the issue of our attraction. I don't know why I'm uneasy. I feel guilty but I haven't done anything.

Not yet.

And it's that qualifier that has me on edge, wishing he'd hurry up and get the hell out of here.

"Thanks. You have no idea how badly I need this." He downs the wine in a few gulps then stares at the empty glass, and me.

I sit and he places his glass on the coffee table, then braces his elbows on his knees, staring at my photo-covered mantel.

"Sorry for turning up here like this but I didn't want to drive around when I was angry and I couldn't go to Mom's so…" He trails off, like it's the most natural thing in the world to pop in when we both know it's not.

"So you came here?"

My incredulity is audible and when he lifts his head to finally look at me I don't like what I see: a startling mix of regret and confusion and hope.

I don't want any part of this. No matter how much I want to hug him to make it all better. It doesn't take a genius to figure out he's probably had an argument with Ashlin. But I can't be his go-to person. Like all married couples, this can't be their first argument and he must have other places to go.

I fidget on the seat, knowing I have to tell him to leave but too polite to be blunt. He takes my silence as permission to continue.

"I can't do this anymore. Live with Ashlin. Pretend like we're a couple." He drags in a deep breath and blows it out, the worry grooves bracketing his mouth deepening. "We're over."

He needs to leave. Now.

But as he continues to stare at me with that shell-shocked expression tinged with hope, it's my turn to tip wine down my throat. I drain the glass, place it on the table, and try to surreptitiously scoot away from him.

"I'm not the person you should be confiding in, Justin, and we both know it."

His eyebrow quirks, annoyingly rakish. "Why?"

If he wants me to spell it out he'll be waiting a long time. I won't play this game. It's fraught with danger and can only end badly.

I shake my head. "You should go."

I make a move to stand and he grabs my hand so fast I tumble back down, much closer to him this time. I'm almost sitting in his lap and it's too much.

"I need you, Ria. Please."

He squeezes my hand tighter, beseeching me to understand. I don't want to. Because I know if I open my heart to this man even a little I'm in grave danger of making a mistake I'll regret.

"You're hurting, I get that." I speak softly, trying to sound calm when I'm a mess inside. A confusing riot of emotions centered on how damn good it feels having him hold my hand. "But whatever you think you're doing here, it's not right."

He tries to intertwine his fingers with mine. "I need a friend, that's all."

Bull, and we both know it.

"Justin, listen, I can't—"

He kisses me, his lips warm and commanding. I gasp in surprise and he takes it as an invitation to invade my mouth. His tongue sweeps in, taunting mine and for an insane moment I give in to temptation.

It's hot and frantic and so damn sexy I may die as our tongues tangle and we moan into each other's mouths. Exactly as I imagined it would be: explosive and passionate and a prelude to so much more.

His hands are on me, one on my butt, the other slipping inside my singlet, palming my breast. My skin is on fire, making me writhe.

I groan when he tweaks my nipple, rolling it between his thumb and forefinger with just the right pressure. Sensation streaks lower, pooling between my legs, making me want to clamber all over him.

When he starts to push me back against the sofa and I feel how hard he is, reality crashes over me.

No way in hell I'm having sex on my sofa with my daughter sleeping in the house.

The moment the thought pops into my head I'm even more ashamed. What would I do if Shelley wasn't here?

I struggle beneath him and push him away. "Justin, we can't."

He stops and crazily I miss his touch when he slides his hand out of my top and readjusts the strap. Hooking his finger into it, sliding it up slowly until it sits on my shoulder. It's an oddly tender gesture and I feel tears prick the back of my eyes.

"I should apologize for that," he says, staring at me with such intensity I can't look away. "But I won't, because I'm done with the lies."

He shrugs, like it's no big deal we almost devoured each other a few moments ago. "I've lived my entire life according to other people's expectations. Being the perfect eldest son, getting the perfect marks, the perfect business degree, stepping into the family business. Marrying a woman from similar social circles. Being a good husband, a good dad…"

He trails off, his audible anguish making me want to hug him so I sit on my hands instead.

"But I can't keep up the pretense any longer. I'm sick of being unhappy all the damn time." He runs a hand over his face. It does little to erase the sadness. "Were you miserable before Grayson left?"

I rarely talk about my marriage with anyone, least of all Grayson's family. After he left, May had berated him publicly in front of her other kids, leaving them under no illusion Grayson had been at fault and had always been flaky. I got the feeling her youngest son had embarrassed her by abandoning his wife and child and that's why she stuck by me. The Parkers have standards to uphold and Grayson had fallen well short, if May's disgust was any indication.

Justin, Trent and Shamira had always been supportive after Grayson left. Christine didn't particularly care. Ashlin had implied I wasn't woman enough to hold onto a Parker man, like it was my fault Grayson had fled to get away from me.

"Miserable? No." I shake my head, hating that over five years have passed but thoughts of Grayson still have the power to make me doubt myself. Could I have done anything different? Could I have tried harder? Could I have seen the signs of his withdrawal? Could I have guessed his sordid secret if I'd looked hard enough?

"I thought we were okay. We hit a rough patch like all couples do when Shelley was little but we worked through it." It had made us stronger, or so I thought. "I think he tolerated his job at the company out of loyalty to the family and I could never understand why he didn't want to do more with his IT skills, but I thought most of his dissatisfaction stemmed from his job, not me. He spent way too much time at work the last month before he left and I resented that, more the workload than him though."

Justin stares at me with open curiosity. "So you didn't hate each other before he left?"

"Far from it."

Heat creeps into my cheeks at the memory of exactly how normal our marriage had been, right until the day he left. We'd made love the night before and it had been slow and sensual and incredibly tender. He'd spooned me as usual. We'd slept; I'd heard him tending to Shelley's breakfast the next morning like he usually did. I had no idea he was about to walk out our front door and never return.

Or the secret lifestyle he led that must've left him so guilt-ridden he had to leave.

"Grayson's an idiot for leaving you," he says, sounding fiercely protective, making me want to be near him again. "To be honest, I was always a little jealous of him."

He glances away, embarrassed. "Jealous of the obvious affection between you two while my marriage has always been… strained."

I have no idea how he's lived with Ashlin this long but it's not my place to say. Not when it can be misconstrued. I can't be the reason he leaves his wife and I need to make him understand that.

"Why did you finally decide to end your marriage tonight?"

He drags his gaze back to meet mine and it's surprisingly clear, not in the least tortured like it was earlier.

"I already told you, I'm done with the lies."

I have to ask, even though I may not like the answer. "I hope it has nothing to do with me, because we can't be together—"

"I did this for me. And I'm not a complete idiot, despite acting like it by giving in to impulse and pawing you."

The corners of his mouth lift in a rueful grin that's endearing. "I wouldn't leave Ashlin and come straight to you for anything other than solace. And it certainly wasn't my intention tonight to… you know." A faint blush stains his cheeks, making him appealingly vulnerable. "I really couldn't think of anywhere else to go so I came here. Just to chat, offload, whatever." His blush deepens. "Have I fantasized about kissing you? Hell yeah. Countless times."

Something shifts in his eyes, the hazel darkening to burnt toffee. "And I've fantasized about doing a hell of a lot more, but I know I have to deal with my shit and not expect anything from you."

Relief filters through me, tinged with something else. Disappointment. He's right and has articulated why we can't be together but I know I'll never forget that kiss and how he made me feel for an all too brief moment.

"Sounds like you have it all figured out."

I don't mean to sound flippant but a small part of me wonders if he'll really go through with this. Leaving Ashlin, divorcing, living with the scrutiny that's bound to come. Justin revels in attention and a messy Parker divorce won't be good for his image.

"I don't have a frigging clue, actually, but I'm getting there." He stands and holds out his hand.

I should ignore it but I'm weak and I want to feel his touch one last time before he goes. I place my hand in his and he pulls me to my feet. We stand there, two feet apart, too close, not close enough. My heart races as he lifts his free hand and cups my cheek.

"The end of my marriage has nothing to do with you, Ria. And I won't put you in an awkward position again. But if at some point in the future when all this crap is behind me and I ask you out, what will your answer be?"

I want to say yes. I want to snuggle into his arms again.

I settle for resting my cheek in his hand so I don't have to shake my head.

My answer is no. It will always be no. It has to be.

CHAPTER THIRTEEN

SHAMIRA

Some couples sleep in on a Sunday. Trent and I are up before dawn because he likes helping me set up my stall at whichever market I'm visiting. I've told him repeatedly he doesn't need to help me set up and hang around to sell. He never listens. He's sweet like that. One of the many reasons I love my husband.

When I first set eyes on him I never expected to fall in love. I'd envisaged a lifetime of faking it: fake smiles, fake hugs, fake sex. It wouldn't have been hard. I'd been doing it for years before I met him.

But Trent Parker has an inherent goodness that shows in so many ways and within six months I'd fallen for him. He's chivalrous and sweet and kind, so it's imperative he never discovers what I did.

I haven't slept well. The fact Ashlin taunted me with my past yesterday sits like a weight on my chest, making breathing difficult at times. I can't afford to lose Trent or risk telling him the truth. So I'm stuck in a strange limbo, fearful every time the phone rings or there's a knock on the door.

The thing is I don't think Ashlin has as much to lose if I spill her secret. She barely talks to Justin anyway so him discovering her treachery probably won't change things. They obviously stay married for appearances and perhaps the kids, so Justin learning she cheated may not register. Who knows, they could have an open marriage and he sleeps around too. But if she tells Trent my secret… I will lose him. And he's everything to me.

"All set up and ready for business." Trent slips his arm around my waist and squeezes me tight. "I'll grab that spare box of handmade soaps from the car and be back in a minute."

"Thanks, and I'll get our drinks."

"Make mine a coffee and not one of those soy turmeric lattes you guzzle by the gallon." He laughs, drops a kiss on the tip of my nose and releases me.

I watch him lope away through the early morning crowd, his long, easy stride quintessentially Trent. He's easy-going, totally happy in himself and with his life, at complete odds with the rest of his family. Thankfully we won't have to see them for a while, before May commands us to attend an afternoon tea or an interminable dinner in a month or so. I admire her efforts in trying to keep her family close, when most of us don't want to be in the same room as each other.

Determined to enjoy today and try to forget about the dramas of yesterday, I rearrange my relaxation blends with the prices facing out, the faintest waft of lavender instantly calming, and stick the 'Back in 5 minutes' sign on the front of the stall.

The coffee van isn't far from my stall so I can keep an eye on merchandise as I grab our drinks. Thankfully, the queue is short and I'm almost at the counter to order when a shadow falls over me, blocking out the sun.

I don't think anything of it until I hear a too-close voice murmur, "Hello, Mira."

I stiffen, turn slowly and lock eyes with my past.

I can't remember his name but I remember the leer and the cold, flat, eyes. A shiver of repulsion ripples over my skin and I resist the urge to rub my arms.

I'd hoped this day would never come. It's why I avoid the famous Esplanade Market near home, for fear remnants of my past may appear. Eltham is far from Donvale Heights. It should be safe. It isn't.

I have to escape. I can't risk him seeing my stall and, in turn, saying something to Trent when he returns. Besides, my husband will take one look at me and know I'm freaked out. My skin's clammy and my cheeks are ice-cold, meaning I'm probably pale and gnawing at my bottom lip like I usually do when I'm worried.

Mustering my old acting skills I put on a blank face, like I don't have a clue who he is.

"Do I know you?" I will my heart rate to slow down while glancing around for the quickest escape route.

"Cut the crap." His voice is the same too, low and guttural, like he swallows cut glass for breakfast and washes it down with a bourbon chaser. "I certainly know *you*."

The way he says 'you', ugly and possessive, brings back more memories. They crash over me in a stifling wave and I'm drowning: this creep abusing me, the perpetual onion odor that clung to his clothes and seeped out of his skin, the sly way he left bruises where no one could see.

Nausea rolls over me and I sway a little. "You're mistaken."

Those soulless eyes fix on me and as I take a step back, I glimpse Trent strolling through the crowd, a large box of my soaps in his hands, hands that will never touch me again if he discovers this prick used to.

When Trent reaches our stall, he'll see me and come over. I can't have him anywhere near this awful reminder of my past. If he hears one word from this creep… My heart stops. I can't let this cretin ruin my marriage and my life. So I do the one thing to ensure they don't meet.

I turn and run.

I dart through the crowd in the opposite direction of Trent and our stall, planning to circle back around to the car once I lose the creep. I dart a glance over my shoulder when I'm far enough away, relieved to see he's not giving chase and is stalking in the direction of the toilet block.

I don't stop running until I reach the car, relieved to find it unlocked. I duck into the back seat and sag in relief, knowing it's temporary. I have to get away from here. Now.

I fire off a quick text to Trent to meet me at the car. He arrives in under a minute, concern creasing his handsome face. When he sees me cowering in the back seat, he opens the back door and slides in beside me.

"What's going on? I saw some guy standing too close to you in the coffee line—"

"I need you to pack up the stall."

"What?"

His incredulity is warranted and I reach for yet another lie.

"That guy's an ex. I had a restraining order out against him years ago. I don't want him anywhere near me so I can't hang around, I'm too shaken."

I cling to my husband's arm and widen my eyes, hoping he'll see the genuine fear and act accordingly.

Predictably, he doesn't let me down. "Okay, but we need to talk about this later."

We will. I'll spin more BS and he'll believe me. He always does.

It makes me feel even worse because this considerate, affable guy doesn't deserve a seasoned liar like me.

CHAPTER FOURTEEN

ASHLIN

Justin didn't come home last night.

We've had fights before. Rip-roaring slanging matches that always end with him stomping out like the spoiled brat he is. But he always slinks back during the night and in the morning pretends like nothing happened.

Not this time.

I'm still scared after his taunt that I could lose everything so I do my best to ignore the terror, channeling my anger instead. I'm furious that he hasn't even sent a text. Nobody treats me like this.

"Mom, we're going to be late for pony club," Jessie whines, her eyes wide and beseeching. It gives me a jolt, because I do the same thing when I want to get my way.

"You're not going," I snap, hating how my daughters visibly recoil at my raised voice. "Your father's out and I've got things to do."

"But we love pony club." Ellen's bottom lip wobbles and I waver for a second. It's not fair that the girls should have to pay for their parents' screw-ups. My life may be empty but my precious girls are by far the best part of it.

From the moment the obstetrician handed each of them to me I'd fallen in instantaneous love, the kind of all-consuming love I'd never come close to experiencing before. The curtain shielding my bottom half so I couldn't witness the C-section had made me feel detached from the whole birth process, but the moment I'd cradled my babies I'd felt a soul-deep connection in a way I'd never anticipated.

I used to stand next to their cots for hours, watching them sleep, wondering how someone as shallow as me could produce two such wonderful human beings. Justin would join me at times and we'd stand in comfortable silence, his hand holding mine tight, exchanging the occasional wondrous glances. Those had been some of the best times in our marriage.

"Where's Dad? He'll organize things for us," Jessie says, and just like that my resolve hardens and the anger is back, flaring into a burning ball lodged in my chest.

"You're not going and that's final," I yell, snatching my phone off the marble island bench in the center of our monstrous kitchen.

The girls stare at me in round-eyed silence and I curse under my breath, stomping into the butler's pantry so they won't see how close I am to crying. I rarely shout at my girls and I hate seeing their frightened expressions. They don't deserve to bear the brunt of my foul mood.

I need to think. It's the nanny's day off and our usual babysitters aren't available. I know because I've already tried contacting all five of them earlier. I can't be stuck here all day with the girls. I'm brittle and they'll sense something's wrong, and I don't want them knowing how bad things are between their father and me.

I need to get out of here and I'm desperate, so I contact the one person guaranteed to make time for them.

I scroll through my contacts and hit the call button for May.

She answers on the third ring and I exhale.

"Is everything all right with the girls?"

No greeting. No platitudes. Just an assumption I'd never ring unless something is wrong with her precious granddaughters. A fair guess, since I can count on one hand the number of times I've called her.

"The girls are fine, May. Actually, that's why I'm calling, to ask if you can mind them for a few hours."

Shocked silence greets my request and I hurry on, injecting sweetness into my voice when all I feel like doing is screaming.

"I apologize for the short notice but Justin is busy, I can't get a sitter and I've got errands to run."

I inexplicably brace, like I expect a stray lightning bolt to strike me down for the monstrous lie.

"Sure, that's fine, Ashlin. I'm home all day so drop the girls off any time."

The tension drains from my body and I prop against the upright freezer. "Thanks, May, we'll be there within the hour."

"See you then." May pauses, like she wants to say something else, so I hang up before she can.

My hands are shaking and I have no idea if it's because of my deception or relief.

"Girls, go get your things, you're going to your grandmother's." I re-enter the kitchen and they haven't moved, both still staring at me like they expect another verbal explosion, so I beckon and they rush into my open arms. I squeeze them tight, wishing I could protect them against everything, but my eyes burn with tears again so I release them and half turn away. "Quick, I haven't got all day."

They scamper toward the stairs and I follow at a more sedate pace. I've already showered, slathered scented body lotion all over and slipped into a new nine hundred dollar lingerie set: black lace, with crisscrossing straps that emulate peepholes.

While the girls are upstairs getting ready, I fire off a text.

CHANGE OF PLANS. C U IN 30.

The response is fast as usual.

I'LL BE WAITING.

I could've dropped the girls off and made him wait the hour I'd texted earlier. But what's the point? Whenever I see him, it'll be the same result. A quick fuck to get back at my husband.

I don't even enjoy the sex all that much. He is a selfish yet skilled lover and I usually get off. But he gives me so much more. Attention. Compliments. Validation. He makes me feel beautiful and wanted in a way I haven't felt since the early days of my relationship with Justin.

Justin.

Where the hell is he?

My thumb hovers over my phone screen. I could call. Or text. But he's the one who threatened to upend my life and he's the one who didn't come home last night.

He can go screw himself.

The girls come rushing down the stairs, designer backpacks filled to the brim with whatever stuff they deem to take to May's. I know they're into electronics these days and despite hearing about a strict screen time regimen from other mothers I'm almost grateful for the 'babysitter' aspect they provide. I let the nanny be the bad guy and limit their onscreen access after school during the week. On the weekends I'm lax, with Jessie spending too much time on her state-of-the-art smartphone and Ellen playing games on her tablet. I often wonder what parents did before the invention of electronics when they needed some time out.

When the girls catch sight of me at the bottom of the stairs their steps slow. They wear matching wary expressions and guilt swamps me for being such a lousy mother, palming them off to their grandmother. Thankfully they love visiting their grandma more than pony club so they won't give me grief over that.

"Ready to go?" I inject false enthusiasm into my voice.

They're not buying it, as their expressions don't change. At that moment I waver. What am I doing? Is this really the life I want to lead, trying to hurt my husband as much as he's hurt me? I'm desperate for attention, desperate to feel wanted. He'll hate that the girls have had to miss out on pony club so he'll feel guilty. He'll initially blame me, but I know he'll feel bad about not coming home last night and then we'll make up. It's what we always do. I create an argument, he fires up, then we move on, with me once again validated in craving attention no matter how warped. With how angry he was last night, who knows, coming back from this doozy of a bust-up might save our relationship.

I adore my girls and I consider calling May back to cancel. But I glimpse the way Jessie's glaring at me, like she can see right through me, and I know I'm not capable of faking a good mood for them for the entire day.

"Will Shelley be at Gran's?" Ellen skips the final step to land in front of me.

"I doubt it," I say, ushering them toward the mudroom. "Get your shoes on and let's go."

The girls hardly say a word on the drive to May's and I'm glad. I usually enjoy listening to them prattle about boy bands and the latest fashion fad, but I'm on edge today. The sooner I drop them off the better.

"Where's Dad?" Jessie asks as I pull into May's expansive driveway.

"Out," I say, making it sound like he's on Mars and never coming home.

"Out where?" Ellen sounds scared, and I inwardly curse my inability to hide my animosity toward Justin.

I swivel in my seat in time to see the girls mouth something to each other, making me feel an even bigger ogre, so I reach for some semblance of normality. "Time to go see your grandma."

When they get out of the car I open my door and beckon them in for a hug.

It's too brief and when they disengage, I say, "I'll be back in a few hours."

They shrug into their backpacks and I add, "Have fun."

Ellen manages a wave and a half-smile while Jessie's coolly assessing stare is way too mature for a girl her age.

The front door swings open and May comes out. She raises her hand, like she's waving me over. That's my cue to leave.

I slam my door shut, reverse quickly, put the car into gear and don't look back.

CHAPTER FIFTEEN

MAY

After the girls rush past me and into the house, I stand on the front porch watching Ashlin speed off like she has a plethora of demons on her tail.

What kind of a mother drops her children off without any instructions? Have they eaten? Do they have homework? What time will she be back?

I shake my head and close the front door. I shouldn't be surprised. Ashlin is the most self-centered, narcissistic person I know, all about her looks and projecting an image. Though considering how much time she spends with Jessie and Ellen, ferrying them around, watching their sports, demonstrating obvious affection, she loves her daughters, but I wonder if her hectic social schedule is often at the expense of her marriage. She's inherently selfish and I should know, considering I'd been married to Percy for several decades. He'd been an absentee parent, too busy with the business and his mistresses to pay much attention to his children. Thank goodness we could give them money and the choices our fortune afforded them, because we were lousy with the emotional support.

At least Ashlin is better than me in that regard. I didn't realize exactly how woeful I'd been in the mothering stakes until I watched Ria and Ashlin with their girls. It's obvious when they look at their daughters, the tender glint in their eyes, that their daughters are the center of their universe. I'm filled with regret that I'd palmed off my kids to better carers than me when they were young while I focused on building the family fortune. I missed out on so much…

"Gran, we're starving," Ellen yells from the kitchen.

Guess that answers the question of whether the girls have eaten or not.

As I head for the kitchen, I glance at the upstairs landing. Christine hasn't risen yet; hasn't made a sound actually. I'm not sure whether to be worried or relieved.

I already contacted Doctor Limstone this morning and he assured me he'd have a place organized at the rehab center as soon as possible if he thinks Christine needs it. It doesn't surprise me. Money talks and the exorbitant fees at the exclusive center can only be afforded by the rich and famous.

"Gran, can we make pancakes?" Jessie's bellow echoes through the long hallway and I smile. Time with my loud granddaughters is exactly what I need today. And it will be nice for them to spend time with their childless aunt.

Not that Christine expresses much joy at seeing the girls when we get together but I hope my granddaughters' enthusiasm will rub off on my daughter.

"Pancakes it is," I say, entering the kitchen to find the girls have already lined up flour, sugar, eggs and milk on the bench.

Ellen brandishes a wooden spoon and Jessie points at a mixing bowl, standing at the ready next to the ingredients.

"We didn't think you'd say no once you saw how organized we are." Ellen's guileless grin warms my heart.

"Do I ever say no to you?"

I tug on Jessie's ponytail and ruffle Ellen's hair as I slide between the girls. Jessie opens her mouth to answer and I jump in. "That's a rhetorical question."

Ellen's forehead crinkles. "What's that?"

"Something you ask that you don't really need answered." I pass the measuring cups to Ellen.

"I think Mom does that all the time." Ellen sounds forlorn. "She never wants to hear what Dad has to say."

I stiffen, hating how my daughter-in-law's selfishness affects her children.

"Mom's in a bad mood today," Jessie adds, surprising me with her bluntness.

As the youngest of the two girls, Ellen often blurts out exactly what she thinks. Jessie rarely talks about her mother and I wonder how much my eldest granddaughter picks up about her parents' troubled marriage.

"Probably because Dad didn't come home last night." Jessie's glance darts away, furtive, and her face reddens. "I wait up for him most nights, just to make sure he gets home okay. But I didn't hear him come up the stairs last night."

Jessie's calm pronouncement lingers in the ensuing awkward silence as Ellen's eyes widen. "How come?"

"How do I know?" Jessie rolls her eyes. "They probably had another fight."

Ellen nods, her expression serious. "They shout in the car when they think we can't hear." She nibbles on her bottom lip. "I don't think they like each other very much."

My heart clenches with worry for my girls. But a small part of me can't help but hope my son's marriage to the avaricious Ashlin has finally come to an end. She'd once been the perfect match for Justin, his equal in every way, but my priorities have shifted lately and opened my eyes to those around me. If something's broken, maybe it's not worth fixing.

I've never broached the subject directly with Justin but every time I see him—at work when I'm at corporate headquarters, at one of my soirees or when we cross paths when I see the grandchildren—I can't remember the last time he looked happy. The company continues to flourish, his children are content, and the Parker family is fine. So it isn't these possible stressors making him miserable. It has to be his marriage.

I've also seen how he lights up around Ria—making a beeline for her at our family gatherings, taking an interest in her job, paying attention to Shelley—and while I'm far from a romantic and can't contemplate the gossip frenzy that would ensue if anything ever happened between my eldest son and my youngest son's ex-wife, I wouldn't mind seeing the two of them together some day. Besides, once the company is sold, the focus will shift off the family and a union between them won't garner so much attention. Justin deserves better and so does Ria. If my son's marriage has truly ended, I'll wait the required time and then will have no hesitation in nudging him toward Ria.

Ensuring the Parker fortune stays within the family, one way or another.

Lost in my musings, I feel a tug on my sleeve. "Gran, did we make you sad, talking about Mom and Dad?"

Annoyed at myself for letting my mind wander at a time I should be reassuring the girls, I drape my arms over the girls' shoulders.

"You can talk to me anytime about anything. You both know that, right?"

Their solemnity breaks my heart as they give the barest of nods.

"As for your parents, adults go through rough times. It doesn't make them love you any less." I squeeze their shoulders. "We all love you."

They snuggle into me and I hug them tight, wondering why I can express emotion so easily with these girls when I couldn't with my own kids.

I blame myself for my fraught relationship with my children, blame my lack of interest in them from the time they could walk. Having four children hadn't been my choice, Percy had seen to that.

Even when I'd been exhausted, he'd insist on procreating to continue the family line. He'd always wanted at least three boys to carry on the Parker name so thankfully when Grayson was born he'd lost interest in me as a brood mare and had taken a mistress. We'd moved into separate bedrooms and it had stayed that way until he died. I'd done my duty bearing heirs to his massive fortune and my feigned frigidity ensured our marriage remained frosty, just the way I wanted it.

Though seeing the insight Jessie and Ellen have regarding their parents' marriage, I wonder if my children had seen more than I'd given them credit for. Maybe I shoulder some of the blame for my children's dysfunctional lives.

Jessie pulls away and glances at me with tear-filled eyes. "Can we call Dad?"

"Absolutely," I say, glad for the distraction from my self-flagellating thoughts and releasing the girls to pick up my cell from its charger.

"Put it on speaker," Ellen demands, visibly brightening when I tap Justin's name in my contacts list.

"I will, sweetheart, but let me talk to him first, okay?"

I have no idea what kind of state Justin will be in if he hasn't made it home last night and I don't want the girls being further traumatized. They've probably witnessed enough angst between their warring parents to last a lifetime. At least Percy and I had kept our arguments civil, reserving our icy low tones and hissed insults for behind closed doors.

The ringtone is loud in my ear as the girls practically hang off me. When the rings click over into his mail service, I see the disappointment on the girls' faces.

"Justin, it's Mom. Please give me a call when you can. I have the girls here and they'd love to talk to you."

I add the last bit on purpose, in case Ashlin is off doing something she shouldn't, which is more than likely considering the rumors.

I like gossip. I like knowing things. It gives me power. But hearing talk at the office centering on the company's accountant and his fling with the boss's wife last year had left me wary. Parker Partnership has a multi-tiered managerial structure so I'd assumed it had been one of those bosses, until I'd heard direct reference to Ashlin and realized by boss they meant Justin.

Then lately there've been other rumors, about Ashlin and a major competitor. It doesn't bode thinking about. Initially appalled, my disgust that her behavior could threaten the biggest deal the company has ever contemplated soon gave way to hope my son would end his marriage once and for all. Now, maybe my wish has come true.

"Where do you think he is?" Ellen's bottom lip wobbles and tears fill her eyes.

The last thing I want is a crying jag so I reach for a guaranteed distraction with kids: food.

"How about we concentrate on whipping up a batch of pancakes and try again later?"

Jessie, older and wiser beyond her years, nods solemnly. "Good idea, Gran."

A discreet cough sounds from the doorway. "Did someone say pancakes?"

"Auntie Chrissie!" Ellen runs across the kitchen and flings her arms around Christine's waist. "We're having pancakes. Want to help?"

"Only if I get to eat the biggest stack." Christine's curious gaze meets mine, and I wonder how much my daughter has overheard.

"I'm pretty hungry," Jessie says, allowing her aunt to give her a quick hug before making room for her along the island bench. "If you're eating a big stack, we'll have to make heaps."

"Sounds doable to me." Christine winks at me and in that second, with my daughter wearing a casual black sundress scattered with poppies and a sunny smile, standing between the girls and looking at home with a whisk in her hand, I almost forget her problems.

"Why don't you guys make the pancakes and I'll rest my old bones over there?"

Christine snorts. "There's nothing old about you."

"Yeah, Gran, you still go to work," Ellen pipes up. "Other grannies use walking frames and smell funny and don't have big parties."

"I'm glad I don't smell," I say, my granddaughter's innocence easing some of my anxiety regarding Christine's addiction and the state of Justin's marriage. "Now less talk and more action, please. Those pancakes won't cook themselves."

"Gran's a bit of a slave-driver," Christine says, in an exaggerated whisper. "We better whip these up fast."

I sit on my favorite striped armchair, in the nook between the conservatory and the kitchen. Sunlight dapples my skin, highlighting its thinness on the back of my hands. No matter what my granddaughters say, I'm getting old. I don't fear it, or death for that matter. What I hate is the thought of the millions I've worked so hard to secure for my family being frittered away. I also hate losing control, which means I need to take steps if Justin's marriage is in fact imploding.

The girls buzz around Christine like the bees I keep at the far end of the garden, eager and happy in a way I haven't seen in a long time. They flick flour and swipe each other's noses with batter, giggling and whispering. Christine, too, appears in her element. She should have this. Children. Family. Love.

I glance at my cell, which remains annoyingly silent. I hope Justin is okay. I close my eyes, imagining how things will change if Ashlin is no longer a member of this family. The monthly gatherings I insist on will be less tense, that's for sure. My daughter-in-law has a way of homing in on a person's weakness and prodding at it. Not that she ever dares taunt me, the woman values her wealth and status as a Parker too much, but I've seen the way she baits Ria on regular occasions and I don't like it.

Ashlin is prominent in Chicago's upper echelon and she flaunts it. Unfortunately, a Parker divorce will catapult the family straight to the top of the gossip columns. But I'm not averse to shifting blame where it's due and if Ashlin dares breathe a bad word about Justin or the family, I'll have no compunction in spreading the 'truth' about her rumored affairs. I know influential people who owe me favors and they'll have a field day besmirching Ashlin so Justin will come out of a divorce appearing vulnerable and sympathetic rather than weak. And leave Ashlin without the sizable alimony she'd be counting on. Oh yes, I can definitely manipulate the situation to benefit the Parkers and ostracize Ashlin once and for all.

"Come and get it, Gran." Jessie touches me lightly on the arm and I open my eyes, surprised to find the table set, a tall stack of pancakes in the middle surrounded by a variety of toppings: a bottle of maple syrup, a small container of chocolate chips, a bowl of strawberries.

"Did I fall asleep?" I never nap, especially not in the mornings. Then again, I hadn't slept much last night, worrying about Christine. And now, mulling the possibility of an impending divorce in the family, with all the resultant implications, might've made me nod off.

"You were snoring like a bear, Mom." Christine smiles, a genuine smile that takes years off her forty-something face.

"Don't be ridiculous, I don't snore." I stand, determinedly ignoring a persistent twinge in my right knee, and join them at the table.

"Keep telling yourself that." Christine passes me the pancakes first. "Age before beauty."

Ellen groans. "Great. That means I get to eat last."

We laugh in unison and I feel the residual tension finally seeping away.

I manage to eat one pancake, another surprise considering I subsist on one cup of coffee a morning and have for years. Being a Parker wife came with expectations and I'd initially skipped breakfast to maintain my figure, keeping up the tradition once I joined the company because I wanted to be one of the first in the door every morning. While Percy meandered into the office mid-morning, I'd be there at eight sharp, relieved to escape the morning dramas of getting the kids to school, happily assigning the arduous task to nannies.

Employees respected my diligence, while friends admired my dedication to work when I didn't have to. I'd cultivated an image as a professional, hard-working, corporate woman while being the perfect hostess and mother at home. The latter had been an illusion, because I'd been wound so tight I couldn't relax enough to eat and lately, with my plan in motion, those old tensions are resurfacing.

We eat and make small talk, the girls regaling Christine with tales of their school, friends and favorite ponies, their laughter infectious. Not once does Jessie glance at her phone, which seems perpetually attached to her hand most other times. Not once does Ellen poke or jibe at her sister, which usually happens when I see them together. And I catch Christine cast wistful glances at her nieces several times over the course of demolishing the pancakes.

When we finish eating, the girls clear away—another miracle— and ask if they can go outside to check on my bees. I'm a keen apiarist, yet another thing Percy had scoffed at. I'd often wished he were anaphylactic like Ria—who never ventures further than the hedge near the pool-house because of her allergy to them—so a sting could've been fatal years before the heart attack that finally set me free.

"Sure, but don't get too close to the hives."

Jessie rolls her eyes. "We know, Gran. You've only told us a hundred times before."

"And we're always careful," Ellen adds, screwing up her nose. "Besides, I'm scared of bees and I'd never go near them."

"Okay then." I wave them away, half expecting Christine to escape with them.

However, Christine doesn't move and watches the girls scamper off while nursing her third coffee of the morning. When the glass door leading from the conservatory to the garden closes behind them, Christine sighs.

"They're good girls." Her tone is soft, wistful, as she stares into her coffee.

"No thanks to their mother." I sound snippy but for once I don't care.

"Ashlin's a good mom but a bit self-absorbed." Christine shrugs. "I've met worse."

I don't want to waste time discussing Ashlin when it's a rarity to have my daughter here for breakfast. "I worry about you, Christine," I murmur, encouraged by witnessing her softer side with the girls and wanting to see her happy.

A wry smile twists her mouth. "I'm a big girl, Mom. I can take care of myself."

"Can you?" I lock gazes with my daughter, daring her to look away, relieved when she doesn't.

"Haven't we already talked about this last night?" Christine pales and her hand trembles as she places her mug on the table. "Give me a break."

The sharpness in her tone can cut glass and I choose my next words carefully. "As a concerned mother, I can't help but worry. The lifestyle you lead is damaging you—"

"Concerned?" Christine snorts, her shoulders squared for battle. "Admit it, you're a control freak. You can't stand the thought of any of your children leading their own lives." She grips the table so hard her knuckles stand out. "I moved to New York to get away from you. Grayson bolted despite having a family. Trent married a woman the complete antithesis of you. Only Justin is your lapdog and if he has any sense he'll cut the apron ties sooner rather than later."

I should be immune to my daughter's barbs. It isn't like I haven't heard similar before. But this time I won't let it affect me or make me back down like I usually would. Today, I have to confront this.

"Those regular withdrawals you make from the family account," I say, willing my voice not to quiver. "They're too large for alcohol, so there's more you're not telling me, isn't there?"

She blanches, making her eyes pop, stark and desperate.

"There was a news item this morning, about a prominent judge OD'ing," I say, ensuring my tone remains judgment free while my heart pounds with the implication my daughter could be in over her head. "She would've scored her drugs from reputable sources and yet—"

"Stop." She glares, defiance and fear in her gaze. "Well done, Mom, intrepid detective." Sarcasm drips from every word as she slow claps. "Fine. You want the truth? Yeah, I'm using your precious money to buy drugs. And do you want to know why I take drugs? Because I get off on the power trip, knowing I'm doing what I want to my body when I want because I can. I know what I'm doing, so stop worrying about me."

Christine's frankness startles me into silence as I battle a sudden wave of nausea that she could be a drug addict as well as an alcoholic, and Christine takes advantage of it. "Just because I've agreed to stay here for a few extra days doesn't mean you get to have a say in my life."

"It's motherly concern," I snap, instantly regretting my outburst when Christine's expression closes off. "I'm not judging you, but I'm worried, so please promise me you'll go see Doctor Limstone today."

Christine's lips compress in a mutinous line and I know I'll beg if I have to. Having my suspicions confirmed has sent me into a tailspin. I've been a terrible mother and I need to help my daughter battle her addictions; it's the least I can do. "Just promise me, Chrissie?"

After what seems like an eternity, Christine's expression softens. "I promise, Mom."

To my surprise, Christine stands and moves around the table to bend down and give me an awkward hug. I have no idea if I've made headway, but for now, it will have to do.

CHAPTER SIXTEEN

RIA

I need to clear my head. After last night's interlude with Justin, and the amount of time I've spent contemplating whether or not to try to contact Grayson, I'm exhausted. Spending a Sunday with my daughter trawling her favorite part of Chicago is guaranteed to take my mind off everything.

"Mom, can we go to the lakeside park?" Shelley tugs on my sleeve as we stand on the corner of Auckland Street, gazing at the crowds streaming in and out of the amusement park.

"Not today, sweetheart."

The last thing I need is a ride on a roller coaster when I already feel like I'm on one permanently at the moment. "How about a cake instead?"

While my daughter is well behaved on the whole, she does have the occasional meltdown and I'm hoping she isn't about to now. I'm on edge after the emails yesterday and Justin last night and I crave a smooth day without any angst.

Thankfully, she only pouts for a moment, before nodding. "Can I have two?"

"We'll see." I tug the end of her braid. "Poppy-seed and orange flourless slice for starters?"

"Yum." She rubs her tummy and bounds ahead of me a few feet, zeroing in on our favorite cake shop. In a street famous for its delicious baked goods, my daughter already knows her mind.

We've sampled quite a few courtesy of May only serving the best at her gatherings and she has excellent taste. I hope my daughter's logic will extend to all areas of her life and she won't make the same mistakes I did.

I let out a heartfelt sigh and Shelley immediately stops. "Are you okay, Mom?"

"Never better." I flash a dazzling smile, mentally chastising myself for inadvertently letting some of my internal angst over Grayson show even for a second. "I'm just craving a piece of that cake."

She buys my excuse but skips back a few steps to slip her hand into mine. "We're almost there. Come on."

She practically drags me into the cake shop, whose window display never ceases to tempt me to try something new. Cannoli, croissants, vanilla slices, apple crumbles, chocolate mousse, *mille feuilles* and countless other delectable goodies piled high on trays, encouraging prospective diners to press their noses against the glass and try not to drool.

I place our order—the usual poppy and orange cake for Shelley, a modest chocolate cannoli for me—and step aside. The place is packed and I scan the crowd, oddly paranoid. Receiving those emails regarding the Parker women has done it and while I wasn't included it doesn't make me feel any safer.

"Mom, they called our number." Shelley is staring at me and I have no idea how long I've been pondering.

I take our cakes and guide her out onto the sidewalk. Sundays are popular in beautiful Donvale Heights and I feel claustrophobic for a moment, surrounded by locals and tourists swarming the streets. Backpackers mingle with bohemian Michigan inhabitants, buskers with yummy-mommies out for a stroll. It's the place to see and be seen and I usually love the cosmopolitan vibe. Not today.

"There are no seats." Shelley's nose crinkles. "Shall we eat by the lake?"

"That sounds lovely—"

"Or we can go visit Auntie Shamira." Shelley hops excitedly from one foot to the other. "I love her shop. Can we go? Pleeeease?"

I can never say no to my daughter, particularly when it comes to family, not when I already feel guilty for her not having her father in her life anymore. Not that I had any say in the matter. Grayson left me but I know if he hadn't I would've kicked him out the moment I received that incriminating photo. So I nod.

"Okay. Though she's probably busy and won't want us distracting her."

Shelley ignores my warning, hooks her arm through mine and all but drags me around the corner into Fitzroy Street, where Makes Scents takes pride of place halfway up.

I'm not into the nebulous holistic medicine Shamira practices: reiki and spiritual cleansing and whatnot. But her oil blends have helped me relax at the end of a hard day and I know she does a roaring trade. Her shop is surprisingly classy, without a lot of the hippy paraphernalia that categorizes similar stores in trendy Brunswick where we live, a few suburbs away. Handmade soaps, candles and oil blends are prominently displayed, with an intoxicating scent of lavender and peppermint hanging in the air.

We eat our cake outside before Shelley presses her nose to the glass and cups her hands either side of her face. "I can't see her."

"Maybe she's out back…" I trail off as I catch sight of Shamira, hidden behind a Japanese screen in the far corner of her shop, drinking out of a silver hip flask.

She's furtive, her gaze darting around, like she expects to be accosted at any moment. It makes me wonder. Is this how she copes with her secret all the time? The one that would send Trent into a tailspin if he discovers how far his wife has gone to not give him the child he so desperately wants?

I hate how I saw that photo and read the evidence of what she did in those emails. I like Shamira. We're friends and knowing her darkest secret does not sit well with me. Though a small part of me wishes she'd reached out to me fifteen months ago when she obviously needed help the most.

To go through what she had alone… it's heartbreaking and I want to rush into the shop and hug her tight.

With how I'm feeling, coming here is a bad idea but before I can dissuade Shelley she's already barged through the beaded curtain and entered the shop. Swallowing my trepidation I follow, glad the shop is half full and we're not the only ones in here.

"Aunty Shamira," Shelley calls out when she catches sight of her, and waves.

Shamira's head jerks up, her eyes round and startled, until she sees Shelley. With a deft flick of her wrist she pockets the flask in the loose folds of her emerald kaftan and comes toward us, a warm smile on her face.

"How's my favorite niece?" Shamira envelops Shelley in a welcoming hug, at complete odds with how Ashlin treated her yesterday. Her simple affection goes some way to easing my distress at knowing her secret and how shocked I am that she'd perpetuate such a monstrous deceit on her guileless husband.

Trent is a gentle giant who idolizes his wife and I've always liked him. Alongside May, he welcomed me into the Parker family with open arms years ago and hasn't changed, despite my divorce from his fickle brother.

"I'm good." Shelley pulls back and grins, her sweet, open expression making my heart clench. My daughter is so innocent for her age and I hope she stays that way for as long as possible. "But I bet you say that to Jessie and Ellen too."

"Maybe." Shamira winks and tugs on her ponytail, and Shelley giggles.

"Can I look around?"

Shamira nods. "Sure."

I add, "Be careful," out of habit, but I needn't worry. Shelley is a child respectful of boundaries. Whether at home or at school, she's a stickler for rules and always does the right thing. She gets her over-cautiousness from me and I wish sometimes she'd be more adventurous. Soft women get trampled on, strong women earn respect. I learned that the hard way.

"She'll be fine." Shamira's smile is tremulous as she watches my daughter get lost in a world of dream-catchers and lavender pillows and I know she'll be a great mom when she has kids.

I've never seen her be anything other than loving toward her nieces and you can't fake that kind of caring. Kids are like animals. They know instinctively who to trust and Shelley openly adores Shamira.

I hate knowing her secret and wish I'd never laid eyes on those stupid emails.

"What are you guys doing here?"

"Those cakes around the corner." I pat my stomach. "We can't resist."

"I'm glad you popped in…" Shamira trails off and her shoulders droop, like she's carrying an invisible weight.

"Everything okay with you?" I touch her arm and she stiffens, confirming what I already know. She's far from all right and considering what she's hiding I don't blame her.

To her credit, she doesn't fake bravado. "It's been a rough morning."

For a moment I wonder if she's told Trent the truth, before dismissing the idea. If she had, she wouldn't be here in the shop. She'd be holed up somewhere far from here after Trent turfed her out.

The thought saddens me. "Anything I can do to help?"

She hesitates, as if genuinely weighing up my offer, before shaking her head. "Thanks, but this is stuff I have to deal with on my own."

I can't help but make the connection between her moroseness and her secret I'd discovered in that email. Is this the reason she's so down? The truth hovers on the tip of my tongue. I want to tell her I know what she's done and that it's okay, I won't judge her for it. I want to make it better for her, to offer my support and say she's not alone. Not because I condone what she's doing but because she's obviously struggling and she's a friend as well as family.

"Do you think Ashlin's becoming more spiteful?"

Shamira isn't prone to gossip so the fact she's brought up Ashlin's name around me is unusual, let alone labeling her as spiteful.

"She seemed more moody than usual at the party," I say, offhand.

That's me, queen of the understatement.

"She's horrible." Shamira shudders, worry clouding her eyes.

"Did she say something to upset you?"

"You could say that." Shamira gnaws on her bottom lip, her gaze darting around, as if she's said too much.

I touch her arm. "Whatever it is you can tell me. I'm discreet."

I have to be, considering I'm privy to many of this family's secrets, however unwittingly.

"You can't tell anyone." She stares at me, trying to convey a message I have no hope of understanding. "I really need to talk to someone…"

"You can trust me." I try to make her smile with a boy scout salute. It doesn't work.

"I know I can." She gives the briefest nod, as if coming to a decision. "I guess it's my fault. I confronted her at the party yesterday."

"About what?"

She toys with the fringe on her kaftan sleeve, fraying the cotton. "I think she's having an affair with the CEO of Goodware Corp. I saw them being cozy outside a hotel. Justin deserves better and I thought if I confronted her she'd show some regret, maybe admit she'd made a mistake and want to make amends with Justin. Instead, she threatened me."

If Shamira notes my lack of surprise at Ashlin having an affair with a major business rival she doesn't show it. In fact, her brow is so deeply furrowed I know there's more bothering her than discovering the extent of Ashlin's treachery toward Justin.

"With what?"

I think I know and if Ashlin has information about what Shamira's done, she'd definitely use it against her.

"Things I've done in my past…" She trails off, a blush staining her cheeks. "You know I grew up really poor?"

I nod, somewhat relieved Ashlin doesn't know everything about Shamira, and she continues. "Back then, I did what I had to in order to survive. But I've moved on since. All my family are dead, I don't have any friends, so I escaped that world and don't regret it."

Anger sparks her eyes. "Then this morning I ran into a man from my past. Considering Ashlin's threat, it seems too coincidental?" She shakes her head. "The timing is making me nervous."

"But how would Ashlin know anyone from your past?"

"Who knows, but I wouldn't put anything past her." Tension brackets her mouth. "It's seriously freaking me out and I had to lie to Trent about it." Her fingers continue to fiddle with her sleeve. "I'm not proud of things I've done in my past. But I left that life behind a long time ago and if Ashlin has somehow found out about it and opens her big mouth…" She shakes her head. "I'll lose everything."

Okay, so Ashlin doesn't know about Shamira's more recent deception but my relief is short-lived. While I can't begin to fathom what Shamira did in her past, it must be bad if she's this anxious by Ashlin knowing about it.

My inner journalist wants to probe Shamira for answers. What else has she done? Why is she so bothered? But she would've told me if she wanted to and I can't pry, no matter how much I want to. She's obviously living with regrets and considering what happened with Justin last night I know all about making wrong decisions,

decisions that will complicate the dynamics of this family, choices the Parkers might not be able to come back from.

"Hey, it'll be okay." I give her a brief hug, offering a trite response I don't believe myself. Because if Ashlin divulges the truth about Shamira's past it can cause irrefutable damage to this sweet woman's marriage. "I take it she blackmailed you into silence? You keep her secret, she'll keep yours?"

Shamira nods, her expression worried. "I want to tell Justin, I really do, but I can't."

"You may not have to."

The words pop out before I can censor them and she quirks an eyebrow. "What do you mean?"

"Justin has left her." I sigh, wishing I'd kept my lips zipped.

Round-eyed, Shamira leans in closer. "Do you think he knows about the affair?"

"I think he's tired of his marriage in general."

I deliberately keep my response vague, not wanting to delve into how much I know and how I came by the information.

"Smart move on his part." She shrugs and her expression clears somewhat. "I guess I don't feel so bad now, knowing about the affair and not being able to tell him."

She thinks she's safe. But I know better. The revelation in that email is a hell of a lot more damaging than anything in her past.

"This could be bad for you," I say, needing to choose my words carefully. "If Justin leaves her she won't care about the affair coming out, meaning she could blurt the secrets of your past to be vindictive?"

Shamira pales, her dark eyes too large for her face. "Do you think she'd do that?"

"She might." I pause, desperate to offer a solution without divulging how much I know. "There's another way you can circumvent this. Cut off the potential threat." I take a deep breath and blow it out. "Come clean to Trent. Tell him everything you've ever kept from him. Before he finds out from someone else."

I eyeball her, willing her to understand I'm not just talking about the past. That she needs to tell her husband the truth about what she did fifteen months ago or risk losing him.

"I can't do that." She shakes her head, lips compressed into a mutinous line. "He'll walk."

"It's the only way to ensure you can't be threatened."

Once again I want to tell her what I saw in that email. I want to warn her that the perfect life she's built with Trent can come tumbling down if her secret is exposed. But Shelley calls out to her aunt, brandishing a daffodil silk eye mask, and the moment is lost.

"Thanks for listening." Shamira squeezes my hand. "I'll think about what you said."

She leaves me standing there and as I watch her goofing around with my daughter, putting the eye mask on and pulling funny faces, I hope she tells Trent the truth.

Before someone else does.

CHAPTER SEVENTEEN

ASHLIN

Justin hasn't called me back.

I left four voice messages earlier and he's ignoring me. He never does that, no matter how I behave. My anger has faded, as has my desire to punish him by meeting up with Aaron today. Bad move. Monumentally bad. This thing with Aaron has run its course and I need to get out. I'm no longer feeling powerful, a woman in control of her sexuality, able to wield it as I see fit, reveling in the attention of a man.

As I lie next to Aaron in an uncomfortable bed in the poorly frequented Starlinton Hotel, I feel... sordid.

I've disregarded my conscience for too long. I'm selfish and trying to ignore how much I'm hurting Justin and affecting my kids hasn't done me any favors. I can't shake the feeling I'm standing on a precipice and about to fall off.

It's unnerving. I'm confident in my own skin, in my life. But Justin's uncharacteristic threat that it can all be taken away has lodged deep. He's said outlandish things before during our arguments and I'm certain this will be yet another one of those occasions, but what if I'm wrong?

I can't be divorced. Considering May's new financial constraints she'll ensure I get next to nothing in alimony; she has friends in high places and will find the best attorney to screw me over. Besides, divorce won't suit me. My image is everything. The perfect life, envied by many. It's the only way I can deal with my inherent emptiness, pretending I have everything when in fact I'm lonely, craving affection like I have my entire life. Nobody sees the real Ashlin. They see a rich bitch, shallow and narcissistic, because that's what I want them to see. And it irks that no one, not even my husband, has ever taken the time to delve beneath the surface and see the real me.

"Hey, beautiful, ready for round two?" Aaron caresses me from shoulder to hip, a move I usually find arousing. He's skilled, I'll give him that. He's an expert with his hands and his tongue, as I've discovered over our six-week affair. Good-looking men are usually selfish but Aaron always makes sure I orgasm first. It's one of the few things I'll miss.

I brush his hand away. "I can't. I have to go pick up the kids."

"They can wait." He rolls toward me and I avoid staring at how ready he is. Always up for it.

"Actually, they can't." I slide out of bed, clutching the top sheet to hide my nakedness. I usually strut around, confident in my body. I should be, I pay enough for it. But I can't shake this odd vulnerability making me want to bolt and leave this mess behind.

"Hey, what's up with you?" He frowns, not at all uncomfortable lying sprawled on the bed, exposed. "You're usually insatiable."

I can't dump him naked so I quickly dress, craving a shower to wash my shame away but desperate to escape more. My hands shake as I zip up my jacket, fear coursing through me.

I may have played this all wrong. What if this time I've pushed Justin too hard and he walks away for real?

I sling my bag over my shoulder and head for the door. "This has been fun, Aaron, but we're done."

He sits upright, a frown marring his exceptional looks. "What?"

"You heard me." I need to make this short, sharp and clean. "Don't act so outraged. You're banging anything that walks these days so I'm sure you won't miss me."

A smug smirk curls his lips. "Babe, come on, we're great together. You know you want me."

The cockiness I initially found endearing is now abrasive. "We're done. Don't contact me again."

I slip out the door before he sees the tears burning my eyes. Not for him, never for him. The sadness clogging my throat is for my stupidity and how I've risked everything for nothing.

I reach my car when the text comes through.

HEY ASHLIN,
CATCH UP FOR COFFEE?
SHAMIRA & I MEETING @ 3 @ CERES.
IF FREE, JOIN US.
RIA

I'm flabbergasted. It's been a long time since Ria reached out to me. She used to invite me to impromptu catch-ups all the time but I'm guessing my constant excuses and shitty behavior put paid to that.

It's not like I don't appreciate the effort, I do, but we're nothing alike and the more time I spend in her company the more inadequate I feel. She's smart and independent and manages to make motherhood look easy while juggling a full-time job as a single parent. She's never been nasty but I see the way she looks at me, how she assesses my designer fashion and accessories with an all-encompassing stare that never fails to leave me feeling lacking somehow.

So I hide my insecurities.

It's stupid, as I don't have many friends. And both Ria and Shamira are inherently nice women. But I'm scared of letting them get too close because women have a tendency to talk and I don't want to bond in case I inadvertently blurt out how unhappy I am.

They're Parkers and ultimately their loyalty lies with May. She controls everything and I'd hate to think of the matriarch learning of my weakness. She's the kind of woman to use it against Justin in some capacity. She's already on some weird kind of power trip after that announcement at her birthday party about cutting us all off financially so I don't want to give her any more ammunition.

My cell buzzes again because I haven't tapped the message to remove it from the home screen. I stare at it, indecision warring with common sense. I'm feeling lousy after my stupid, petty revenge session with Aaron and I should head home. But a tiny part of me yearns to be included and with Ria reaching out after how badly I've treated her, I feel obliged to accept her invitation.

I fire back a short reply and get into my car before I change my mind. I duck home for a quick shower and it only takes ten minutes to reach Ceres, an understated upscale café not far from my house. Feeling ridiculously nervous, I enter the small café, immediately comforted by the tantalizing aromas of imported coffee beans, vanilla and cinnamon. They do great lattes and muffins here and I'm surprisingly hungry as I wend my way through the tables toward the back, where I spy Ria.

She's staring at her cell, a frown creasing her brow as she scrolls through something with her finger. Her forehead wrinkling annoys me because she's obviously so confident in her own skin she doesn't use Botox.

When I reach the table I clear my throat and she glances up, her frown clearing, a tentative smile curving her lips.

"Hey, Ashlin, glad you could make it."

"Thanks for inviting me." I sound stilted but if she picks up on my nerves she doesn't show it. "Have you ordered yet?"

"No, I was waiting for you and Shamira, but she just texted saying she can't make it so we should go ahead."

My momentary relief at not having to make small talk with the hippy vanishes as I realize it's now just Ria and me, making conversation all the harder.

"What are you having?"

She looks ready to protest but I'm still standing so it makes sense I order at the counter for us.

When she doesn't answer, I say, "Their lattes are great and the blueberry muffins are delicious, so I've been told."

"That sounds good, thanks."

This time her smile is more genuine and I relax a little. "Be back in a sec."

I feel her stare boring into my back as I make my way to the counter and after I place our order, pay and grab our table number, I quickly glance at my watch, wondering how long I can leave the kids in May's care without her questioning me as a mother any more than she already does, and what would be the minimal time spent here before I can beg off our coffee date and escape.

Ria must be thinking the same thing because as I return to the table she's staring at her watch and I can't help but laugh.

"Planning a quick getaway, huh?"

"The truth is I only have an hour so I can't stay long."

"Let me ask you this." I sit and place my handbag on the empty seat beside me. "If it was Shamira here instead of me, would you still be wanting to leave so soon?"

To her credit, she doesn't lie. "Maybe."

This time we both laugh and it feels good. We'll never be close but I'm glad I made the effort to come today, especially after the fight with Justin last night and me foolishly running to Aaron this morning.

"Is everything okay?"

I blink, hoping she can't read half of what I'm feeling on my face. "Why do you ask?"

She hesitates. "Because you look… tired."

"Rough night."

I'm saved from elaborating by the fastest barista on the planet, with a waitress bringing our lattes and muffins to the table in record time.

Ria taps a sugar sachet against her fingertips several times before tearing off the top and tipping granules into her latte. That annoys me too, the fact she has sugar when I can't look at the stuff without worrying about doing an extra hour's cardio at the gym. The muffin is an anomaly for me but I need the pick-me-up.

"Can I ask you something?"

She nods as she stirs her coffee. "Sure."

"It's been a while since you've invited me to anything so why today?"

She wriggles in discomfort before lifting her head to look me in the eye. "Because I want to ask if you have any enemies."

"Enemies?" I parrot, sounding like an idiot. "What do you mean?"

"Have you received any emails, messages, that kind of thing, threatening you?"

"No…" I trail off, remembering her comeback at May's party after I'd taunted her about her job. I assumed Shamira had voiced her suspicions to Ria too and that's why she'd fired back at me. But is there someone else who knows about my affairs?

"What's going on?"

The hesitation is there again, but she shakes her head. "Nothing. I just wonder if the Parkers are a target sometimes."

"Tall poppy syndrome, you mean?"

"Something like that." She shrugs and sips at her latte. "Being prominent isn't always a good thing."

"Tell me about it," I mutter, knowing firsthand the scrutiny that comes with being part of a recognizable family. For me, living under a microscope started well before I married into the Parkers, with being a Garner earning just as much analysis. When I wasn't striving to live up to my parents' high expectations I'd be pretending to ignore the envious stares of the girls at school. Being part of a distinguished family wasn't all it was cracked up to be and I'd always felt alone even when surrounded by people because I never knew who I could trust. Did friends truly like me or were they impressed by my family's name, prestige and wealth?

Now, with Ria's cryptic comments about being targeted, I wonder what's going on. Starting up with Aaron, Justin's biggest competitor, had been all about getting back at him for ignoring me; a childish, idiotic action of a woman who should know better. Now that I've ended it, I hope I haven't potentially caused more problems, though Aaron is too self-centered to strike me as the jealous type. He will have no shortage of women filling his bed.

But Ria is asking me about threats for a reason and it has me worried.

"Has someone threatened you?"

"No." She eyeballs me with a clear gaze. "But I think we all need to be more careful."

Her warning strikes me as odd but before I can ask more, her cell rings. She glances at the screen.

"It's Shelley's dance instructor, I have to get this."

I nod, devour my muffin and quickly finish my coffee as she answers the call. I don't deliberately eavesdrop but I can't help but glean from her responses that Shelley's up for some kind of award and they want Ria to be there.

When she stabs at the disconnect button, the corners of her mouth curve upward in a soft smile and in that moment I realize how pretty she is.

I can see what Justin sees in her.

She's the opposite of me.

Ria is beautiful in a natural way. Her make-up is understated, her sorrel brown hair untouched by dye. She's the antithesis of my tattooed eyebrows, eyeliner, lip-liner and artfully streaked blonde. She's also way too nice, so is it any wonder my husband is drawn to her when I've done my best to push him away for the last twelve months or so?

Ridiculously, tears well in my eyes and I blink them away. My throat feels tight and my chest aches. I've done this to myself, to my marriage. Me. I've allowed my insecurities to fuel my self-sabotaging tendencies and ruin everything.

"Hey." She lays a hand on my forearm. "I know we've never been close but if you ever want to talk, offload, whatever, I'm around, okay?"

"Thanks." I manage a weak smile, wishing I'd done a lot of things differently, like allowing this woman into my life a little.

Being estranged from my only sibling means I should've made a bigger effort to get to know my sisters-in-law. But I like being the noticeable Parker woman, demanding all the attention, and it looks like I expected the same in my marriage and it hasn't done me any favors.

She removes her hand from my arm. "Sorry for bailing on you but I have to go."

"That's fine, I have to go too."

We stand simultaneously and pause, awkward, unsure whether to hug or air-kiss. Impulsively, I lean forward and wrap my arms around her in the briefest of hugs.

"Thanks again for inviting me."

"My pleasure," she says, staring at me in wonder as we step back, like she can't quite believe I'm being this nice. "Take care, okay?"

"You too."

I let her walk ahead of me before gathering my handbag to follow, because for the second time in as many minutes I feel the inexplicable urge to bawl.

CHAPTER EIGHTEEN
SHAMIRA

I've managed to avoid Trent the whole day. First by making a phone call to a garrulous supplier on the way back from the market ensuring I avoided further questioning, and later by helping out in the shop even though I hire extra staff on a Sunday. He's been holed up in the den as usual, listening to music, chatting online with fellow guitar aficionados. I'm glad of the reprieve.

It had been nice having Ria and Shelley drop in; they provided a temporary distraction from the thoughts whirring through my head like one of the spinning color wheels I stock. I'd been glad to accept Ria's invitation for coffee at Ceres after she dropped Shelley at dance class but had later reneged when she'd mentioned inviting Ashlin too.

I know Ria. She's a peacemaker and after what I'd told her, she couldn't help herself. She envisaged Ashlin and me hashing out our problems and moving forward for the sake of the family. But I can't, not without coming to grips with what I'm going to tell Trent.

In typical laid-back Trent fashion he hasn't hounded me. But I know once I enter our apartment he'll ask me about what happened at the market this morning. Pity Ria didn't accept my invitation to come back for dinner. I could've done with the buffer.

I like Ria. She's genuine in a family full of fakes. I'm the biggest phony. Maybe she's right. I should tell Trent the truth, all of it. But the thought of his reaction leaves me cold. He's relaxed and loving but I can't bear the thought of seeing his acceptance turn to disgust.

That's what scares me the most. Not the potential loss of luxury: this apartment, my shop, the safety of knowing where my next dollar is coming from. But the certain derision I'll face, the same pitying stares I'd had to put up with for many years, making me feel worthless and ugly… that, I can't tolerate.

I still can't get over the bizarre run-in with the man from my past the day after Ashlin threatened me with exposure. I'd discounted it as a coincidence, but if her marriage is over, as Ria said, I wouldn't put it past her to ruin mine for the hell of it.

I'm apprehensive that he'll find me again and this time he'll tell Trent everything. But I used a false name back then so the odds of him tracing me here are minimal. Unless Ashlin is behind the whole thing and tells him… crap, I can't keep going around in circles like this, obsessing about something I have no control over. I need to focus on more important things, like ensuring my husband doesn't find out the rest.

I take several deep breaths, inhaling and exhaling with slow precision to steady my nerves, before opening the front door. I spy him immediately, sitting in front of the TV, idly flicking channels. Not a good sign. Trent rarely watches television. Even when he's bored he'll rather strum his guitar or listen to music than watch TV.

"Hey," I say, slipping off my sandals inside the door and padding toward the kitchen. "You hungry?"

"Not really."

He finally lifts his head to glance my way and I see it: the wariness in his eyes. Like he knows I'm hiding something.

"I'll make an omelet."

Usually he'll help me beat the eggs or chop the onion. He doesn't move from his slouch on the sofa.

"Ria and Shelley stopped by earlier. I asked them to come back later to eat with us but Ria wanted to get Shelley home after dance class to get ready for school tomorrow."

"She's a good kid." His expression softens like it always does at anything child-related. "How's Ria?"

"Good."

Though I'd glimpsed something, a touch of anxiety that made her appear fragile. I know the feeling. But I have my own problems to deal with so I hadn't delved. I feel bad because we're friends and I should've dug a little deeper. It's been too long since our last girls' night out and I should rectify that. Ria is smart and funny and laid-back; nothing like the rest of the Parker family.

His eyes narrow slightly and I know what's coming before he opens his mouth. "So tell me about that ex at the market this morning."

Even though I expect it, his question winds me. My lungs seize and I'm breathless, willing the spots dancing before my eyes to disappear. I put down the whisk before it clatters to the floor from my nerveless fingers. I've mentally rehearsed a spiel but delivering it is a different matter.

Feigning nonchalance, I force myself to eyeball him. "Not much to tell. I lived near that market for a while, he was a local, we went out a couple of times and he became obsessed. A bit of a stalker, really. So I took out an intervention order and that was the end of it."

Though the falsities tumble from my tongue like the truth, the enormity of lying to my husband lodges like a weight on my chest, heavy and stifling, and I surreptitiously drag in deeper calming breaths.

Doubt flickers in his eyes. "So it's just a coincidence he turned up at the market this morning?"

"I hope so, because if he deliberately tracked me down I'll have to go to the police." I'm digging myself in deeper with every lie and I'm drowning, floundering, out of control, willing my husband to let the subject drop so we can get back to being the great couple we are.

He waits a few moments, mulling my response, a groove slashing his brows. "Let's leave it for now but if you see him hanging around, let me know."

"Absolutely." I breathe a sigh of relief but it's short-lived when he continues to stare at me with an intensity that unnerves.

"Is there anything else you need to tell me?"

I still, every muscle in my body stiffening with dread. My heart's pounding at the thought he might suspect I'm lying but I school my face into a blasé mask. "What do you mean?"

His frown deepens and the glint of suspicion in his eyes has me holding my breath. "You really freaked out this morning. I've never seen you like that. I get the feeling there's more to this than you're telling me."

He's a smart guy, my husband. I stare at the bowl of barely beaten eggs, my appetite gone. He hasn't accepted my excuse, not completely. It looks like all I've succeeded in doing is buying time.

I need to tell him. It's the only way for us to have any chance of working through this; the only way for him to have a smidgeon of forgiveness. But I can't tell him today. I'm drained. Besides, I need him in a good mood, not defensive and suspicious, though he has every right to be. Plus I need to mentally rehearse exactly what I'm going to say.

"We all have a past," I say, sounding oddly breezy, my fake chirpy tone completely forced and designed to end this interrogation. "But for now, I'd rather concentrate on the present, which involves wine, an omelet and you, not necessarily in that order."

His frown eases and his eyes clear as his mouth curves into the lopsided smile that warms my heart. "I may have a piece of that omelet after all."

"Done." I resume whisking, glad that my hand doesn't shake and relieved he's dropped this for now.

But cooking our favorite quick and easy dinner does little to soothe the fear eroding my confidence, making me doubt I'm doing the right thing in living a lie.

CHAPTER NINETEEN

ASHLIN

After the unexpected coffee date with Ria, I should pick up the kids and head home. But I'm still feeling fragile and can't face my girls or my bloodhound mother-in-law. I know May. She won't be happy I dumped the girls and ran. She'll want to pry and I'm not up to an interrogation, not when I'm feeling this vulnerable and likely to blurt things I shouldn't. Ria broke down some of my defenses and I need time to re-erect them.

Dumping Aaron is the right thing to do but I can't shake the foreboding I've seriously messed up this time. Does Justin know? Is that why he didn't come home last night? I'd never seen him so mad and while I'd deliberately goaded him into losing his temper like I sometimes do after I've imbibed too much alcohol, I hadn't expected that kind of comeback.

What if I've ruined everything?

I should've asked Ria how much she knows and if so, has she said anything to Justin. Then again, she doesn't seem the type to interfere. I've been awful to her for years and she hasn't returned the favor, why would she start now?

As much as I act jealous in front of Justin, I've never seen her behaving untoward with my husband. She's not that type of woman. But as I drive aimlessly along Lakeside Road and through the side streets of Ash Park toward May's, I'm at a loss.

So I ring Justin again.

"Hey, it's me. I'm okay, the girls are fine, but we missed you last night and this morning. Could you please call me back? And I'm sorry for acting like a bitch."

Tears burn my eyes and I end with, "I really am sorry, for everything. Call me."

I stab at the disconnect button on the steering wheel and thump it with my other hand. That message bordered on pleading. I'm never subservient or apologetic so I hope he knows I mean it. I have so much to be sorry for; it's a start. But calling him does little to alleviate the persistent dread eroding my self-control.

Hating the tightness in my chest, I slide the window down for air. I hear the roar of a powerful engine and glance in my rearview mirror. A black sedan is close behind me. Too close. I can't see a face behind the lowered sun visor but they're tailgating me.

"Idiot," I mutter, slowing down deliberately so the moron can pass. That's all I need on this crappy day, a road rage incident.

The car pulls out to pass, speeding up until it is level with me. I don't want to see some punk's middle finger so I avert my gaze and look straight ahead. To see a minivan coming in the opposite direction, lumbering along in the direct path of the sedan.

I brake, giving the sedan room to pass. But the moron panics and swerves into me, pushing me off the road. I overcorrect, spin and hear the squeal of brakes a moment before there's nothing but blackness…

I rarely dream but today is different. I'm floating on a cloud with strings attached to my wrists as if a giant puppet master is controlling me.

Everything's a blur, a haze, and it's somewhat comforting.

I hear voices. Jessie and Ellen whispering. Unusual for my girls, who like to talk loudly in an effort to outdo each other. I hear Justin too, talking in a hushed tone. Why can't they speak up? I need to hear if they're talking about me. But why would they do that? I'm the perfect wife, the perfect mother, aren't I?

The voices sharpen, clarify and the haze fades as I open my eyes. The first thing I see is an IV pole to the right and Justin standing next to it, his face a study in misery.

"Hey, it's just a dream."

I manage a smile but my mouth hurts, like I've crunched down on metal. My jaw aches, my lips feel tight, even the inside of my mouth feels like I've been grinding my teeth all night. I prod at my teeth with my tongue, tentatively exploring, only to find even my tongue is tender. Bizarre.

"Mom, you're awake!" Ellen appears in my line of vision and I'm confused, because tear tracks stain her cheeks. My girls rarely cry. They get that toughness from me and I'm proud they don't show their emotions like some other young girls do. Showing weakness is never good. People don't respect you if you're timid.

"Of course I'm awake." The words sound funny and that's when I realize my ears are sore too. They feel bruised, which is totally weird. And my jaw hurts even more as I talk. "Is it time for school yet?"

Justin leans forward and places a hand on my arm. I like it. He doesn't touch me very often. "Ash, you were in a car accident. You're in the hospital."

"Don't be ridiculous," I snap, sounding more like myself than that weak, nebulous dream voice. But as I try to sit up, pain rips down my spine and I moan.

"It's true, Mom. An ambulance brought you here and everything." Ellen peers at me, worry lines marring her smooth brow. Jessie stands close behind her but doesn't speak. She hates hospitals and looks seriously freaked out, her eyes wide, her lips compressed, her skin as pale as the beige wall behind her.

"Ambulance?" I don't remember anything since the hotel. And Aaron. Oh no... "Was I alone in the car?"

"Of course." Justin casts me a quizzical glance, but I glimpse the flicker of suspicion and the trepidation churning my gut intensifies. I could explain away the odd questions, blame it on the accident and the fact I must've sustained a god-awful bump on the head if my jaw feels this bad, but Justin isn't an idiot and I need to stop treating him as such. "You'd dropped the girls off at Mom's this morning. Then just over an hour ago you were found wrapped around a tree in Ash Park."

"I—I—can't recall much…"

A lie, because it's all flooding back: spending the morning with Aaron to get back at Justin. Dumping him. Meeting Ria for coffee mid-afternoon. Driving around aimlessly. Virtually getting pushed off the road by a maniac.

"There weren't any witnesses but the police said that according to the tire tracks on the road you could've swerved to avoid a cat or dog, lost control and hit the tree." Justin sounds so solicitous I'm tempted to keep up the forgetful charade.

He hasn't spoken to me with genuine concern for a long time. It gives me hope we can get past this. If he didn't care he wouldn't sound so apprehensive and that means there's still some deep-seated emotion between us that can be salvaged.

I need to make changes, starting with fighting to save my marriage.

"Some of the family are outside if you're up for visitors?" He touches my hand, the briefest, lightest brush before removing it and I stifle the urge to reach out and hang on tight. "Ria's picking Shelley up from dance school and sends her best. We've all been worried about you."

I hate anyone seeing me at my lowest, but I remember the fear of Justin not returning my calls, of his threat that everything I have can be taken away from me, and I decide to play nice with his family.

"Sure, let them in." I struggle into a sitting position, gritting my teeth against the flare of pain in my back, like someone has stuck a red-hot poker in my neck and skewered it all the way to my butt.

"The doc can up your pain meds if you need them?" Justin studies me with an intensity that soothes better than any analgesic.

My husband is looking at me again, really looking at me. Maybe this accident will be a turning point for us?

"I'm okay for now." I smile at him, trying not to wince. Even my face hurts, from my brow to my cheeks and lower, like I've gone a few rounds with my kickboxing instructor and lost.

He looks uncomfortable in the aftermath of my uncharacteristic smile, considering I'm usually glaring at him. "Jessie, tell everyone they can come in."

My daughter practically runs to the door. If she has her way she'd keep running. She hates doctors and hospitals. Not that she's had much contact with both, thank goodness. She'd had a dislocated thumb as a toddler, had come to visit when I'd had Ellen and a badly sprained ankle at eight. Each time she'd been jumpy and pale, demanding to go home. I must get her out of this silly funk. How will she ever undergo a cosmetic procedure if she can't abide this environment?

May, Trent, and Shamira file into the room, staying near the door and well away from the bed. Good. I don't need their false concern.

May steps forward, her expression serene. I give her points for not pretending like she cares. "You gave us quite a fright. How are you feeling?"

"I've been better." I give a gentle tug on the IV line attached to the back of my wrist for emphasis. "But whatever they're giving me through this is good stuff."

The rest of them force polite laughs, seemingly content to let May be their spokesperson. "Well, if you need anything, don't hesitate to ask. The girls can stay with me while you're recuperating."

I glance at Justin and raise an eyebrow. Why aren't the girls staying with him at home?

He looks away quickly. "Thanks, Mom. The doc says Ashlin's just in for observation and should be out of here within a day or two."

That short? So much for playing the sympathy card. If I were in here longer it would give me some much-needed time to work on my marriage; to spend some time with Justin, be looked after by him. Daily visits from Justin would be a good start toward regaining some kind of connection.

"We'll be fine." May slips her arms around Ellen and Jessie's shoulders. "You focus on getting better."

Shamira and Trent nod, and I'm struck by their spinelessness. Considering my last conversation with Shamira at May's birthday party, they're only here for appearances. Everyone's always trying to stay on May's good side and for what? By her grand announcement at her party she's cutting off the family money anyway and doling out a small wage like we're kids who should be grateful for pocket money.

I'm sick of all the kowtowing and pretense. I yearn to tell them exactly what I think. I settle for an exaggerated moan that has Justin leaning over me in an instant.

"You okay?"

I nod and my wince from the pain isn't faked. "Just sore. But I'm pretty tired. I think I need to rest."

"You heard the patient." Justin draws himself up and faces his family. "Thanks for coming but Ash is tired."

I'm not sure if it's the strong painkillers making me slow on the uptake but I see an odd glance I can't fathom pass between him and his mother, like he's trying to convey some kind of private message. It annoys me, that even when I'm lying at death's door—slight exaggeration, considering my injuries can't be that bad if I'm out of here in a day or two—he's looking to his mother for guidance.

"Get well soon, Mom." Ellen blows me a kiss and Jessie merely nods. I understand her animosity. I abandoned them this morning, never returned to pick them up and now this.

Or maybe she understands far more than I give her credit for and knows I've driven her father away, maybe for good?

The Parkers mumble a collective goodbye and May ushers the girls toward the door where she pauses, her gaze sweeping between Justin and me. She wants to say something, I can feel it, but thankfully her lips compress and then she's gone.

Leaving me alone with my husband.

"I better let you get some rest too." He edges away from the bed like he's scared I'll grab his arm and won't let go.

"I think someone tried to run me off the road deliberately," I say, wanting him to stay. I need to make amends and there's no time like the present to start. "There was a black sedan tailgating me. Then it pulled alongside me, trying to pass I assume, but then it swerved into me."

His eyebrows rise and he stares at me with blatant skepticism. "The police didn't say anything. They saw your tire marks in a skid, with no evidence of foul play."

His eyes narrow, like he assumes I'm lying for the attention. So I let it go rather than reasserting my conviction that I'd been run off the road.

"Is the car wrecked?"

He nods, continuing to stare at me with suspicion. "If you wanted a new one, all you had to do was ask."

I don't smile at his wry response. He's given me the perfect opening to address our on-going issue of poor communication. "Would you have listened though?"

My broaching the proverbial elephant in the room startles him and he takes a few moments to respond.

"Look, this isn't the time to discuss anything," he finally says, dragging a hand through his hair, a sure sign he's rattled. Nothing fazes Mr. Perfect. He takes everything in his stride. Except a wife he doesn't notice most of the time and only then to berate me.

"Where were you last night?"

The question pops out before I can censor it and he reacts like I've prodded him with a Taser, jolting before he stiffens, tension making his neck muscles rigid.

His expression closes off and he takes a step back. "We don't usually share where we've been or who we've been with." Disgust curls his upper lip and I know I've made a mistake in confronting our latent resentment now. "Why would you ask me now?"

My heart stops. The way he's staring at me, with derision… he suspects I've been lying to him, that I'm hiding something. This is the time I need to grovel, to apologize, to say something to save my marriage, but my thoughts are too fuzzy and I'm exhausted, the pain in my head intensifying the harder I try to think clearly.

"Can we talk about this later?" I press my fingertips to my temples and throw in another moan for good measure. "I feel like I've been run over by a bulldozer."

He gives a curt nod, like he can't wait to get out of here. "Rest. I'll visit in the morning to see how you're doing."

"Thanks for being here." I reach out, my hand hovering halfway between us.

He glances at it and I will him to take it. After what feels like an eternity his fingers brush mine before his arm falls to his side and he strides away.

I guess it's more than I deserve considering my behavior.

I pin my hopes on it.

It's a start.

CHAPTER TWENTY

MAY

The girls are subdued when we make it back to my place, after a brief cheer-up stop at their favorite ice creamery. I know they're worried and I've done my best to reassure them. But for now, I need some time alone with my son.

Christine meets us as we enter through the back door. "How's Ashlin?"

"Mom's good, though her face is kind of bruised," Ellen says, shrugging out of her jacket and hooking it on the stand. "She needs to rest so we're staying here."

"That's good." Christine opens her arms to the girls and they rush into their aunt's arms, making me wonder anew why my daughter hasn't prioritized having children.

"Girls, do you want to have a swim? The pool's warm, or maybe a game of tennis?" I stare at Christine over the girls' heads, trying to convey my need for privacy. "Your father and I have some work to discuss."

Christine mouths "okay" and gently propels the girls toward the back door again. "Everything we need is in the pool-house so why don't we take a dip?"

I touch my daughter's arm as they pass. "Thanks for this."

"No worries." Christine smiles and jerks her head in the direction of the hallway. "I just heard a car pull up, that must be Justin."

I nod. "Something's going on between him and Ashlin and I intend to get to the bottom of it."

Christine hesitates, unused to offering me advice. "Be gentle with him, Mom. Boys aren't as tough as girls."

Don't I know it. My son is a pushover when it comes to his wife but the frostiness I observed at the hospital gives me hope. He'd barely touched Ashlin and his concern had seemed muted, like he'd been there out of obligation. I know he hadn't been home last night and that might mean their marriage is in serious trouble.

I quash the instant flare of pity. My son will be better off without that woman but I can't help but feel sorry for my granddaughters who will be caught in the crossfire of divorce. And I'll have to speak to him about timing: with me selling the business, discretion is paramount. I won't have my son or his avaricious wife derailing my plans.

"I like having you here," I say, pleased when Christine enfolds me in a brief hug.

She laughs off her uncharacteristic expression of sentiment. "Don't get used to it."

I smile, grateful I've made some kind of breakthrough with my daughter and hoping it lasts when she returns to New York. "You're welcome here any time. This is your home."

Christine waves as she exits the back door, passing Justin on the way in and pausing to give her brother a hug. He doesn't seem surprised or bothered that she doesn't ask about Ashlin's wellbeing. Then again, I know why he stays in a dead-end marriage—for the sake of his girls—and I admire him for it. Hadn't I done the same for my kids to preserve the Parker image of perfection? I'd hazard a guess Justin's marriage is bliss compared to what I'd endured with Percy.

"Hey, Mom." He kisses my cheek but his heart isn't in it. I can see the dark shadows under his eyes, the tension bracketing his mouth. My son has something on his mind and I have every intention of getting to the bottom of it.

"The girls are outside, having a swim with Christine," I say, curious to see if he'll rush out to avoid having a discussion.

When he gives a brief nod and sits at the table, I have my answer. "I'll see them in a bit. Thanks for looking after them."

"Anytime." I busy myself at the espresso machine, giving him time to articulate what's bothering him.

Out of all my children, I've always been closest to Justin. As my eldest I have a special bond with him and it flourished when I appointed him CEO of the company. Percy had put a lot of pressure on him and I'd hated it. I often wonder if Justin would be happier doing something else rather than stepping into a CEO role he'd been groomed for by a demanding father. I guess I'll soon find out. Once I sell the company, Justin will be free of familial obligation. I'll be free too, to enjoy my grandchildren, the only good in my life these days. And if Justin divorces Ashlin, my time with the girls will increase tenfold. I can't wait.

"Is everything all right—"

"It's over between Ashlin and me."

My strong, brave son speaks so softly I wonder if I heard correctly and his revelation isn't a figment of my wishful imagination.

I pick up the coffee cups and turn, trying to get a read on his mood. He appears stoic, like the end of his marriage isn't such a big deal. But I glimpse genuine pain in his eyes and I mentally curse that woman who's done this to him.

"I wondered if something was going on when Jessie told me this morning that you hadn't come home last night, and then when you didn't return my call."

He grimaces. "Sorry about that. I needed some time to myself, to get my head straight."

"You know I'll support you in any decision you make." I place the coffee cups on the table and sit next to him. "Where were you last night?"

"I checked into a hotel." His furtive glance away makes me wonder what he'd been up to and with whom. "When we got home from your party, Ash started up as usual and I couldn't take it anymore." He blows out a breath. "So I went to Ria's."

Before I can comment, Justin continues. "I needed someone to talk to."

He folds his arms in a classic defensive posture and I wonder what really happened at Ria's.

"Did she help?"

He shrugs, his insouciance annoying but I know better than to push my stubborn son for answers. "Ria's great. She's objective and that's what I needed last night."

I accept the dig. I've never hidden my dislike for Ashlin and had been dropping veiled hints ever since Percy died and the expectations on the Parker family had automatically lessened.

"You like her." I throw it out there, wondering if my son will have the guts to acknowledge his attraction to his brother's ex-wife.

Anyone with eyes in their head at my party would've seen the two of them, chatting and laughing as they went into the kitchen to get the cake.

Is Ria the reason my son has finally made this tough decision?

I trust Justin enough that he won't rush into anything with Ria. And as I catch him staring out the window to watch his daughters, adoration in his eyes and a soft smile curving his lips, I know he won't do anything to hurt them.

"Ria is... special." He rubs a hand over his face. It does little to erase the stress lines grooving his brow. "But I'm not a complete moron. I know the company can't afford a scandal at the moment and I'd never do anything to hurt the girls. Though I wish you would've told me about the changes to our financial arrangements..." he trails off, hesitant to say more, before continuing, "and I know from what you've been alluding to the last few weeks that there's a chance the company could be sold—"

"I'm sorry for not discussing it, but I wanted a concrete offer before coming to you." I clear my throat, somewhat embarrassed. "I didn't want you worrying about being ousted as CEO until I had something official to present to you. Not that you won't get a similar position elsewhere with your credentials and name—"

"Relax, Mom, it's okay, I'll be fine. And I won't do anything to spoil your grand plans."

Relief filters through me. "I'm glad you're going to wait until the divorce comes through to make a move."

To his credit, he doesn't feign ignorance; he knows exactly what making a move means and on whom. He doesn't seem particularly surprised at my bluntness either but he glances away, like he can't face my scrutiny. "There's no other option."

I want Ashlin expunged from the Parker family, but I can't help but think it will benefit Justin if Ashlin is standing alongside him whilst I sell the company. Until the deal goes through, I won't allow anyone to jeopardize it.

If Justin and Ria eventually decide to do something about their feelings, I know people will talk. Gossip will be rife, but it can be managed. I tolerated my fair share of gossip being married to Percy and it hadn't harmed me. I'd been above it all, stronger than anyone gave me credit for. The company had been my focus and it still is. I'd do anything to keep the family's fortune safe for my grandchildren.

"I'm proud of you." I squeeze his shoulder and release it. "You've made a tough decision."

Justin appears startled, his eyebrows rising. "No lecture? No judgment?"

I shake my head. "Not from me. Your girls adore you and that won't change. We'll fight for full custody and—"

"Whoa, slow down." Justin holds up his hands. "Let me discuss this with the family lawyer first."

My surprise gives way to dismay. Surely he won't leave his girls in the hands of that woman? "You don't want full custody?"

"Of course I do," he snaps, regretting his outburst as his shoulders slump. "Sorry, it's just that I need to get all the facts before I make any big decisions."

"Bit late for that, considering you're ending your marriage," I say drily and he shoots me a filthy look. "Look, Justin, I think this is a good move, finishing with Ashlin. But you know what she's like. She won't give up the prestige of being a Parker easily. She'll fight it with everything she's got. So make sure you get all the legal advice you need before telling her."

He nods, a thoughtful expression on his face. "You think this will get nasty?"

I refrain from rolling my eyes, just. "It's Ashlin. What do you think?"

He scowls and scrubs a hand over his face again. "You're right. I'll see the lawyer first thing in the morning."

He pauses, as if hesitant to say more. "Ashlin mentioned that she thought someone might've run her off the road. She was strange with me in the hospital…"

"You know your wife better than anyone. She'd say anything for attention, especially if her marriage is in trouble." I snort. "What do the police think?"

"That she lost control after possibly trying to avoid an animal and hit the tree."

I compress my lips, knowing silence will convey my opinion of Ashlin's fanciful notions much better than anything I can say.

"I'll move my stuff out of the house while she's in the hospital, then wait till she's home to tell her it's officially over."

"Sounds like a plan." I don't want to interfere more than I have to but my son deserves more than what his wife has dished out lately and I've held my tongue long enough. Now that his marriage is over I have no reason to pussyfoot around the unsavory topic of his wife's alleged infidelities. "I won't make it into the office tomorrow, I'd rather stay home and be here for the girls before and after school. So after you've seen the lawyer can you please fire Russ?"

A slight frown crinkles his forehead. "Why?"

I clear my throat. I don't want to hurt my son but he's been oblivious for too long. Either that or he's chosen to turn a blind eye to his wife's foibles for the sake of his children but in leaving Ashlin he's finally come to his senses and he has to know. "There've been rumors circulating. About Russ sleeping with some of the female staff and uh… your wife."

He almost upends his coffee cup by jerking forward, his shock genuine. "What the fuck?"

Justin never swears in my presence, and that alone shows how oblivious he's been. Has he really never noticed her absences, wondered where she was or what she was doing? His surprise quickly gives way to anger as he blanches, his mouth twisted with bitterness, his eyes hardening.

"It could just be rumors but I've heard enough over the last few months to think we can get a better accountant."

"Done."

I watch his anger drain away, replaced by a mixture of sorrow and confusion in his readable eyes. I hate seeing my son in pain but if it's for long-term gain—namely being free of Ashlin—I'm all for it.

Justin glances at his watch. "I want to spend some time with the girls before heading home to pack."

"Go ahead." I wave him away, my heart lighter that my son has confided in me about his smart decision. "And if you need anything, don't hesitate to ask."

"Thanks, Mom."

He leans down to envelop me in a brief hug, before heading out the back door, leaving me cheerier than I've felt in a long time. Justin divesting himself of a wife bringing disrepute to the family can only be good.

He's made a selfish choice for once, a tough decision, and that can only bode well when he's forced to strike out on his own. Because I lied to him earlier, when I expressed my confidence in him. He may have the credentials and the Parker name backing him when he has to find a new job, but I wonder if he realizes how much I actually do at the company. And I have a sneaking suspicion Justin will be as much of a letdown as the rest of my children when it comes to making something of themselves without relying on my money propping them up.

As for his forbidden feelings for Ria… well, I'll deal with that complication when it happens.

CHAPTER TWENTY-ONE

RIA

Shelley's curled up in bed, reading, when my cell rings.

It's Justin.

I hate the flair of excitement low in my belly. The sudden surge of anxiety makes me study the screen like a teen expecting a call from a popular boy.

It's probably nothing. I assume he's calling to update me on Ashlin's condition because I couldn't make it to the hospital. But after last night I know that whenever he calls or whenever I see him nothing will be the same again.

He kissed me. He groped me.

I let it happen.

Worse, I enjoyed it.

Rolling my shoulders to quell the nerves, I hit the answer button.

"Hey, Justin, everything okay with Ashlin?"

I deliberately use her name. His *wife*. Remember her?

"She's fine, thanks for asking."

I hear a sigh, like he's dealing with some heavy stuff. "How are you?"

I can do platitudes. Mundane small talk is safe and far from forbidden memories of that kiss we shared. "All good here."

"I'm packing my stuff to move out," he blurts, and I hear relief in his voice. "I'm telling Ashlin it's over."

I could say so much: is he sure he's making the right decision, has he thought how this will affect his kids, does he realize she probably won't make this easy for him?

I settle for, "Ending a marriage is always difficult."

"Or in this case long overdue."

He's bitter and angry, his voice tight with it. I don't envy him having to go through a separation. Grayson may have broken my heart but in a way he'd done me a favor by making a clean break. I may have craved closure at the time but not seeing him again after he walked out made it easier somehow.

"I've had a long chat with Mom, she knows everything." He pauses, as if choosing his next words carefully. "She told me there've been rumors about Ash having an affair with Russ, the accountant at work."

I wince and stare at the ceiling. I've seen the proof firsthand in that email I received, along with evidence of a more recent indiscretion that can have diabolical consequences for the company if she's swapped pillow talk with the competition.

I mumble a noncommittal response and thankfully he continues. "She doesn't tell me she's screwing around behind my back, but she says crazy stuff like she thinks someone tried to run her off the road." He sniggers. "That's Ash, always wanting to blame someone else for the havoc she causes."

I stiffen as a trickle of dread runs down my spine. Had Ashlin's car accident actually been a veiled attempt on her life?

In that moment, I wonder if those emails had been some kind of warning?

I'd assumed the information in them could be leaked in an effort to damage the family. But what if it was something more, an actual physical threat?

"That's a pretty big accusation. What did the police say?"

"That she probably swerved to avoid something on the road and hit that tree. There were no scratches or dents on the driver's side so she wasn't forcibly pushed off the road."

His answer doesn't settle my nerves. Another car wouldn't have to touch Ashlin's to run her off the road. Pulling alongside and mocking a swerve would be enough to do that.

"Whatever happened, she's lucky she's okay," I say, sounding suitably solicitous. "When's she coming out of hospital?"

"Tomorrow or the next day, according to the docs." He sounds exhausted, like it's the last thing he wants. "Which means I have to get back to packing."

"Sure."

"I've rented a short-stay apartment in the city."

I have no idea why he's telling me this. It's not like I'll be dropping in for coffee anytime soon. Now more than ever I have to keep my distance. The last thing I need is speculation that I caused the breakdown of his marriage.

"I hope it all goes smoothly." I sound ridiculously upbeat, my false perkiness grating.

"Ria?"

How could him uttering one word affect me so deeply, the low rumbling reaching down deep and tweaking my long-buried crush?

"Yes?"

"Thanks for listening."

I want to say "anytime" but I don't want him to call, to discuss his marriage ending or anything else. I need to maintain my reserve, to resurrect those barriers I've worked hard to maintain before that kiss.

"Bye." I hang up before he can say anything else, feeling foolish and cruel.

All Justin probably needs is a friendly ear, someone to offload to. Pity I can't be that person. It's dangerous, knowing Justin is a free man now. Technically he's still married and that status won't change for a year, probably longer if Ashlin draws out the divorce as I expect her to. Her acrimony will know no bounds.

I can't think of him as single. Because I may be tempted to go against every sense of self-preservation I have, every part of me screaming that our attraction can't go anywhere, even when he's free.

Besides, I have more important things to worry about, like Ashlin's claim she'd been run off the road and the possible connection to the threatening emails I'd received. In my line of work I'm always taking seemingly random facts and making links, and even the subtlest ones often lead to a story. In this case, I can't ignore my gut: if Ashlin says someone ran her off the road, she'd been deliberately targeted, and that could mean danger for Shamira and Christine, who also featured in those revealing emails.

The thing is, why? Who would want to harm my sisters-in-law?

I have to find a clue, something that will help. I grab my laptop from the coffee table and flip it open. I open my inbox and study the saved emails. I scrutinize them carefully, looking for the slightest hint to the identity of the perpetrator, but come up blank. And no further contact from Lars means I have to do the last thing I want to.

I have to try to contact Grayson.

My fingers tremble as I quickly pull up the game I know he used to frequent, a worldwide phenomenon housed on a server hosting billions. I've avoided it for the last five years despite enjoying the mindlessness of playing it with him when we'd been married, on the off chance I'd recognize Grayson's username and be tempted to reach out.

Because that's the kicker in all this. Despite Grayson abandoning us, despite that awful photo implicating him in a sordid life I knew nothing about, at times I wonder where he is and what he's doing. I'm proud of myself for never giving in to the temptation of discovering his whereabouts. I've got contacts, it could've happened. Instead, I'd focused on becoming a strong, independent provider for my daughter, a woman who doesn't need a man in her life. But if someone is targeting this family, it only makes sense I reach out to the one man who has the skills to find out who's doing this. I won't have Shelley potentially threatened by some faceless enemy with a weird vendetta against the Parkers and if I need to swallow my pride to ask Grayson for help, I'll do it.

I'm counting on the fact my ex is a creature of habit and that once I get into the gaming site, I'll spot one of his favorite usernames. I log on and I'm into the gamer program in under thirty seconds. I scan an endless list of names of players who've been online in the last few hours. Nothing leaps out at me and my eyes start to blur as name after name scrolls across the screen.

I scrub a hand across my eyes to clear them and that's when I see it.

A goofy name I'd often tease him about.

It has to be him.

At least, that's what I hope.

I copy and paste the accompanying email address into my contacts and quickly exit the site.

The chill invading my body intensifies as I type a brief email to the man I hoped to never see again. I have to consider it may not be him so I keep it brief. I'm in trouble. I need his help. Urgently.

I consider deleting it for several long moments, before remembering Ashlin's suggestion she'd been run off the road. If she'd been deliberately targeted…

There's too much at stake. I need to find whoever's behind those bizarre threatening emails, so I hold my breath and click send.

CHAPTER TWENTY-TWO

SHAMIRA

Trent lets me have a lie-in on Monday mornings because he gives an early guitar lesson at the local high school and I don't open the shop until ten. He's always quiet, tiptoeing around, ensuring he doesn't wake me. Today, it's irrelevant. I haven't slept all night. While he snored his usual low-grade rumble after we made love, I lay awake in bed staring at the moon-dappled ceiling, rehashing the weekend and Ria's suggestion I tell my husband the truth reverberating in my head until it's all I can think about.

She made it sound so easy. Tell him before Ashlin does. But what if Ria's wrong about Ashlin's marriage ending? What if I can still salvage this? If there's the slightest chance I don't have to tell Trent everything, I'll take it.

I can't bear the thought of his disgust when I divulge the truth about my past, about how I deceived him yesterday. Worse, what I did over a year ago… One lie upon another and so it goes on.

I wait until I hear the front door click and give Trent a ten-minute head start before leaping out of bed. I don't bother with a shower. I have to get to the hospital.

A long forty-minute ride in peak hour traffic later and I'm at the private hospital in a leafy Rockland Grove street, standing outside Ashlin's door. She's sitting up in bed, staring blankly at the TV mounted on the wall. I hate hospitals and I don't blame her for looking bored out of her brain. I'm guessing what I have to say will liven up her day.

Taking a deep breath, I knock and enter. "Hey, how are you feeling?"

She raises an eyebrow and looks me up and down. "Better than you if your dress sense today is any indication."

Typical Ashlin, judgmental and condescending, and I waver. Maybe I made a mistake coming here to reason with her? Then I think of Trent and his utter devastation if he discovers the truth from her.

I have to do this.

"Don't you like stripes and spots?" I do a little twirl, making my ankle-length black and white striped skirt flair at the hem, while lifting my arms so my red and navy spotted A-line top can flair too. "It's a fashion statement."

"More like a fashion disaster," Ashlin says, eyeing me dubiously. "What are you doing here anyway? You made your obligatory five-minute visit yesterday."

Ignoring her sarcasm, I edge closer to the bed. "I need to talk to you."

"About?"

"My past."

Her eyes narrow, the gleam unmistakably shrewd and calculating. She should look vulnerable with that big bump on her head and a burgeoning bruise around her right eye. Instead, she looks plain nasty.

"I'm hoping you'll do the decent thing and keep the information to yourself, even if you have no reason to do so now."

Ashlin stares at me with confusion so I rush on. "I mean, if you're getting a divorce it doesn't matter if Justin knows about your affair or not, but you have to understand that I love Trent and I want our marriage to stay solid. You telling him about my past will only hurt him—"

"What did you say?"

I'm so hell-bent on getting my spiel out I miss the color leaching from her face, leaving her as pale as her sheets. Her fingers clutch at the top sheet, bunching it into wrinkles. Her mouth gapes in horror, her eyes round and panicked.

"With Justin leaving you, I assumed you'd get a divorce…" I trail off, knowing I've made a massive blunder and so has Ria.

By her wide-eyed shock and pallor, Ashlin doesn't know about Justin leaving. And I've ruined everything.

"I'm sorry—"

"Shove your apology up your ass," she hisses, some of the color returning to her cheeks. "Where did you hear that crap about Justin leaving me?"

I flounder, not wanting to get Ria into trouble but needing to give her something to get myself out of it.

"Ria mentioned something—"

"I should've known," she spits, tiny specks flying from her mouth. "She's always had the hots for my husband."

"That's not fair." I'm honor bound to defend Ria because she'd be the last woman to steal anyone's husband, especially not her sister-in-law's. "Don't shoot the messenger. She wouldn't have said anything unless she'd heard it elsewhere."

"Like from Justin, you mean?" Ashlin sits up, surprisingly mobile for someone whose face looks bashed in.

Increasingly uncomfortable, I shift from side to side. "I don't know what's happening in your marriage and it's none of my business, but you can't tell Trent about—"

"Just leave," she says, collapsing back on the pillows like this is all too much. "Why shouldn't I tell him, so I can ruin your marriage like you've ruined mine?"

The woman is delusional. I haven't wrecked her marriage. From her selfish behavior she's done a fine job of that herself.

"I get it, you're feeling fragile, but please don't tell Trent—"

"I'm not fucking fragile!" she yells, her skin a weird mottled crimson as she jabs a finger in my direction. "I'm sick of this family and all the bullshit that goes with it. My marriage isn't over so you can tell the lot of them exactly that."

She jabs her finger again before her arm falls to the bed, lifeless. But her eyes haven't lost their fire. She stares at me with so much hatred I inadvertently take a backward step.

"As for Trent, I can't wait to get out of here to tell him exactly who he's married to."

There's nothing left to say. I tried. I failed.

She's left me no choice.

I have to tell Trent the truth about my past before Ashlin does.

CHAPTER TWENTY-THREE

ASHLIN

I wait for my husband to visit, nerves making me pluck at the bed sheets, change channels aimlessly and drink too much water, wishing it were vodka. My chest is tight and my skin clammy. I know he'd been angry the other night, but divorce?

I'm such an idiot. I've pushed too far and it's going to take a monumental effort to get him to change his mind. He's as stubborn as his mother and once he makes a decision he's immovable. He'll be in at eleven this morning, which gives me time to formulate a plan. It's simple, really. Play the dutiful wife, repent, and change, willing to do whatever it takes to get the spark back.

Justin is weak. He pretends to be the big man in the family, the alpha taking care of his pack, but he's a pussy. I imagine he's been mouthing off to someone, probably his mother, about our argument the other night and good old May has mistaken his whining for a declaration of separation.

The old bat would love that. I see the way she looks at me these days, like I'm a scourge on the Parker name. It wasn't always like that. In the early days she valued my money and connections as a suitable partner for her precious son. When Percy had been alive she'd been different, more deferent and respectful of my status as Justin's wife. Now, I catch her staring at me with ill-concealed dislike.

Like she knows about my indiscretions.

I assume if she did she would've confronted me so maybe my guilt is morphing into paranoia. Whatever it is, I'm sure May is the one spreading rumors about me and Justin and when I'm out of this prison I'll tell her to mind her own business. She must've mentioned it to Ria, who told Shamira. Irrationally, I'm a tad hurt Ria hasn't come to see me, considering our improbable bonding session yesterday. Though she did text late last night expressing her concern and asking if I needed anything. Not that I ever would ask her but I kind of like the semi-truce we've established.

I shouldn't have been so mean to Shamira earlier too. It wasn't her fault she'd inadvertently dropped a bomb on me, but calling me fragile put me on edge. And I'd never tell Trent about her past. The first time I'd threatened her I'd been fueled by too many champagnes and the shock of being put on the spot by her accusations. Today, I'd been reeling from the D word to do anything other than retaliate.

It's stupid, that even with my life teetering on the edge of imploding, I'm projecting my usual tough exterior, when nothing can be further from the truth. I'm a mess at the thought of Justin leaving me, my carefully constructed façade open to speculation and ridicule.

Why the hell had I thought that by sleeping with Russ and Aaron I'd feel better about myself? I hate being insecure and needy, and both men had snuffed that out in me for a brief period of time. I didn't want them, though. I want my husband to want me. But if what Shamira said is true, I've lost him.

I glance at the clock on the opposite wall. It's ten forty-five and Justin is likely to be early. I buzz for a nurse, waiting the requisite sixty seconds before buzzing again.

What seems like an eternity later a nurse barely out of grad school breezes into the room, way too chipper with her inane grin. "What do you need, Mrs. Parker?"

"My handbag is in the cupboard. Can you get it for me please?"

She blinks, like I've encroached on her valuable bedpan time. "Is that all?"

Her sunny smile vanishes, replaced with a disapproving glower as she hands me the bag. "We have many patients requiring urgent care, you know."

I raise an eyebrow at her haughty attitude. "And you know that my family paid for the new wing of this hospital and we technically fund your wages too?"

She's pissed so I flash a sickly sweet smile. "That's all for now."

She stomps out without another word and I unzip my bag, thankful I always carry make-up with me. I saw the family staring at my bruises yesterday. Nothing a little concealer won't fix.

However, as I glance in my compact mirror, I'm horrified by the massive purplish-black bruise around my right eye and an unsightly lump on my forehead. I look awful. But as I take a foundation stick out of my bag, I have second thoughts about prettying up for Justin. I look more vulnerable with evidence of my accident and that may elicit more pity than trying to put on a brave face.

I stuff the foundation, powder compact and lip gloss back in my bag and place it on the sliding table next to my bed just as there's a knock on the door. My heart races and I drag in several calming breaths before calling out, "Come in."

Justin pushes the door open and enters the room. He doesn't look happy to see me. He has this odd expression, halfway between hopeful and resentful. It alerts me to the fact that Shamira's right: my marriage is in serious trouble and if I don't play this right his threat, that I'll lose everything, is in dire danger of coming true.

"Hey, husband. How are you?" I smile and he practically recoils. The smile may have been overkill, as these days we rarely make eye contact. It saddens me that we've come to this. I hadn't given it much thought over the years as our relationship deteriorated, having witnessed my friends' marriages going through a similar decline. Men earning a squillion, their trophy wives happy to fake happiness in exchange for a cushy lifestyle. It's the norm in our social circles.

But I've been a fool accepting our ailing marriage as normal.

I can lose everything.

"I'm fine. How are you feeling?" He approaches the bed like a recalcitrant kid being beckoned by a nurse for a vaccination.

He doesn't want to be here.

And right then, I know I'm in trouble.

He doesn't want to be around me, he can barely look at me, and when Justin makes up his mind about something… I'll need to pull off the acting performance of my life to salvage this disaster of my own making.

"I'm still battered and bruised but getting there." I straighten my shoulders and fake a groan. "I want to be home as soon as possible though, so hopefully tomorrow."

He looks panicked at the prospect and I can't shake a growing sense of impending doom.

"No need to rush it." He props against the chair next to my bed, making it clear he's not staying long. "The girls are fine, by the way."

He sounds judgmental and annoyed. I don't blame him, I should've asked about the kids first. My girls are the best thing in my shallow life but I'm so rattled by Shamira's revelation about the demise of my marriage that all I'm focused on is assuaging Justin. I'm hell-bent on saving my marriage and while I love the girls and miss them terribly, right now my priority has to be ensuring I don't lose my husband. They'll thank me some day. It will affect them too. They need their parents together and to remain in the trusted Parker circle.

"I'd planned on calling them after school so I can talk to them in person," I say, adding, "I'm sure May's doing a great job looking after them."

"She is." He makes a grand show of looking at his watch. "I need to head into the office."

"And leave me here by myself?" I attempt another smile, coyer this time, and his lips compress in an unimpressed line.

"You said you're fine. Just rest up—"

"But we never talk anymore, not without the girls around, so why don't you stay awhile?" I pat the bed, expecting him to capitulate like he always does. We've done this dance for years.

Not today, apparently, as he stares at me with complete disinterest. Then he laughs. A harsh, raucous sound devoid of amusement and it raises the hackles along the back of my neck.

"Stop that," I snap, before inhaling through my nose and blowing a slow breath out of my mouth to calm down.

"Why? It's funny." He gestures at the spot I patted on the bed. "The fact you want me anywhere near you these days is laughable. Especially when you've spent years trying to push me away."

He's mad as hell. He may be grinning like an idiot but I hear the anger in his voice, restrained, but there all the same. So I try to placate. I never back down but I'm willing to try anything at this point. He's disarming me by not conforming.

"Come on, honey, we've been under the usual stress parents are—"

"Cut the crap," he says, his upper lip curling in a sneer. "What have you got to be stressed about? You have a nanny to look after the girls. You have a chef to prepare those calorie-controlled meals you're so fond of, and you spend your days flitting between cafés and cosmetic surgeons."

He finally steps closer but I glimpse the vein bulging at his temple, indicating he's furious. Startling, because Justin rarely loses his temper. "That's when you're not fucking other men, apparently."

I let out a gasp before quickly schooling my face into a mask. But it's too late, he's seen my slip-up and he's going to use it against me.

"Don't be crass." I need to salvage this by lying. "I don't know who you've been listening to but you know there are always rumors floating around our social circle. Heck, if I believed half of what our so-called friends tell me I'd think you've slept with every employee at the company."

"Don't patronize me." He shakes his head, the uncharacteristic sneer making him look plain mean. "Besides, I don't care who you've screwed or how often. That's not the reason I'm ending this marriage."

I feel the blood drain from my face, leaving me slightly woozy. My momentary swoon is real but like everything else about me Justin thinks it's fake. I try to formulate a response, something classy and nothing like the loud 'fuck you too' reverberating through my head.

"I was going to wait until you got out of hospital to tell you but I can't go through this charade any longer." He eyeballs me, daring me to disagree. "We're over, Ash. We've been over for a long time and I can't stay in a toxic relationship any longer."

I feel the rage bubble up within, desperate for an outlet. But if I lose it now I'm playing into his hands and I won't give him the satisfaction.

"All marriages go through rocky patches. This is one of those—"

"I'm so tired of this." He pinches the bridge of his nose and when he looks up, I see the defeat in his eyes. Like he's gone ten rounds with a prizefighter and lost.

I think I prefer his anger. Because seeing that defeat means he's truly given up, like the weariness has seeped inside and can't be dislodged.

"Let's not drag this out any longer than we have to," he says, his voice croaky. "I'll move out citing business reasons so as not to disrupt the girls' routine. We'll stay together in name because of the company and we'll keep the divorce under wraps while the business is in flux but you need to hire a lawyer so we can keep this civil and—"

"Fuck you!" I yell, finally losing the tenuous control of my infamous temper that probably got us into this situation in the first place. "You can't get rid of me that easily—"

"Watch me," he says, his tone so soft, so lethal, that at first I miss the subtle threat.

But his eyes don't lie and I shrink back against the pillows as he glares at me with blatant animosity, his hands curled into fists by his side.

Justin isn't a violent man but in that moment, with his loathing chilling me from a few feet away, I think he's capable of anything.

CHAPTER TWENTY-FOUR

MAY

"You're a miracle worker." Christine stares at me in wide-eyed wonder as we stroll along Chapel Street, something we haven't done since Christine was a child.

Back then I enjoyed parading my beautiful children along Chicago's hippest retail strip. I reveled in the compliments from strangers and silently wished my mother had been as proud of me when I'd been little. Instead, she'd been a chilly woman, a hands-off mother who barely hugged me, let alone held my hand if we were out in public. She chastised me constantly for not being good enough: an average horse rider, a terrible ballet dancer, and never thin enough. I may not have been the best mom with my kids but I wasn't half as bad as the tyrant who raised me. I hadn't mourned her death when I'd been twenty-four. Leaving me her fortune was about the only motherly thing she ever did of any value.

Today is like taking a step back in time as Christine links elbows with me, as if she's proud to be seen with her mother, a rare occasion indeed. Ever since she divulged the truth about her drug taking, we've bonded somehow. I've done my best not to mention it and she seems more relaxed around me because of it. Not that I'm under any illusions; she faces a tough road ahead and she'll want to go it alone without any intervention from me. But for now, I'm enjoying spending time with my daughter for the first time in many years and hopeful that our relationship moving forward has changed because of it.

"Miracle worker?" I play dumb but know what Christine is referring to. I've been beaming all morning because of it.

"I know going to rehab and aiming for a fresh start is what I need." Christine rests her head on my shoulder for a moment, a rare display of affection that brings a lump to my throat, before straightening. "I've been in denial and you gave me the support I needed to admit what was happening, so that's definitely some kind of miracle."

"You have no idea how happy I am." I'm eternally grateful my daughter has finally seen sense and wants to take control of her life again. "So Doc Limstone did a real number on you, huh?"

"He did, major scare tactics, but I needed the wake-up call so I gave him the go-ahead to book me into rehab." Christine falls silent for a moment, before continuing. "Does this mean you'll be checking up on me constantly after I'm out?"

I shake my head, wishing I could steer my daughter toward a less dangerous pastime but knowing the decision has to be Christine's ultimately. "You know how I feel. I had to intervene, but now I'm trusting you to make smarter choices."

Christine winces. "Nice guilt trip, Mom."

I smile and stroke my daughter's cheek. "That's what mothers are for."

The fact I can have this discussion with Christine makes me euphoric. Having her home this time stabbed at my conscience and I'm glad I finally spoke up. I should've done it a long time ago.

We reach the end of the block, where Chapel Street intersects with Lake Road, a bustling hub of cosmopolitan Chicago that I love. "Is it okay if I do some more shopping and meet you back home?"

I nod. "Go ahead. Shall I leave the car?"

"Don't be silly, I'll get a taxi." Christine bends down to kiss my cheek, another rare sentimental gesture that lightens my heart. "See you later."

I watch my statuesque daughter walk up Chapel Street, her long strides eating up the pavement, the epitome of a confident woman in her designer jeans, flowing blouse and leather jacket. I don't want to question if my daughter is really doing better, because I know firsthand how confidence can be a sham.

Most people see me as an assertive control freak. When I walk into a charity luncheon, people accede to me. When I stride into Parker Partnership headquarters, employees are deferent and respectful; while some appear terrified. I'm used to commanding a room and everybody in it. With wealth comes power and I've been lucky enough to have both for a long time, well aware that so much of being a Parker is about how you present yourself, with poise, with your head held high.

Had my only daughter been compelled to turn to drugs to achieve the same empowerment? It makes me wonder: did my domineering ways have something to do with that? Had my cold and indifferent manner affected my daughter? It isn't the first time the thought has crossed my mind. If a simple shopping trip after spending a few days with me alleviated Christine's tension, it jolts me into thinking that maybe I could be one of the reasons behind my daughter's drug habit.

And it doesn't sit well with me.

How much attention had I lavished on all my children over the years? How many times had I delved into their lives to really get to know them? Percy hadn't liked emotions and would go to any lengths to avoid them; as parents, we'd been too distant from our children.

Our regular get-togethers I organize now are nothing more than smoke and mirrors, showing a united front, presenting a unified public image and a way for me to assert control. Providing them access to the family fortune has been my way of showing them I care. But out of all my children, only Trent seems happy and well adjusted, and I hate to admit that I could be partially responsible for the dysfunctional rest.

I'd put up with Percy's overt disdain for so many years and know I may have treated my kids the same way. I can't change the past. I can't change their childhoods, but I can try to be a better mother now and that's the real reason I reached out to Christine this time and asked her to stay.

Being a matriarch comes with responsibilities and I take mine seriously. I've failed with my children and I'll be damned if I'll fail again.

It's why taking care of my granddaughters has become all-important to me.

It's my only chance at redemption.

Thoughts of my family and Christine's addiction drain me and I'm eager to get home and enjoy a last hour of peace before the girls get home. With Jessie and Ellen at school and Christine out for a few more hours, I can savor the usual silence of my home.

I take a left off busy Lake Road and into the quiet side street where I parked, already envisaging a steaming cup of Earl Grey and a handmade shortbread from Saks, when a heavy weight hits me between the shoulder blades and propels me forward.

I stagger and put my hands out to prevent falling. Off-balance, I tumble forward, catch my foot on the sidewalk and sprawl on the grassy strip, landing heavily on my wrist.

Pain shoots up my arm and I cry out, my vision blurring as I glance up in time to see a person on a bicycle pass without stopping. I can't tell if the person who bumped me is a man or woman as they're wearing one of those stupid unisex hoodies. And they're moving fast, like they can't wait to escape.

I try to struggle into a sitting position but the pain in my wrist snatches my breath, so I lie still for a moment.

"Are you all right?" A young mother pushing a stroller stops to help me up, concern creasing her brow. "I saw that guy run you down."

"I'm sure it must've been an accident." I try to move my wrist and bite back a cry of pain. I don't have time for a broken wrist and I'll be royally pissed if some idiot cyclist has done this.

"Didn't look that way to me." The mother points to my wrist, which has already swelled. "Do you need me to take you to the ER to get that checked out?"

"No, I'm fine, and thanks for your help."

The mother nods but eyes me with worry, while I mull what she said. It doesn't make sense that anyone would try to deliberately target me. I don't have enemies. Jealous rivals in the business arena, yes, but I've had those for years. Why would some idiot on a bike run me down now? This woman is mistaken. Some are prone to dramatics and I have no time for it, never have.

I grit my teeth against a stab of pain in my wrist and allow her to help me into a sitting position. I'll be fine. I need to be, because nothing will derail my plans for the company and my family.

CHAPTER TWENTY-FIVE

SHAMIRA

My feet drag as I enter the apartment. A potent mix of fatigue, guilt and anxiety runs deep, making me weary to my bones. I can't do this anymore; live a lie. Besides, Ashlin has taken any choice I have out of my hands.

I have to tell Trent the truth.

Now.

I called him on the way home from the hospital, asking him to meet me here. I worried Ashlin may have called him first but he'd sounded his usual upbeat, chipper self. Besides, delivering devastating news over the phone isn't her style. She'd want to do it in person so she can see the havoc she wreaks firsthand.

His early-morning guitar lesson had finished and I caught him on the way to his favorite secondhand store, which he visits weekly in the hope of finding old vinyls, instruments or anything to remotely do with guitarists.

I admire his passion for music. It translates to all areas of his life, including me: undeserving, unreliable, unremarkable me. I hide it from him, my insecurities, but soon he'll know and my life as I know it may be over.

The launch of my new digestive elixir is tonight and I'm not sure whether to cancel or brave this out. May insists PR is good for business but I'm feeling wretched. Some of the family have RSVP'd: May, Justin and Ria. Christine is minding the kids. The shop will be packed with interested, eager customers and usually I'd be in my element, waxing lyrical about my concoctions and their health benefits.

After I tell Trent the truth about my past, tonight might not even happen. Our marriage could be over. He's a placid guy and he loves me, but can he forgive me for withholding the truth all these years?

I shiver and rub my hands over my arms. It does little to eradicate the chill invading my body and making my teeth chatter. I cross to the kitchen, grab a bottle of brandy I use for cooking, and take a swig straight from the bottle. The liquor burns my throat and I cough and splutter before taking another, hoping it will warm me. It doesn't and as I recap it and shove the bottle back in its cupboard I hear the front door open.

"Everything okay?" he calls from the entryway as I brace, knowing that nothing will be okay again.

"Thanks for coming home." I glimpse his startled expression as I run toward him and fling myself at him, wrapping my arms around his neck and burying my face in his chest. I inhale, allowing the familiar fragrances of his musky aftershave and faint body odor to calm me. Today, they don't work and my heart pounds as I slowly pull away.

"You're scaring me." He drapes an arm across my shoulders and leads me to our worn suede sofa, one of our favorite spots for making love.

Sitting here should comfort me, should provide me with some sense of belonging. Yet as my pulse races all I feel is confidence-shaking trepidation.

"I have to tell you something." I swivel to face him so our knees are touching and I reach out to clasp his hands. "It's irrelevant to our marriage now and doesn't change a thing but I think it's time you know the truth."

His mouth flattens, his eyes a scary, flat blue. "Have you cheated on me?"

"God no, nothing like that." My grip on his hands tightens and thankfully he doesn't pull away. "It's about my past."

His eyebrows raise a fraction. "Is this about that guy from the market?"

"Partly." I take a deep breath, feel my belly expanding in the perfect yoga breath, and huff it out slowly. It does little to calm my rampaging nerves. "That creep wasn't an ex. He was a client."

"Client?" he parrots, confusion creasing his brow.

I wait, unable to articulate that I used to be a whore, and I see the exact moment he computes what I'm saying as wariness, tinged with repulsion, sparks in his eyes.

"You know I didn't grow up like you. My mom got sick, a virus the local public health clinic couldn't deal with, and I hated watching her go downhill. If we didn't enter the private system we would've had to wait six months for an appointment with a specialist so… I had to get the money."

Heat flushes my cheeks while the rest of me remains chilled to the bone. "There were always grubby guys living in the flats who'd pay for favors. But the money was never enough for Mom's care so I ended up doing more…" I trail off, hating how my husband's handsome face appears to collapse in on itself: his sunken cheeks, his hollowed eyes, his downturned mouth. He appears to age before my eyes and disgust churns in my gut: I did this to him.

"You were a *hooker*?" He yanks his hands out of mine and I let him, the pain in my chest so deep, so agonizing, I can't breathe for a moment. "Why didn't you tell me?"

"Because it would've changed everything," I whisper, wishing I could turn back time to a few weeks ago before I'd seen Ashlin cheating on Justin, before I'd confronted her, before this. "I fell in love with you so quickly and deeply, I couldn't believe you felt the same. Then there was the whole drama of being accepted into your family because of my poor background, I couldn't imagine them knowing what I'd done and the repercussions for you."

He shakes his head, the longish hair I love so much brushing his collar in a soft swoosh. "But you could've told *me*. You could've trusted *me*." He thumps his chest so hard I jump. "I adored you from the first minute we met and I've trusted you ever since. Why couldn't you trust me?"

"I do, baby." I reach for him but he leaps to his feet and starts backing away, staring at me like I'm a monster.

"Why now?" He crosses his arms and glares at me with ill-concealed dislike. "Why tell me now?"

"Because we don't lie to each other and I hated having to do it at the market."

It's the partial truth, because if he finds out Ashlin knew about this before him, he'll go ballistic.

"We don't lie to each other?" He barks out a laugh devoid of amusement. "Yet that's what you've been doing to me for years…" He's furious, bristling with it as he stares at me with disgust. "The thing is, if you'd told me, I would've still hated it but I would've understood. What you did for your mom… having to go through all that… it's awful." I see a momentary flash of compassion before he shakes his head, anger replacing the understanding in his eyes. "Yet all I can think now is how long did you fuck other guys for money?"

I cringe at his outburst. Trent rarely swears, his gentleness one of the many qualities I love.

"Eighteen months," I say, my voice quivering with shame. "But Mom got the help she needed and she recovered, so while I hate what I had to do I didn't regret it at the time."

His defensive stance didn't soften. "You told me she died before we met."

"She did. Of a heart attack a month after she got the all-clear from the specialist."

I'd been catatonic for weeks after, rallying against a god I didn't believe in for making me endure an endless string of sleazy men only to take Mom from me regardless.

Trent will never know he's the reason I picked myself up and wanted a better life, that I'd targeted him at that pub. That I'd become the woman he wanted so I could put the past behind me. That even now I'll do whatever it takes not to upset the status quo; that I'll do anything not to disturb our tranquil marriage.

I've told him enough truths for one day.

"I love you and this doesn't change anything." I stand and take a step toward him, like a handler approaching a skittish colt. "Now that you know I hope we can move forward—"

"I need some time to process." He spins away and almost staggers toward the den where he'll retreat into his music.

I yearn to reach out to him, to touch him, to comfort him.

Instead, I let him go.

He slams the door and a few moments later I hear the weird synthesized sounds of his online music. He's been tinkering online a lot lately. In fact, he's playing a lot less and focusing on the strange world online. I don't understand the attraction. I love listening to him strum as he hums, writing songs at random or playing old classics. It's soothing. But the weird sounds online are jarring.

He turns up the volume and the loud twangs of a fake electric guitar make my ears ache. I can't stay here, waiting for him. He's not a talker. After our rare arguments, he always shuts me out then later pretends nothing has happened. I doubt that will happen this time but on the upside he hasn't kicked me out. In fact, apart from his initial shock, he took the news better than I anticipated.

The volume increases to a screech and I cover my ears. I'll head downstairs to the shop and lose myself in ensuring everything's ready for tonight. Immersing myself in the familiar will be soothing.

I also need a distraction from the other more harmful secret I'm harboring, the one I can never tell him because it would finish us.

CHAPTER TWENTY-SIX

RIA

Shelley is excited about the prospect of spending some time with her cousins this evening and I'm relieved. As much as I love my daughter she's overly exuberant in Shamira's shop at the best of times and I don't want anything to ruin my sister-in-law's launch tonight.

Shamira is fragile. I've never seen her so defeated, as she'd been the other day at her shop. I also assume she hasn't told Trent the truth about her past yet because if she has I doubt the launch would go ahead.

While she hadn't told me exactly what she'd done to survive in the past I can guess. Growing up a foster kid, being shunted from home to home, I'd seen my fair share of what some people do to make ends meet. I'd been one of the lucky ones, landing with an older couple in my teens, where I stayed until I met Grayson.

But other foster kids hadn't been so lucky, trapped in a system that didn't favor anyone. Some had ended up on the streets, doing whatever it took to survive.

It's interesting, that her past hadn't been in that email, yet her more recent indiscretion had? Then again, medical records are irrefutable whereas there'd be no solid proof of her previous life: cash transactions and men who didn't want to be identified. What I want to know is how Ashlin found out? Hiring a PI to discover dirt on her family members would be the kind of underhanded thing she'd do.

But whoever sent those emails to me had dirt on her too?

The whole convoluted rigmarole makes my head ache and as we wait for May's front door to open I hope that for a few hours tonight I can forget the entire mess. Surprisingly, Justin answers the door and my stupid heart gives a betraying leap.

"How are two of my favorite ladies in the world doing?" He does a funny little bow and Shelley giggles.

"Uncle Justin, Jessie and Ellen are your two favorite girls."

I note she doesn't add Ashlin to the mix. She's smart, my daughter, has probably picked up on the vibes her aunt exudes no matter how hard I've tried to shield her.

"They sure are, but I can have plenty of favorites." He bends down to hug Shelley and an unexpected lump forms in my throat.

Justin is a kind, lovely man.

And one hundred percent off limits.

Our eyes meet over Shelley's head and I see something in his steady gaze that makes me want to turn around and run before we fall into this forbidden thing any further than we already have.

"The girls are waiting for you inside." He releases Shelley and she runs off without a backward glance, leaving me feeling gauche and awkward, before he says, "How are you?"

"Fine."

I sound too perky and try not to cringe.

"I told Ashlin it's over."

He sounds relieved and nothing like a man who's walked away from a thirteen-year marriage and may harbor regrets.

I want to ask a multitude of questions. How did she take it? How are you feeling? What happens from here? But I don't want to appear too invested, so I settle for, "How are you holding up?"

"Good." He jerks his thumb over his shoulder. "Better than Mom after the morning she's had."

"What happened?"

A sliver of foreboding pierces my false cheeriness. The possibility of Ashlin being deliberately run off the road hot on the heels of those threatening emails has me in a funk and I'm on guard.

"Some idiot on a bike practically ran her over." He beckons me inside and I grit my teeth as a waft of his aftershave tickles my nose.

"Is she okay?"

He nods. "A badly sprained wrist, according to the doc."

"Lucky she didn't break any bones."

"Yeah, especially considering the woman who witnessed it thought it was deliberate."

I stumble and his hand is under my elbow in a second. "What do you mean?"

"Mom said it was an accident, but the woman who used Mom's phone to ring Christine said it looked like the cyclist tried to mow her down."

While Justin's touch discombobulates me, I've never been more grateful for his steadying hand. This doesn't make any sense. I know someone has it in for my sisters-in-law if those emails are any indication, and someone may have targeted Ashlin, but now May too? I'd seen nothing in those emails referencing my mother-in-law being in danger, so what the hell is going on?

"That's awful," I finally say, when I catch Justin staring at me. "Does she really want to come tonight?"

"Says nothing will keep her away." He rolls his eyes. "You know Mom. Admitting weakness isn't her style."

I almost confide in him then. I need someone else's point of view that I'm not crazy in imagining someone has this family in their sights. But I know deep down why I can't.

It's obvious: the one person whose life would become easier if Ashlin is out of the picture is Justin.

It's a truth I don't want to acknowledge, a supposition more than likely based on reading one too many thrillers. But if anything happens to Ashlin, Justin would be the primary suspect and if he really wished to harm her why separate now and throw extra suspicion on himself? Besides, my fanciful theory is flawed: he'd never harm his mother deliberately.

No, I'm way off base, but I can't ignore a sliver of doubt… how well do I know this man and can I really trust him?

"Are you okay?" His grip slides from my elbow to my upper arm, where it tightens, lingers, making my skin prickle with unease.

"I'm fine." I ease my arm away and feel oddly relieved. "Is May in the conservatory?"

"Yeah. Christine's got some board games set up for the girls."

"I'll just pop in and say hi before we go—"

"Are you sure you're okay?"

I bite my bottom lip from blurting exactly how not okay I am and give him a blasé wave before heading toward the conservatory.

First Ashlin, now May. I wish Grayson would hurry up and respond to my email because something is off in this family and I need to discover what the hell is going on before I'm next in the firing line.

CHAPTER TWENTY-SEVEN

MAY

"Are you comfortable? Is there anything I can get you?" Ria continues to fuss around me, despite being told several times on the drive over and for the last half hour in Shamira's shop that I'm fine. I don't like people hovering over me and Ria has been more than attentive, while ignoring Justin.

I have no idea what's going on with those two but Justin seems exceptionally casual around Ria and Ria appears standoffish and jumpy. I should be glad Ria isn't as loose and amoral as Ashlin, obviously keeping her distance from Justin because of his recent separation, but one of these days I'll have a quiet word with Ria and voice my approval of a potential match with my eldest son in the distant future.

"Go and mingle, I'm fine." I wave her away, glad to be left on a stool behind the counter, where I can rest and observe in peace. Rest because my wrist continues to throb despite the painkillers I've downed and observe because something's amiss with Shamira.

My daughter-in-law usually thrives on this kind of evening, launching a new product, content in an environment she loves, glowing as she takes center stage. Not tonight. Ever since I walked in with Ria and Justin I knew something's amiss. For one thing Trent isn't buzzing around his wife like he usually does and for another Shamira sports a pallor that makes her look ill.

They've obviously had a falling-out and I sigh. I couldn't be happier for Justin finally leaving Ashlin but I like Shamira. The free spirit is good for my softer son. Besides, with Grayson botching his marriage to Ria, Justin about to be divorced, and Christine perpetually single, I want one successful union in this family.

I watch Shamira drift through the crowd, offering tiny shot glasses of some hideous green concoction she made for gut health. I prefer a straight double malt whiskey before dinner every day to keep my gut healthy but I'll keep that gem to myself. Shamira smiles but it doesn't reach her eyes and her gaze constantly darts around the room, seeking Trent, who seems content to talk to everyone but his wife.

They've definitely had an argument, a rarity with those two. I hope they resolve it quickly. I raise my good arm to get Shamira's attention but my daughter-in-law doesn't see me. She's doing a round of the room, commanding attention like any Parker woman worth her salt. The crowd is eclectic; a combination of Chicago's elite prepared to pay anything for the latest health craze, to locals wearing tie-dyed loose T-shirts over brightly colored leggings. Shamira chats to them all, but her conversations are brief and her smiles are forced, I can tell. When there's a brief lull, she scuttles toward a far table where she's lined up bottles to refill the shot glasses.

I watch her pour a black liquid into the glasses before ducking down to where she stocks her personal supply. Shamira rarely gets sick and proudly attributes it to her home remedies that she swigs at various intervals throughout the day. Personally, I'd rather drink anything other than Shamira's concoctions, going by the look and smell, but if it keeps my daughter-in-law healthy who am I to judge?

Shamira uncorks a silver bottle, her favorite. No one touches it, not even Trent, as Shamira has told us all on several occasions. She says it's her magic elixir of youth. I think it stinks like mowed grass mixed with fertilizer.

Shamira takes several sips and screws up her nose before tipping the entire bottle down her throat. She pulls a face and I bite back a smile. That foul stuff obviously tastes as bad as it smells. Shamira straightens and resumes filling the remaining glasses. She works too hard, that girl. I wave again, trying to get her attention, but Shamira picks up the tray filled with glasses and takes a step forward before swaying, stumbling and righting herself.

Something's wrong and I stand, ready to help. But I watch, helpless, as Shamira staggers a few steps as if in slow motion, before she crumples to the floor.

I cry out but the crash of glasses has already garnered attention. Ria and Justin are nearby and kneel beside Shamira, checking her pulse and her breathing.

I stride over, holding out my good arm to part the gathering crowd. "Give her some space," I bellow, waving my arm around, cursing the throb in my other arm in its annoying sling. I kneel next to Ria. "Is she okay?"

Ria's stricken gaze focuses on Justin. "Call an ambulance. Now."

I back away as I catch sight of Trent pushing through the crowd, his eyes wild.

"Where's my wife?"

I try to lay a comforting hand on his arm but he brushes me off, distraught as he spots Shamira lying unconscious on the floor.

"What the hell happened?" He kneels beside her, tears in his eyes as he grabs her limp hand.

No one answers so I feel compelled to divulge what I'd seen. "She drank one of her concoctions, then keeled over a few seconds later."

"I always said that health stuff will kill you," Justin says, his lame attempt at humor earning a scathing glare from Trent and a disapproving shake of the head from Ria.

Justin winces. "Sorry, that didn't come out right." He lays a hand on his brother's shoulder. "She'll be all right, probably overtired and has fainted."

CHAPTER TWENTY-EIGHT

SHAMIRA

There's a hair on my left cheek and it itches.

I'm exhausted. So tired even my eyelids feel heavy, like they're pinned down with weights. My heart has felt heavier every time I've tried to catch Trent's eye tonight and he's ignored me.

At least he came to the launch. He didn't help me or speak to me, waiting until the first guests filtered in before switching off his music and coming downstairs. He looks like he hasn't slept in a week but I know that's not true. I only told him the truth this morning. But he looks disheveled, with his crumpled shirt half hanging out of his pants, the sleeves rolled up at mismatching angles and he's missing a sock.

No one comments because he's his charming, laid-back self, to everyone but me. I pretend it doesn't bother me, putting on a brave face for the guests, giving my welcome speech, handing out free samples. But I'm gutted inside, unsure of everything.

Will he wait until everyone leaves before kicking me out? Will he speak to me again or will he want to handle everything through lawyers, like I imagine Justin and Ashlin will?

I lift my hand to swipe away the hair on my cheek and that's when I realize my eyes are actually closed and I haven't been imagining the heaviness in the lids. I crank them open with difficulty. They feel raspy and dry, like they're stuck together with glue. When they fully open, I see Trent, his face mere inches from mine. He doesn't look mad. He looks relieved. Earnest. Dare I say it, happy?

"Thank God you're all right." He leans forward to brush a gentle kiss across my lips. "You gave me one hell of a scare. Don't ever do that again, okay?"

"Wh-what happened?" My lips feel as dry and stuck together as my eyelids. Anticipating my needs as always, he slips a straw between them and I suck gratefully, the cold water filling my mouth and trickling down my throat, easing the tightness.

He glances away, as if he doesn't want to tell me, and that's when I realize something else. I'm in the hospital. When I wiggle my hand I feel the tug of a tube stuck in it.

"Was there an accident at the launch?"

"Something like that," he finally says, the tenderness in his tone almost undoing me. "Do you remember what happened?"

I screw up my face. It hurts. Like I've walked front-on into something and I'm bruised. "Not really. I think the launch went well but I was tired so I had some of my energy blend."

He nods, his grave expression alerting me that I may not like what he has to say next. "You passed out. The ambulance brought you here. Toxicology ran some tests. You had a high level of acetaminophen in your blood."

"What the heck is that?"

"They call it APAP. It's found in some pain relieving medicines, cough mixtures, stuff like that. It's okay in small doses but can be lethal in large doses."

My head aches. I can't understand what he's saying. "So how did it get inside me?"

I glimpse something in my husband's eyes I've never seen before: fear. "There were traces in your energy blend bottle."

He lets the implication sink in and it takes a moment before I realize the truth.

"Someone tried to *poison* me?"

"We don't know, but it looks that way." He shrugs, seemingly helpless. "Unless you accidentally did it yourself? I don't know what you use in that blend and the pharmacist said you could've inadvertently topped up too much of one substance, causing an imbalance and possible reaction?"

It's bullshit and we both know it.

Though I had been distracted after I'd told him the truth that morning. Maybe I blended too much of something… though I've never heard of APAP and doubt I can manufacture it by mixing basil, cinnamon leaf, lemon and a mint infusion.

Which means someone added it my drink, but who?

The prime suspect is Ashlin, considering how I blabbed about her impending divorce this morning before she'd heard the news from Justin, but she hadn't been there. Which leaves a bunch of strangers and paying clients, and family. My mother-in-law likes me, as does Justin and Ria. Only my husband has a reason to dislike me at the moment. But to resort to poisoning me to teach me a lesson? It's ludicrous. Trent is the most relaxed, caring man I've ever met. He adores me.

Has the revelation about my past pushed him too far? If so, I can never tell him what happened to our baby when I fell pregnant.

"I use all natural ingredients. I doubt anything I mix can conjure up poison out of thin air."

I'm subdued, confusion exacerbating my doubts about my stalwart husband.

"But even natural substances taken in wrong dosages can be toxic. At least, that's what the pharmacist said," he adds, like he's nervous I'll think he's way too knowledgeable and somehow blame him.

Right now, I don't know what to think. Except that I can't trust anyone, even my own husband.

"I'm tired." I close my eyes, hoping he'll take the hint.

Thankfully, he does. "You rest up and I'll be waiting right here when you wake up."

He takes hold of my hand, the rhythmic sweep of his thumb on the back of it so familiar my eyes sting. I should feel comforted and relieved that he's touching me again.

I don't.

I feel nothing but trepidation that someone wants to do me harm and I'm clueless as to who it is.

CHAPTER TWENTY-NINE

RIA

I'm at May's, waiting for news. Trent preferred we didn't go to the hospital and I can understand. He loves Shamira so much, they're an insular couple who live in a bubble, content to be independent from the rest of the family outside of May's gatherings.

By his attentiveness when she collapsed I assume she hasn't told him everything yet. In a way I'm glad. She needs him by her side to deal with whatever this is. It was terrifying, seeing her unconscious on the floor, then being carted off by the paramedics. That had been fifty-five minutes ago and while he'd texted May to say Shamira had regained consciousness, we know nothing about why she'd passed out in the first place.

"The girls are awfully quiet," May says, glancing at her phone rather than me.

"They're watching online videos."

I don't let Shelley watch them as a rule but Jessie is physically attached to her smartphone and right now I'm happy to keep the peace. I'd wanted to take Shelley home but she hadn't wanted to cut the evening short so rather than cause a ruckus I agreed to stay for another hour. Surely we'll have news of Shamira by then.

As if wishing for it has conjured it up, May's phone rings and she snatches it up and presses it to her ear.

Her expression is grave as she answers it. "Trent, how's Shamira?"

Christine rushes into the room, a deep frown slashing her brows. While we don't see each other very often I'm glad she's stuck around longer this time. It's good for my daughter to spend time with her aunt, to place value on family even if her father is gone.

I see May's eyebrows shoot up toward her hairline.

"Are you sure?" she says, her mouth opening and closing like a goldfish, shock widening her eyes. "Uh-huh. Okay. Well, give her my love. Ria and Christine send theirs too."

We both nod vigorously as May continues. "If you need anything, don't hesitate to call, regardless of the time."

She hangs up and lets the phone clatter to the table, like her fingers have lost all feeling.

"What's wrong?" I sit forward, increasingly worried when May doesn't respond for a moment.

"Mom?" Christine perches on the arm of May's chair and lays a hand on her shoulder.

May gives a little shake, like she's trying to clear her head. "Trent said they ran tests on Shamira at the hospital and the toxicology report indicates she had a high level of some kind of painkiller in her blood."

"That's not good. Maybe she popped a few before the launch and it interacted with something she drank?"

It sounds farfetched as I say it because Shamira has been blending concoctions for years and would know what herbal remedies interact with medicinal stuff. She's fastidious that way, always recommending her clients consult with their doctor before consuming her mixtures if they're on any medications.

May shakes her head, concern pinching her mouth. "No, that's not it. Traces of the painkiller were found in her drink bottle, the one she uses all the time for her energy blend."

Christine straightens and comes to sit next to me, facing May. "What are you saying?"

I know before May opens her mouth to respond and I clamp my lips shut before I blurt can't they see someone is targeting this family?

"It looks like someone tried to harm Shamira deliberately." May's voice sounds squeaky and she clears her throat. "I can't believe it."

Christine shoots me an incredulous look, as if she doubts her mother's sanity. "Are you sure?"

May nods, worry lines bracketing her mouth. "The main thing is she's going to be fine. Trent said they're keeping her overnight for observation and she'll be home tomorrow."

"I'm glad she's okay." I sound trite but what can I say? That I think there's something sinister going on? That I'm increasingly worried Shamira's the third woman in this family to be targeted and I'm terrified I could be next? Or worse, my daughter?

This is the perfect time to find out what everyone knows but I need to lead into it gently.

"You don't think…" I trail off, knowing I may sound crazy articulating my suspicions out loud but wanting to alert these women to be on guard. "I mean, this is the third Parker in this family to end up in hospital over the last week. Don't you find it odd? Have either of you received any threatening emails or messages, anything like that?"

Christine shakes her head and May stares at me like I'm mad. "I've received nothing like that. Besides, I tripped after an irresponsible cyclist bumped me and the woman who witnessed it overreacted, and Ashlin ran off the road. How can those two accidents be linked to what happened to Shamira?"

So that means I'm still the only Parker woman who received those emails. It doesn't make sense and I'm annoyed that May's dismissive of my suspicion so quickly. She also disregarded what that woman saw when the cyclist ran her down. I know she's practical and logical in everything she does, but considering an alternative isn't out of the realms of possibility. "Ashlin said she thought someone deliberately ran her off the road."

May makes a scoffing sound but Christine stares at me with open curiosity, like she's considering my theory and can't dismiss it.

"Until we know more about how Shamira ingested that chemical mix, I don't think we should speculate," May says, frowning at me, disapproval for my supposed fanciful notion heightening the color in her cheeks. "For all we know this incident with her is an accident too and there's no point looking for conspiracy theories that aren't there."

I want to blurt the truth: about the revealing photos in those emails, about the secrets hidden by this family, about everything. But I have no proof yet and until I do I can't go making wild accusations that will ostracize me from this family when I need them most.

Feigning submissiveness I nod, but Christine is still staring at me, like she knows I'm hiding something.

Shelley runs into the room and skids to a stop when she sees our somber expressions. "What's wrong?"

We haven't told the girls about Shamira, not wanting to worry them unnecessarily. But I don't lie to my daughter and I'm not about to start now.

"Aunt Shamira fainted at her launch and she went to hospital for a check-up, but she's fine." I stand and slip an arm around my daughter's shoulders. "We're going home now, sweetie."

I mentally will her not to protest because I need to get home and see if Grayson has contacted me. With May in denial that the family is under attack, it's imperative I discover who's behind those threatening emails and I need Grayson's expertise. It irks that I've had to reach out to the man who'd hidden a whole other life from me before absconding and who's been an absentee father who doesn't give a crap about his daughter, but he's a wizard online and right now I need him. Besides, a small part of me is curious to get his take on all this: he's the only one of us who's been out of the Parker bubble for years, yet understands what it's like to be part of it. As much as I hate to admit it, his opinion may be invaluable.

May could be right and these three incidents are unrelated, but after those emails I don't think so. I'm worried about my family.

The moment I heard May say that Shamira had been poisoned an idea flickered to life. What if someone had tried to harm Ashlin and failed? What if that person is targeting others in the family because he's angered by his failure? Is he trying to scare us? Or playing some other twisted game? Maybe he's toying with us, trying to distract us from his real motive? Something company related perhaps?

Whatever the rationale I need to do something. And if I have to chase Grayson to the ends of the earth to get his help, I will. I'm scared.

I need to protect my daughter at all costs and if that means using any methods possible to find Grayson, I'll do it.

CHAPTER THIRTY

ASHLIN

I hate hospitals, and lying around playing up my injuries in the hope the nurses will contact Justin and he'll feel sorry for me isn't working. He hasn't been back to see me since he effectively ended our marriage and I'm tired of being a passive victim. It's not me. I'm gutsier than this and damned if I'll take this divorce lightly. I need to see if he's serious first and then instigate steps to protect my kids and my assets.

I check myself out. None of the medical staff protest. They're sick to death of me if their hostile glares are any indication. Not that I blame them. I've been awful to the nurses and treated the docs like they're incompetent fools who've recently graduated. It's not their fault my marriage failed yet I took it out on them. I'm not proud of the way I acted, both in the hospital and before, when I ruined the best thing to ever happen to me.

I take a taxi home, somewhat relieved when the driver turns into our drive and Justin's car isn't there. Not that I expect him to be home at eleven thirty in the morning but he's full of surprises these days. Especially his overt display of loathing when he'd threatened to get rid of me the last time we spoke.

I've never seen him like that and I can't get it out of my head, how the man I molded for so many years has morphed into a ruthless bastard. I'd almost applaud and say "about time" if his newfound backbone didn't affect me so badly.

I pay the driver, grab my bag and hobble up the drive. My hips ache from where the seat belt dug in during the accident and my neck is stiff and sore but otherwise I'm fine. I inhale the familiar fragrance of jasmine, eyeing the neatly trimmed bushes lining the drive. I usually find the smell comforting, one of the many things that signify home. Today, it's cloying and overpowering, making me want to take pruning shears to the lot and hack them to pieces.

I let myself in, disarm the alarm and head straight for the bedroom. If he's truly left me, he would've emptied the wardrobes like he said. I slowly climb the elaborate wrought-iron stairs that split on a landing halfway, and take the left turn toward our parents' retreat. The first thing I notice is the empty coat stand. It's an ugly thing, dark mahogany that clashes with our white and grey color scheme, but it belonged to his father and Justin wouldn't hear of me throwing out Percival's hideous stand.

He's never used it for coats but sticks caps on the wooden arms. Another thing I despise: grown men shouldn't wear caps, designer or not. Now, the caps are gone and the coat stand is uglier than ever, mocking me in its barrenness.

The first sliver of fear that this divorce malarkey is real pierces my confidence and I practically run into the bedroom despite my throbbing hips. It's pristine as always, the ten cushions in perfect precision on the bed in an arrangement the housekeeper knows I like. But it's her day off, which means Justin hasn't slept in our bed.

I turn to the left, slipping off my shoes and allowing my toes to curl into the thick pile. I love the luxurious feel of expensive carpet beneath my feet, even if I rarely go barefoot at home.

I pad toward the expansive walk-in robes, matching his and hers, large enough to house an entire apartment. As I enter Justin's side all the breath whooshes out of my lungs.

It's empty.

He's taken everything. There's nothing left, not even a tie or a stray sock. My legs give way and I slide down the wall, landing on my butt with a bump that shoots pain straight up my spine. I stare at the empty shelves, the hangers, the shoe racks, finally absorbing the impact that my marriage is over.

Helplessness swamps me. I did this. I pushed and pushed until I left him no option but to leave. I want to cry but I don't. Tears never help anything. Besides, I learned a long time ago to never show weakness and old habits die hard.

I pick myself up off the floor and shuffle back into the bedroom. I need to find my phone and call the best damn divorce lawyer in town. But as I grab my bag I hear keys in the door and my heart gives a betraying leap. I'm pathetic that even now I still harbor hope he won't leave me.

I take my time descending the stairs, not wanting to appear too eager and because sliding down that wall has really jarred my sore back. Just as well, as I hear the raucous voices of my children and my mother-in-law's reserved tones. Not Justin after all.

I'm eager to see my girls but hide my disappointment as best I can that Justin isn't with them as I come down the last few stairs and they catch sight of me.

"Mom!" Ellen flies toward me, her ecstatic expression alleviating some of the darkness in my heart, as she barrels into me and I stagger a tad.

Jessie follows at a more sedate pace, but she hugs me too. "Glad you're okay, Mom."

"I've missed you two." I envelop them in a hug, my throat clogging. I'm never over-emotional and rarely in front of my girls but they are the one good thing in my life and I squeeze them tight.

I lock gazes with May over the girls' heads. Hers is icy and her mouth is twisted in disapproval.

"You should've told us you were coming home today," she says, curt and judgmental.

"Last minute decision." I release the girls, who hover around me rather than run off as I expect. They must've really missed me.

"I was tired of being stuck in the hospital and can recover just as well at home."

May glances around, as if expecting Justin to pop up.

"I took a taxi home." *Your precious son isn't as chivalrous as you think.* "What are you doing here?"

"The girls wanted to pick up a few things to bring back with them to my place."

She's waiting for me to say not to bother, now I'm home they'll stay with me. But I need to source an attorney and have another conversation with Justin, hopefully more civil than the last, and I don't want the girls privy to it.

"Thanks for looking after them." I muster my best subservient voice. "If you could have them for another night or two, it'll give me time to sort things out."

She nods, not surprised in the least by my request, which can only mean one thing.

She knows.

Of course she knows. Justin has always been a mommy's boy and I bet he ran it past her first before telling me about the divorce. Bastard. I imagine May would've done a jig when she heard he'd been contemplating such a drastic step and given him a healthy shove in the direction of the best family specialist lawyer in Chicago.

I hate that a divorce plays right into her hands. She'll be gloating over this, triumphant that once again she'll be the number one woman in her son's life. But I won't let them strong-arm me and I need to let May know that. I'm not some meek idiot they can push around.

I squeeze the girls' shoulders and release them. "Girls, why don't you go grab the stuff you want while I chat with Gran?"

Jessie bounds past me, but Ellen lingers.

She gnaws on her bottom lip, staring up at me with wide, worried eyes. "Why can't we stay at home with you, Mom?"

My heart swells. At least my daughters care about me if nobody else in this family does. I stroke her hair. "Because I'm still sore after the accident and I need more time to recover. But I love you girls and I promise as soon as I'm feeling better you'll be back home where you belong, okay?"

She nods, her eyes solemn and still clouded with concern. "Okay." She wraps her arms around my waist and snuggles, the feel of her familiar hug going a long way to soothe my battered soul. "I'm glad you're out of the hospital. Gran and Aunt Shamira went to hospital too and I don't want anyone else to have to go."

That's news to me and it's only then that I notice a splint-like brace around May's right wrist.

"You're a good girl, El, but I'll be fine." I ease her arms away and drop a kiss on the top of her head. "Off you go and pack some more stuff."

She runs up the stairs, skipping every second one as usual, and my throat tightens further. I'm more fragile than I think if the sight of my girls doing everyday things is making me want to bawl.

I hate how short-tempered I've been with them lately, caught up in my deception with Aaron and harboring guilt over deliberately hurting Justin. My marriage has been in a bad place for so long I somehow ended up blaming it all on him when I know that's not true.

My inherent insecurities have caused this. I've been pushing Justin away for a long time, before he had the chance to do it to me. A stupid, stupid, mistake I'll now pay dearly for.

"We can talk in the dining room," May says, sounding annoyingly imperious in *my* home.

Yeah, she definitely knows and is taking full advantage of the situation.

"What's this about you and Shamira being in hospital?"

She waves away my question with her good hand, like anything I say is of little consequence already. "I had a fall and sprained my wrist."

"And Shamira?"

Her gaze darts away, like she's hiding something. "She ingested something toxic and was unwell at her launch. Probably made up a batch of something without the proper balance of ingredients."

I hate being spoken down to but I'm not really interested in either of them, am only asking out of curiosity, so I shrug in response. I've never been one to offer false platitudes or appear solicitous when I don't give a crap. I have more important things to worry about.

"But you're not interested in the state of our health, are you?" She pins me with a hostile glower I've never seen in all the years I've been a part of this family. "Justin has left you and I want to make one thing clear."

She takes a step forward, invading my personal space, and I resist the urge to shove her out of my face. "You will not drag this family through the mud. You will not taint us in any way or ruin our reputation—"

"And if I do?" I fling back, not willing to be lectured to by her. I've put up with her from necessity all these years and if my marriage is truly over, May High-and-Mighty Parker is one thing I definitely won't miss. "What are you going to do about it?"

"Don't push me, Ashlin." She jabs a bony finger into my chest and I gape in surprise. "You have no idea what this family is capable of when we need to protect our own."

She's full of it and I'm not tolerating her BS a second longer. "Listen up, Mother-in-law dearest. You can't threaten me because I know too much and I'm not afraid to get down and dirty. I know people. People who would find what I have to say about your precious business very interesting."

It's an idle threat because my girls are Parkers and I would never do anything to jeopardize their stake in the family fortune. But I'm sick of this woman bullying me. "So back the hell off."

To her credit she doesn't retreat. I'm the one who's forced to take a step back when I hear the girls clamoring down the stairs again.

I glimpse pure, unadulterated hatred in her narrowed eyes before I spin on my heel and walk away. I need to say goodbye to my girls, then instigate proceedings with a lawyer.

No one intimidates me, least of all my lousy husband and his interfering mother.

CHAPTER THIRTY-ONE
SHAMIRA

Trent is driving me nuts.

I should be grateful he's back to being caring and solicitous since I got discharged from the hospital: tucking extra pillows behind my back, bringing me frequent cups of chamomile tea, stacking new magazines within easy reach. But his constant attention grates; he hasn't mentioned anything about what I told him, and I have no idea if he's playing the doting husband because I'm unwell or because he's forgiven me.

I'm pretty sure if he revealed some dark secret from his past I'd be just as angry. It's like he's forgotten about it though and that's what makes me wary. Is this an act or has he truly moved on and accepted my past?

"Can I get you anything else?" He perches on the end of the sofa by my feet and rests his hand on my lower leg. "Are you hungry?"

"I'm fine."

I don't sound it. I'm snappish and he recoils slightly.

"Sorry, I'm still feeling a tad queasy."

A lie, but I can't tell him the truth; that ever since I discovered I'd been poisoned I've been wondering if he did it.

He had the motivation. He'd been so disgusted with me when I told him about the prostitution… had he wanted to teach me a lesson? To punish me for not telling him sooner?

I don't want to believe it. Trent is a pacifist and always has been. I can't imagine him wanting to harm anyone or anything, let alone me. But I'd lied to him and we all have our tipping point. And he is a Parker after all.

Ashlin is the only other person I suspect would want to harm me considering how our last conversation went but she wasn't at the launch. So who did it? The uncertainty is making me go a little crazy.

"Do you want to take the anti-nausea meds the doc prescribed?" He stands, ready to be of assistance, almost too eager. Trying to make amends for his guilt?

And so the whirlwind of thoughts and suspicion begins again, around and around, making me crave answers more than ever.

"No, I want to rest." I close my eyes, clamping down on the urge to yell at him to leave me the hell alone, but I feel him watching me. It makes me uncomfortable when I usually love being the center of his world.

He touches my toes and I jump, my eyelids snapping open. "What?"

"I want you to know I'm okay with all that stuff you told me about your past." He scrubs a hand over his face; it does little to erase the worry lines furrowing his brow. "I didn't handle it very well and I'm sorry."

He squeezes my foot and a small part of me melts. "When I saw you lying on the floor unconscious, it put things in perspective for me." He comes closer and kneels near me, his solicitousness surprisingly soothing when a moment ago I wanted him out of my sight. "I love you and I'm sorry you had to go through such a tough time. I know how lucky I am, having a privileged upbringing, so I have no clue what I would've done in your situation. And ultimately you saved your mom, regardless for how long, and you should never regret that." He brushes his knuckles along my cheek, tenderness in his eyes. "You're everything to me and I don't want to lose you, ever."

A fine speech that should gladden my heart but all I can think is whether he'd feel the same way if he knew all of it?

I need to tell him.

About the baby.

About the abortion.

About why I did it.

But I can't speak, the truth a constant barb lodged deep, threatening to eradicate my perfect life.

He leans over and slides his arms around me gently, like I'll break. I swallow back tears because while my body is recovering I doubt my heart will ever be the same.

"I'm not going anywhere." I snuggle into his chest, the wool fibers of his sweater tickling my nose.

I mean it, too. I will tell him when the time is right. Then I'll fight for us.

But in the meantime I need to figure out who the hell tried to kill me.

CHAPTER THIRTY-TWO

MAY

I don't take kindly to threats. Percy had been an expert, dishing them out willy-nilly in his quest to keep me under his thumb. I'd grown immune to them after a while, especially after I learned my husband was a spineless bully who liked to talk big but rarely followed through.

I have a feeling Ashlin is made of similar stock, all bluster with not much substance, but I can't take a chance. The company is entering a precarious period and the last thing I need is a bitter, soon-to-be-ex-daughter-in-law wreaking havoc; especially if the rumors are true. I don't like hearing that not only is my daughter-in-law having an affair, but the man she's involved with happens to be Parker Partnership's biggest rival.

I hadn't liked Ashlin's threat, that she knows too much about the Parkers and isn't afraid to get down and dirty. I doubt Justin would discuss too much about the company's day-to-day operations with his wife but Ashlin would've been privy to her husband's phone, his computer, his paperwork at home...

Ashlin could definitely cause trouble for the company and our upcoming plans, which means I need to discover how much she knows from Justin.

With a brisk knock I enter Justin's office. His PA nods, indicating I can go straight through. I don't want to have this conversation, preferring to stay out of the machinations of my son's divorce. But

Ashlin is a scorned woman and her bitterness could spill over. I want to ensure Justin lets her know the importance of discretion at this crucial time. This divorce needs to be kept quiet until the company sale has gone through. It's imperative.

I enter Justin's office and find him staring at the million-dollar view of Chicago's central business district sprawled fifty stories below. He works hard, rarely stops, so to find him looking aimlessly out the window speaks volumes.

"You're distracted." I approach his desk and take a seat opposite. "Want to talk about it?"

He swivels to face me, surprisingly relaxed for someone about to face a she-devil for court proceedings, before sitting behind his desk. "Not really."

"Unfortunately, I think we have to." I clasp my hands in my lap. I often do this when talking to my son so I won't give in to the urge to grab him by the lapels and shake some sense into him. "I ran into Ashlin at the house earlier."

His eyebrows rise. "She's home?"

"Probably discharged herself from the hospital, I didn't ask." I'm many things, a hypocrite isn't one of them. I don't care why Ashlin's home; I don't want her interfering in company business. "She's angry."

He shrugs, infuriatingly calm. "I told her I was moving my stuff out while she was in hospital. I guess she saw I meant it when she got home."

"So that was behind her spiteful outburst."

He frowns and sits forward, the tension of discussing his wife visible in the sudden bunching of his shoulders. "What did she say?"

"Empty threats. At least, I hope so." I search for the right words to probe him for information and finally decide there's no easy way to say what has to be said. "I mentioned to you there've been rumors about her affairs."

"I don't give a f—"

"The rumors imply her latest has been with Aaron Grosber."

Anger darkens my son's eyes and his knuckles stand out where his hands inter-lace on his desk, and I wish I could make this all go away.

"She's screwing around with our number one *opposition*?"

Fury laces his tone and I wonder what makes him madder, the fact his wife is sleeping around or the fact it's with the company's biggest rival.

"Apparently. So when I tried to calm her—" not necessarily true, but Justin doesn't have to know how protective I am of my family and our business, "—she said she knows people and isn't afraid to give them information, which implied she could hurt us in some way. Can she?"

Justin pales and slumps back in his chair, as tightness grips my chest. I've fought too long and too hard to protect the Parker fortune to let some vindictive woman get the better of me. "Tell me what she knows."

"Not a lot, but I have offloaded after work occasionally." He grimaces and scrubs a hand over his face. "I didn't think she was listening half the time. Plus my den's always open so if she really wanted to know what's going on in the company, she could have found… well… anything."

The tightness in my chest spreads and I hope I'm not having a heart attack. My doctor pronounced me exceedingly fit for sixty-four at my last check-up and I doubt having a birthday since would change that. But hearing the possible treachery my daughter-in-law can inflict on the family business certainly does.

"What do you want me to do?" Justin's head falls forward and I hate seeing him so defeated.

He's done nothing wrong. He'd married to solidify the Parkers, a union guaranteed to accentuate his power and standing in Chicago. He'd trusted his wife, invested time and effort into building a family with her. It wasn't his fault Ashlin desecrated her vows and made a mockery of her marriage.

"Play nice. Don't antagonize her. Make sure she knows how important it is to keep the divorce under wraps for now. And for goodness' sake, make sure she can't access anything regarding the company." I sound snippy and try to soften my tone. "I know how you feel—"

"No, you don't. You have no idea what this feels like!" He thumps the desk with his fist, sending documents scattering.

"Actually, I do."

I never tarnished my husband's reputation to our children. He died five years ago, not long after Grayson left, and I'd wanted to put the past behind me and move on. Part of my rationale for selling the company now is to shed the pall Percy cast over me, even in business. I'm ready to make changes, to show everybody I'm no longer a faux grieving widow but a woman in control.

But I know Justin. He'll brood over his decision to end his marriage and will probably blame himself. I don't want that. So I'll tell him the truth about his father in the hope he'll gain some clarity over his own situation.

He pins me with a curious gaze. "What do you mean?"

"Your father had numerous affairs. Too many to count. So I do know what you're going through."

As my son stares at me in shock, I glance down at my lap, surprised to see my hands clasped so tight the knuckles stand out. I force myself to relax. Getting wound up over Percival's antics never serves me well.

"I tolerated him and pretended our marriage was okay for the sake of appearances. And because our significant finances merged when we married, divorcing would've been too difficult." I raise my eyes to meet his. "I don't know, maybe I wasn't as brave as you, and divorce isn't common in our social circle, but that doesn't mean his infidelities didn't matter." I huff out a breath. "I was appalled by his indiscretions but I put up with him."

"I don't know what to say." His gaze darts away, uncomfortable and floundering.

I take pity on him. "I'm only telling you so you don't beat yourself up over ending your marriage. I had no choice. Your father and I both came from prestigious families and understood the need for discreetness in all aspects of our lives. We would never have brought disrepute on the family or the company so I turned a blind eye to your father's infidelities. When he died, it was almost a relief. But you don't have to do that. Once the company is sold you can do anything you want."

His gaze flies back to mine and he eyeballs me with admiration. "You're a strong woman, Mom."

"I did what I had to do." I shrug, like the years of heartache spent with a philandering tyrant meant little. "Which is what you need to do too. Proceed with caution and do whatever it takes to divest yourself of Ashlin without rancor."

He nods, his brow furrowed in contemplation. "I'm taking care of it."

"Good." I stand, relieved Justin accepted my interference and will be on guard moving forward. "One last word of warning?"

He manages a wry smile. "You always get the last word in."

I smile back, hoping he'll heed my advice and not jeopardize everything we've worked so hard to achieve. "Be careful who you trust."

Justin's head tilts to one side as he studies me, but I've said all that needs to be said.

Divorcing a woman like Ashlin, he'll soon discover what I mean.

CHAPTER THIRTY-THREE

RIA

That evening, I sit in front of my computer, knowing what I have to do but too scared to do it. It's easy coming up with a plan. It's the execution that's a bitch.

Grayson hasn't answered my email so now I have to dig deeper. I tell myself I'm doing good asking Lars to hack into America's biggest database via the dark web in order to find Grayson, that I'm doing it to protect Shelley and the family. All very altruistic but how will I explain it to Lars?

There's only so many times "I need this for an article I'm writing" will work. Besides, if Lars is caught, he won't protect me and that could mean prosecution for me too. What would happen to Shelley? But it's the thought of my daughter that's propelling me to do this because I want to keep her safe from whoever is targeting our family.

I'm still not convinced. But I need this information desperately and as my fingers creep toward the keyboard to contact Lars, the doorbell rings. Annoyed by my immense relief, I pad to the door. I open it and shock renders me speechless.

"Long time no see." Grayson, my long-lost ex-husband, offers me the bashful grin I used to love. "Can I come in?"

I want to slam the door in his face. I want to slug him. I want to pummel his chest with my fists for all the pain he caused when he vanished five years ago.

But I'd been about to let a trusted colleague commit a federal offence to locate him so I open the door, biting back my first response of "screw you". He hurt me. Badly. I'd loved him unreservedly and he threw it back in my face the day he walked out of here without a backward glance. As for that photo… no, I can never forgive him for the secret life he hid from me and how it sickened me to see evidence of it.

I follow him into the lounge, hating that he remembers his way around and isn't the least bit ashamed to show it. Worse, I find myself admiring him. He's wearing low-slung denim frayed at the cuffs, a soft cotton T-shirt in the palest blue and sneakers. There's a little extra grey in the soft brown curls skimming his collar and when he turns to face me again I note the fine lines around his eyes and between his brows.

His eyes are the same though, bright blue bordering on aquamarine. Parker eyes, though Justin's are hazel, and I instantly feel disloyal making the comparison even though the man standing in front of me with practiced nonchalance abandoned me and doesn't deserve my loyalty.

"Miss me?"

Damn, his lips quirk in the same laconic way they used to and I feel a lick of heat deep within. Not good.

"What are you doing here, Grayson?" Thankfully my voice doesn't quiver, despite the confusion rioting through me.

"I came because you reached out to me." Concern deepens his eyes to indigo. "Are you okay? Shelley?"

Like it's the most natural thing in the world to ask after all this time. Idiot.

"We're fine." The urge to hit him again is strong but I curl my fingers into my palms to stifle it and tilt my head up to stare him down. "Shelley's asleep and I'd like to keep it that way."

The last thing I need is my daughter being bewildered by a father she can barely remember reappearing out of the blue for goodness knows how long before absconding again.

His expression softens, the flicker of affection in his eyes stabbing at my resolve to tell him to get out when I need him the most. "How is she?"

"Fine," I snap, folding my arms in a purely defensive gesture that will do little if he actually comes within a foot of me.

Because for some unknown reason my body is reacting in a traitorous way, flooding with heat and tingling in places it shouldn't, remembering exactly how good things had once been between us. Annoyingly, my cheeks are burning, a beacon to my irrational physical reaction to seeing him again.

"You look frazzled," he says, his drawl making me bristle with indignation and intensifying the flush scorching my cheeks.

I muster my best disapproving frown. "That's what happens when you show up on my doorstep after five years of no contact."

He has the grace to look sheepish. "I have my reasons."

Is he for real? I want to throttle him for breaking my heart and leaving me a single mom when Shelley needed him most. I see the way she idolizes Justin and Trent, desperate for a father figure when her own doesn't care about her.

"Don't I know it," I mutter, turning away before I say something I'll regret.

Then again, why do I care? I owe this man nothing. He ripped my heart out when he vanished. One minute we'd been happy, the next he'd gone, with no explanation.

Sure, he'd made no secret of his dissatisfaction within the company, but I'd never expected those feelings to coalesce into destruction. Then that photo of him in a compromising position had arrived and I assumed that was the real reason behind his vanishing act. It sickened me, to think I'd loved him, lived with him, married him, when I'd never really known him at all.

After what I'd seen in that photo I should be glad he walked away from our marriage. But he'd shattered our family and I'll never forgive him for it.

"You never would've reached out to me unless it's urgent." He's snuck up behind me and places a hand on my shoulder. Ashamedly, I let it linger for a moment because his touch is so familiar and feels good, before shrugging it off and spinning around. "I'm worried about you."

"Too little, too late." I glare at him, wondering if he can feel the anger radiating off me, making me feel like I'm lit from within. "I have no idea what you're really doing here when you could've answered me online."

I see him hesitate, as if he's contemplating telling me the truth, before he shakes his head. "It's been five years since I left, Ria, and nothing. You could've found me any number of times but you chose not to. So the very fact you did now means something serious is going on and I want to know what."

I should be relieved he's here, that I can show him the evidence and tell him everything in person. But the longer he stares at me with those startling blue eyes filled with concern, the harder it is for me to remember to hate him for destroying us.

I huff out a breath. "I need your help."

"I think I know why."

My eyebrows shoot upward. "How do you know?"

"Because when you reached out I knew it had to be something big so I hacked into your computer," he says, sounding more serious than I've ever heard, his admission rendering me speechless.

"You're shocked." He reaches out to touch my hand and I yank it away, finally getting my head and mouth to work in sync.

"What the hell is wrong with you?" My chest tightens with fury, indignation making me shake. "How dare you."

Even though I'm desperate for his help, I feel violated. Having this man delve into my life without my permission feels dirty. My palm itches with the urge to slap him, when I've never slapped anyone in my entire life.

He drags in a breath and blows it out, shiftiness in his furtive gaze as he looks away. "I saw the emails so I assume that's what this is about."

I don't know him anymore. Considering what I'd seen in that photo five years ago maybe I never did. When we first got together twelve years ago I thought I knew everything about him. How he liked poached eggs on toast smeared with avocado. How he liked lounging on a Sunday night watching reality TV with me tucked into his side. How he liked me on top as many times a week as we could muster.

My cheeks flush again. It must be from aggravation. I need to keep telling myself this.

"You had no right to hack into my computer." I collapse onto the nearest chair, grateful when he keeps his distance and sits opposite me, a coffee table between us.

"I know, but I kind of freaked out when you contacted me," he says, draping his hand across the back of the chair like he used to and once again I'm assailed by memories of a time where I thought this man was my everything. "And for what it's worth, I'm sorry for accessing your computer."

I don't speak, crossing my arms, and he eventually continues. "I'm sorry for a lot of things." He thumps a fist to his chest, over his heart. "Walking away from what we had killed me in here, but I had to. What I was doing left me no choice."

"I don't want to hear it." Bile burns a path up my throat at the thought of what he'd been doing before he left. "Your perversions have nothing to do with me now."

Confusion creases his brow. "Perversions?"

He has the audacity to feign innocence and I almost lose it. I want to rant and rave and fling something at him but I don't want Shelley waking.

"Cut the crap." I drag in a breath, willing my rage to subside. "I saw the photo of you."

He stares at me, surprise widening his eyes. "What are you talking about?"

"You're unbelievable." I leap to my feet and march into the study to grab my laptop. When I swivel to march back into the lounge room, he's behind me and I will my senses not to inhale his familiar woodsy aftershave.

"Here. Take a look at this and tell me I'm imagining you led a secret life behind my back."

I stab at a few buttons and bring up the photo I'd only looked at once when it landed in my inbox like an undetonated bomb five years ago, the day after my marriage imploded.

He leans closer, peering at the photo of him naked and being whipped by a dominatrix, while I grit my teeth at his nearness. "That's not me."

"You're full of—"

"It's shopped," he says, pointing at the neck. "They've inserted my head here and you can't see the join because of the collar."

"Bullshit," I say, but I find my gaze drawn to where he's pointing.

When the photo had first landed I'd taken one glance at it, burst into tears and run for the bathroom where I'd vomited. It had made me sick to think the guy I'd loved, the guy who'd rubbed my feet at night and made me hot chocolates with tiny marshmallows, had led an S&M lifestyle so far removed from our marriage I could barely comprehend it.

It hadn't entered my head the photo could be doctored because he'd already fled our marriage the day before and the photo merely proved why.

"Ria, look at me."

His low, gravelly voice washes over me and I stifle my visceral reaction to lean into him.

"Look at me." He touches my shoulder and I spin away to throw off his touch. "That isn't me. I never cheated on you during our marriage and I sure as hell didn't go in for anything like this."

I want to yell that he's lying, that if he's hacked into my computer he's probably done something to the photo to make it look fake. But I risk a glance at him and see he's guileless, confusion still darkening those memorable eyes.

And against my better judgment I believe him.

"Then why did you leave?"

He startles, like I've electrocuted him. "You think I left because of *that*?"

"Then why else? It's not as if you gave me another explanation," I whisper, not really wanting to hear the answer. Because if that incriminating photo is fake and had nothing to do with Grayson doing a vanishing act, that means him leaving had something to do with me and I can't stomach it.

I'd thought we were a great couple. Sure, we had our problems like any other marriage. We argued, mostly over money and the frequency with which he dipped into the bottomless Parker family account. I wanted to be independent, he was used to having whatever he wanted handed to him on a silver platter. But I could never fault his love for Shelley, and me most days, which made his leaving all the harder to bear. No one understood it. Not even May had an answer for me, which is why she's looked after me all these years.

"I'll try to explain…" He pinches the bridge of his nose, a classic Grayson-ism that catapults me back in time to when I knew the gesture meant he'd be scrambling for excuses. "Back then, you thought I tolerated working for the Parker Partnership. But what you didn't know…"

He scowls and it does little to detract from his handsome face, a face I've explored in exquisite detail with my fingers and my mouth. Damn memories. "I delved into something I shouldn't have and ended up being threatened because of it. A major threat, the kind I couldn't ignore because of what it could do to us."

He drags in a deep breath and blows it out. "I couldn't risk you or Shelley being harmed so I had to leave. That was the price I had to pay to keep you both safe."

I stare at him in disbelief, stunned that the man I'd lived with for seven years hadn't trusted me enough to tell me the truth all those years ago.

"I couldn't tell you. I had no idea who was listening. They could've bugged our computers or cells and I couldn't risk it." He shrugs, like his ridiculous tale straight out of a spy movie means nothing. "They threatened you and Shelley, said I had to leave or else."

I shake my head. It doesn't clear the fog making logical thinking difficult. The enormity of his confession is baffling. "But you could've written down all this stuff to explain. You could've told me!"

"I didn't want to put you or Shel in danger and if I'd told you the truth, knowing you, you would've dug deeper to try and discover who was behind it all." He sends me a pointed stare. "Like you're doing now with those other emails."

Damn him for being right as bitterness tightens my throat. "There had to have been another way."

"Do you think I didn't exhaust every opportunity thinking about how to fix it before I left?" He lays his hands out, palms up, like he has nothing to hide. "I took their threats seriously and they made it clear I had to leave. I couldn't risk exposing you and Shel to any possible danger."

I stare at him, stupefied, that even now he's somehow twisting his own warped motivation and putting it back on us. "How noble of you. I mean, you had other options, like not sticking your nose into other people's business in the first place! Why couldn't you just do your job, stay in line like a good Parker, and ultimately keep us safe?"

My voice has risen and I calm it with effort, not wanting to wake Shelley. "You did general IT work and dabbled in hacking at home. So what made you think you could do stuff like that at work—"

"You're in over your head." His solemnity would be alarming if not for the fact I gave up taking advice from this selfish man a long time ago. "If I hacked into your computer, the bad guys can too so whoever sent those emails is targeting this family for some reason and I don't want you or Shel to be any part of it."

"Too late, considering they only sent me those emails." I eyeball him, staring him down, neither of us willing to give an inch.

"Have you asked the rest of the family if they've received any?"

"Of course, but…" I trail off, knowing I'll have to tell him the rest eventually but still too rattled by his revelations to know what to believe or not. "There've been a few accidents. Ashlin, your mom, Shamira—"

"What kind of accidents?" He pales and reaches out as if he wants to comfort me.

"Ashlin was run off the road and her car totaled, someone on a bike pushed your mom over and Shamira was poisoned."

"Fuck." He drags a hand through his hair and I resist the urge to smooth it down like I used to. "And you think it's linked to those emails you received?"

"Has to be. But there's been no demand for money to keep everything quiet so what's the end game?"

He pins me with an astute stare. "That's why you contacted me, because you've tried to find out who's behind it and you haven't had any luck."

As much as it pains me to acknowledge I need his assistance because I'm failing, I nod. "I used my best contact for online traces but he's come up blank. I need your help."

"I'll need access to your computer—"

"Don't you already have it?"

He has the grace to blush at my direct jibe. "Ria, I was terrified something had happened to you or Shel when you reached out, and that's why I hacked your computer, but I wouldn't invade your privacy again. And I know this is a lot to comprehend but I'm here to help."

"How noble."

I bite back the rest of what I want to say. *Why didn't you trust me enough to tell me what was going on with you back then? Why didn't you love me enough to stick around? Why didn't you have the guts to confront whoever was threatening us rather than running away?*

When an awkward silence stretches between us, he says, "I want to see Shel."

My heart plummets. "No. You gave up parental rights around the time you left without a backward glance."

His eyes darken with a surprising anguish. "I've told you why I had to leave—"

"And I'm not buying it." Fury makes my words fire out like staccato gunfire. "*You* made the choice to dabble in something you didn't understand. *You* brought that danger on us. You want me to applaud your nobility in taking us out of the equation? Here you go." I slow-clap. "But don't for one second think you can waltz back into our lives now and try to pick up where we left off. I need your help but that's where it ends. Besides, if you're back, doesn't that mean whoever you fled from five years ago will know so the danger's still present?"

He's silent, scrabbling for some kind of response that I'll shoot down anyway.

"Just go." I pad to the door and open it, staving off a shiver as a cold blustery wind blows in. Or maybe it has more to do with my fear that Grayson's right: if he knows I'm trying to track down who's targeting the family, maybe the people doing this might too? I'd never put Shelley in danger willingly but what if I already have? "I'll forward those emails and if you need remote access to my PC let me know."

"I'll be staying at Mom's," he says, as he eventually brushes past me and out the door. "Please be careful. We don't know who we're dealing with and until I can trace who's behind this I'm worried about you—"

I close the door in his face, hating that my hands are shaking, hating that he's made me feel something more. Because for those few seconds when he explained that he'd come home to protect me from some unforeseen danger, I felt drawn to him on a level deeper than a residual physical attraction. I felt... *something*, and I don't want to.

Grayson is my past.

Keeping Shelley safe is my future.

That means I need his help to discover who is targeting this family and why, but that's where it ends.

CHAPTER THIRTY-FOUR

MAY

I tuck my granddaughters into bed and kiss them goodnight, when the doorbell rings. Their faces light with hope and my heart bleeds for what these poor kids are going through. They obviously crave attention and affection, and while they're in my care I'll lavish both on them.

"Is that Dad or Mom?" Ellen's expectant expression makes the ache in my chest intensify.

"Don't be silly," Jessie says, sounding older than her eleven years, but the hope in her eyes can't be quelled despite her know-it-all attitude. "We spoke to Dad an hour ago and he said he's still at *work*. And Mom's recovering from her accident so it can't be her."

I don't miss the sarcasm lacing Jessie's voice when she speaks about her father's job. I remember she mentioned waiting up for him every night, so she may resent his long hours at the office. It's not ideal with a custody battle looming in the not too distant future. Considering her age Jessie must've seen and heard things between her parents, and being more astute than Ellen she may be holding a grudge against her father's frequent absenteeism at work. Kids focus on the oddest things because Justin more than makes up for his long hours at the office by spending time with the girls on the weekend. But it sounds like Jessie's feeling particularly vulnerable. I'll have a quiet word with Justin about it.

If Jessie has picked up on the animosity between her parents, it won't be long before Ellen becomes aware of it too. I don't like my narcissistic daughter-in-law but I have to begrudgingly admit she's a good mother who loves her daughters, and hate that a custody battle has the potential to break that bond: the Parker fortune will ensure we don't lose, meaning Justin will gain full custody and Ashlin won't get to see her daughters often. I know what that feels like all too well and I regret not being more present in Christine's life.

This time a knock sounds at the door, a loud, annoying rap. "I think your aunt Christine is expecting a visitor." The fib slides easily from my lips, as I want the girls to get some much-needed sleep. They have dark circles under their eyes, indicating they haven't been entirely comfortable sleeping away from home. I don't blame them, considering Ashlin doesn't believe in sleepovers—at least not with their grandmother—so they rarely stay over.

The doorbell rings again, insistent and annoying.

"Goodnight, girls. I'll see you in the morning."

"It's way too late for visitors," Jessie mutters, sullen now that hope has been dashed, turning to face the wall and pulling the covers over her head.

I agree and wonder who could be on my doorstep at nine p.m. on a weeknight. I don't get many visitors as a rule considering I don't have any friends. Acquaintances impressed by my fortune, yes, but true friends had fallen by the wayside early in my marriage when I became increasingly insular out of necessity. Anyone I got close to, Percival ended up sleeping with and I couldn't tolerate it after the first few indiscretions. It had been difficult enough pretending in front of my children that everything was all right but having to do it in front of the women betraying me had become intolerable.

"Goodnight, Gran." Ellen blows a kiss and closes her eyes, always the dutiful child.

When the doorbell rings for a third time, I wish I'd installed those ugly, monstrous gates Percy had wanted to keep out unwelcome visitors, mutter an unladylike curse under my breath and descend the stairs. Christine has popped out to pick up her favorite ice cream and has probably forgotten her keys. However, when I open the door, it isn't my daughter on the front step.

It's my youngest son.

I gape in shock and cling to the doorway as I sway a little. "Grayson?"

I sound idiotic, saying his name like that, but I'm reeling, having him turn up like this without any warning.

It's been five years since I've seen him and almost that long since he made contact, a brief, hastily scrawled postcard from California that told me next to nothing. My bold, charismatic, charming son who'd been independent since he could walk, who'd always had wanderlust thrumming through his veins, has finally come home and I'm torn between wanting to hug him and throttle him.

He grins, the familiarity of it after all this time so poignant my throat tightens. "Hey, Mom. You don't look a day older since the last time I saw you."

Of course he aims for levity. It's what he does. But I won't put up with it this time, not after I've only heard from him once in five years via a few scribbled words on the back of a flimsy piece of cardboard.

"You deserve a good hiding but we're both too old for it." I open the door wider and beckon him in.

"I missed you too, Mom." He envelops me in his arms and I stiffen, not willing to give in too easily but unable to keep the joy from filling my heart.

My baby has finally come home.

Justin is my staid, responsible son who'll do anything for the Parker name and I admire him for it. Trent is my dreamer and I've never been particularly tolerant of his soft-hearted ways. But

Grayson is my unabashed favorite; at least, he had been before he ran away. He broke my heart five years ago and I never fully recovered. The fact he hadn't come home for his father's funeral didn't bother me as much as his total disregard for his wife and child, and now he's back I'll make sure he doesn't do anything to hurt them again. I'm protective of Shelley and Ria because I feel bad a son of mine abandoned them. Shoddy behavior indeed.

I wriggle a little and he releases me with a chuckle, knowing he's always had a knack for worming his way into my heart no matter his antics.

"Have you eaten?" I usher him toward the kitchen and he falls in step beside me. It has always been the most comfortable room in the house, the one place where all my children gathered regularly. Petty rifts and differences may have kept them apart like most siblings, but they'd always had to eat and the kitchen had been their go-to place growing up. I miss that.

After Percival died, I envisaged moving into another house, something less ostentatious, but had never summoned the energy. At least, that had been my excuse. The real reason becomes apparent as we enter the kitchen and I glimpse Grayson's unguarded expression: pure, undiluted happiness. He too equates this kitchen with home.

"You sit, I'll help myself to a snack."

"Good, I don't feel like fussing over you because you don't deserve it."

He laughs at my disgruntled response, like he can see right through me and knows how I really feel about having him back home. I watch him move around the kitchen with ease, like he's never left, and that damn lump in my throat returns as he makes quick work of fixing a sandwich.

He's aged, with new lines fanning from the corners of his eyes and mouth. He's leaner too, like he's taken up running. It pains me that I don't know what he does these days, for work or recreation.

Is his favorite food still barbecue pork ribs? Does he still favor light beer over full-strength? Is his penchant for dark chocolate over milk as strong as ever?

He's forty soon and I wonder if that has something to do with his sudden reappearance, some kind of midlife crisis that manifests as guilt for his appalling abandonment of his marriage and his child. Or has he caught wind of the impending sale of the company and expects a slice of lucrative pie?

With his upcoming milestone birthday, I can't imagine having four children in their forties when it only seems like yesterday I'd been that age myself. How fast time has passed and how much has changed. I'd had it all figured out back then, how my life would turn out. Pity I got it so wrong.

"Is it okay if I stay here?" He sits opposite me at the immense dining table, his sandwich untouched, as if he made it as a means to delay conversing rather than hunger. "It's fine if it's not, I can go to a hotel—"

"This is your home, of course you can stay," I snap. "But I need to know what you're doing here and why, after all this time."

He shrugs, finally picking up his sandwich and eating half of it before responding. "I had this insane urge to see my family."

A blatant lie. I see it in his inability to meet my gaze when he'd always been one to look me in the eye. My brash, confident boy who never backed down from anything.

"By family, do you mean us or Ria and Shelley?"

"Both." He ignores my sarcasm but nudges his plate aside, the other half of the sandwich forgotten as tension brackets his mouth. "I stopped by Ria's on the way here."

"And?"

"It didn't go well, but I didn't expect it to." He huffs out a sigh, the grooves around his mouth deepening. "Not that I blame her."

"She's a good woman and an excellent mother," I say, wondering if that's the real reason my prodigal son has returned. A sudden hankering to see the daughter he callously abandoned five years ago? A way to make amends? To seek forgiveness?

As to how Ria will react, I can't speculate. She always adored Grayson but he'd broken her heart and she never spoke of him, even on the few occasions when I tentatively broached the subject to ascertain whether there'd been any contact between them. "Don't mess up her life, okay?"

"I have no intention of doing that." He shoots me a scathing glare so reminiscent of the strong-willed child he'd been that my breath catches in my chest. "I doubt I'll be staying around long so I won't disrupt their lives."

"Then why did you come here?" I fold my arms and survey him with the eyes of a mother who doesn't know this man-child anymore, if I ever did. "There's been a lot going on lately and we've got enough to deal with."

"What do you mean?"

Wariness creeps into his eyes as if he actually cares. Harsh, but my inherent cynicism insists there's more behind my youngest child's reappearance after all these years than any real caring for his family.

"There are big changes afoot in this family and it's not a good time for you to show up out of the blue, without any real explanation."

His raised eyebrow mocks me. "What about the rest?"

"Like?"

"Ria told me Ashlin had a car accident, you were almost run over by a cyclist, and Shamira ended up in hospital after being poisoned." His mouth compresses into a grim line. "You're all okay?"

"Obviously." I wave my bandaged wrist at him. "I'm fine, Shamira's okay, and Ashlin sustained minor injuries and is home now, though I'm looking after her girls until she's back on her feet."

His other eyebrow rises. "Where's Justin?"

I hesitate, not wanting to divulge too much about Justin's divorce to a son I can't trust. I still don't know the real reason he's turned up and until I figure out why, I need to be circumspect.

"He's extremely busy at the moment."

A wry grin twists his mouth. "Isn't he always?"

"He's been a rock for this family," I say, wondering if Grayson feels at all guilty for leaving us. "We've got enough going on without adding your hidden agenda to the mix."

He doesn't refute my accusation, which only proves my gut feeling is right. He has a reason for coming home but won't divulge it to me.

When I eyeball him, daring him to come clean, his gaze slides away to fix on some point over my shoulder. "Don't worry, Mom, I'll be out of here in a few days, max."

He sounds lost, like the little boy who'd once run to me when Justin's teasing became unbearable, and I relent. "Stay as long as you like. Just don't stir up trouble with Ria."

He studies me with open curiosity. "You're awfully protective of my ex-wife."

"She's the mother of my grandchild and I care about them."

He doesn't call me on the use of 'care' rather than 'love'. Then again, none of my children have ever heard me use the L word. I'm not prone to grand gestures or emotional declarations. I'm not hardwired that way. Growing up as an only child with parents who barely tolerated each other, followed by my own matrimonial disaster, ensured I don't love anyone much. I like, I care, and that's where it ends. Unfortunately, my kids know it too.

"Is my old bedroom still available?"

I nod. "You don't have a suitcase?"

"I travel light." He hefts a small duffel bag and once again, his gaze shifts, evasive, and I wonder what secrets my last-born is hiding. "Thanks for letting me crash here, Mom. See you in the morning."

He lays a hand on my shoulder, a brief touch that has me leaning toward him a little, before he leaves the kitchen quickly. I hear him clomp up the stairs, the unfamiliar tread of heavy male boots. I've missed him, even if I'd never admit it. Though his sudden reappearance is baffling, yet another odd occurrence within my family.

I need answers but have no idea how to get them.

CHAPTER THIRTY-FIVE

SHAMIRA

If I was sick of Trent's attentiveness when I initially got out of hospital, his constant hovering a day later is driving me nuts: the endless cups of tea, the repetitive asking if I'm okay, the offers to make me a snack. He's being the perfect husband and I should be grateful, but I'm not used to this much attention and it makes me suspicious, like he's trying too hard to make up for something.

"How about a foot massage?" He sits at the end of the sofa and touches my feet, and I grit my teeth against the urge to shuffle away.

"You've been amazing but I'd really like some me-time, so why don't you head off to bed?"

He must hear something in my faux solicitousness because his brow furrows like I've offended him. But I can't take it any longer. His over-the-top smothering is at complete odds with the way he reacted to my revelation about my past and I can't get it out of my head that someone, probably close to me, tried to poison me to teach me a lesson.

"If you're sure?" He stands, towering over me in a way that makes me oddly uncomfortable.

"I'm sure. Thanks." I blow him a kiss but he leans down to brush his lips against mine, but he doesn't linger and I don't prolong the contact like I normally would.

"Don't stay up too late and wake me if you need anything."

I force a smile. "Shall do."

His knuckles graze my cheek in an affectionate gesture he does often. I usually love it. Tonight, I try not to flinch. It's crazy, this feeling that I can't trust him. He's never done anything to make me doubt him before and even now I can't truly believe he had anything to do with slipping those painkillers into my drink. But I'm on edge and feeling vulnerable. I need some space to think this through logically.

"Goodnight," I say as he heads to the bedroom and he raises a hand in acknowledgement.

I wait until he closes the door before flopping back on the cushions. The bed creaks as he settles and thirty seconds later I hear his soft snores. He always falls asleep the moment his head touches the pillow but I'll wait an extra half hour before I go to bed too. I can't face him any more tonight.

My cell buzzes on the side table next to me and I'm surprised to see it's a text from Christine.

R U HOME?

She's never texted me before so I pause, wondering what she wants, before replying.

YES.

IS TRENT STILL UP?

Her response is odd, like she doesn't want to see her brother. In fact, why hasn't she texted him instead of me? It doesn't make sense. I fire back.

NO.

I'M OUTSIDE. NEED 2 C U. URGENT.

This is weird. Christine and I don't socialize apart from family gatherings, so the fact she wants to see me and not Trent at this time of night is bizarre. Not to mention turning up here without warning. All the Parkers have impeccable manners and would never turn up on someone's doorstep without prior notice.

I pad to the apartment door and open it, stunned when Christine staggers in, weaving left and right before she props up against the nearest wall. She's wearing a black hoodie and jeans, matching boots and beanie, when I've never seen her in anything other than designer gear. But her dark outfit isn't as shocking as a burgeoning black eye, a cut lip and bruises that look scarily like fingermarks circling her neck. Her eyes shock me the most: dull, lifeless, like all the fight has drained out of her.

I swallow back the obvious, "What happened to you?" and settle for closing the door before slipping an arm around her waist to help her inside. She leans against me and I lead her to the sofa I've just vacated, where I ease her onto it. She groans, her face contorting with pain as her hips sink into the cushions.

"I'll be back in a minute," I say, scurrying to the kitchen to fix her a chamomile tea and adding a side glass of brandy to the tray.

When I re-enter the lounge room she's tucked into the sofa like she's trying to disappear, her eyes darting everywhere, scared of her own shadow.

"Here, get this into you." I lay the tray on the coffee table, not surprised when she downs the brandy first.

I wait, not wanting to pry but needing to know how I can help. After what seems like an eternity, she begins to talk.

"I guess you want to know what I'm doing here looking like this?"

"It had crossed my mind," I say, with a reassuring smile. "You don't have to tell me if you don't want to but perhaps you'd feel more comfortable talking to Trent—"

"No." Her objection is quick, vehement. "I'm sick of the Parkers judging me."

Ah, so that's why she's come to me. She figures the hippy will be more accepting of whatever or whoever has caused this.

"Do you need medical assistance—"

"No." She shakes her head, before letting out a heartfelt sigh. "Back home, I go to the same people all the time. Vetted guys with regular clientele dealing in high-end stuff."

She announces her drug addiction calmly, like she expects I already know. I don't, but I've done worse than pop pills or snort coke so I can't judge. Now I understand why she's come here and hasn't gone home—she doesn't want her mother to see her like this—and why she asked if her brother is in bed. Luckily Trent sleeps like the dead so won't hear us talking, and wake. Christine would clam up in front of him.

"I know this is a lot to dump on you when we've never been close, but this happened nearby and I thought I could clean up before heading home…" She trails off, shame staining her cheeks crimson. "I'm in for one mother of a lecture from Mom."

Her smile is lopsided but I don't buy her flippancy. She's hurting and considering what I've been through in my past, I can identify.

"You can stay as long as you like." I touch her arm, offering reassurance. "We've all done stuff we wish we could change."

"You're not judging me?" She sounds hesitant, embarrassed, with an underlying hint of defiance.

"I'd never do that." I shake my head and offer her a genuine smile. "Not my style."

"Thanks." She sighs, then winces, wrapping an arm around her middle. I assume it's for comfort before realizing she could be in more pain than I think.

"Are you sure you don't need medical attention? I can get a doctor to do a house call—"

"I'll be fine." She stares at me for a few moments, as if trying to fathom why I'm being so understanding, before she gives a slight nod to indicate she trusts me. "I've had worse."

My eyes widen and she barks out a sharp laugh. "I got into the whole drug scene early, in my late teens. I was stupid then, didn't do careful research like I do now, so ended up mixing with the wrong crowd and copping the odd beating when they robbed me. These days back home in New York I only go to regulars so the risk of this happening," she points to her bruised face, "is minimal."

"So what happened tonight?"

"I'm checking into rehab tomorrow so I wanted one last hurrah tonight." She cringes and defeat makes her slump further into the cushions. "I don't know what I was thinking." She shudders, her eyes darkening, hiding a world of pain, and I want to hug her. But we've never been close and I'm not sure if she'd appreciate any kind of touch right now.

"I just wanted one last chance to feel good, you know?"

She's trying to justify her behavior but she doesn't have to do that with me. I'm the queen of explaining away the things I've done in the past. Not that she knows it, though I did hint at it a few moments ago by saying we've all done stuff we're not proud of. But the less the Parkers know about me the better. Because I have a bone-deep dread that if they start digging around, they won't just discover the truth about my past, they'll find out what I've done in an effort not to have a child.

I risk a quick pat on her hand and as expected, she flinches away. "Stay here as long as you like. No questions asked."

Her eyes fill with tears and she dashes them away with the back of her hand, embarrassment tingeing her cheeks. "You're amazing, you know that?"

"Not really." I shrug, but her praise buoys me. Apart from Ria, who's always been nice to me, the rest of the Parkers don't really acknowledge I exist. I'm the kooky, hippy weirdo to them, someone to be tolerated because I'm Trent's wife. They never *see* the real me, never have. It has suited me because I don't want them delving deeper into my life, but it's nice to have Christine acknowledge I've helped her. "I know what it's like to live with secrets, so take as much time as you like to recover."

She studies me but doesn't ask what I mean, which I'm grateful for. Instead, she snaps her fingers. "You must think I'm awfully selfish. I haven't even asked how you are."

"I'm fine." I gesture at the hallway leading to the bedrooms. "Your brother has been doting on me all day."

"He's a good guy." She shifts a little, as if trying to ease the pressure on her back. "Out of all of us, he's the only one."

Her audible bitterness surprises me. "What about Justin?"

She makes a scoffing sound and a tiny frown slashes her brow. "Justin is a selfish, egotistical narcissist. All he cares about is the Parker Partnership, like Mother. Ashlin may be a cow but I don't know how she lives with him."

"Not anymore." The words pop out and I instantly regret it. The last thing I want is to discuss anything concerning Ashlin.

Christine's eyebrows rise in surprise. "You know about their separation?"

I nod, hoping she won't ask how. I don't want to reveal that I visited Ashlin in the hospital and why. "They haven't looked happy for a long time so I think this is best for both of them."

"How often do you see them?" Her head tilts slightly to the side as she studies me with open curiosity. Damn.

"Every three to four weeks, depending on how often May summons us to keep up the appearance of one big happy family." I hate the Parker functions but put on a brave face for Trent, who loves seeing his family. "She can be very persuasive."

Christine grimaces and this time it's not from pain. "Why do you think I moved to New York as fast as I could after finishing college? I couldn't wait to get away from her."

I feel awkward discussing her mother, disloyal somehow, though I'm not remotely close to May. I get the feeling she tolerates me after being married to her son for years.

"She's always been accepting of me," I feel obliged to say. "Despite where I grew up she's never made me feel second-best."

"That's because she knows she's superior to everybody." Christine sighs and tries a gentle stretch before collapsing back on the cushions. "I know I sound awful, but that's the way Mom is. She loves for appearances' sake and tries to help if it affects the company. She only cares about maintaining the prestige of the family name."

I ask the obvious. "Why did you stay on after her birthday party if you feel this way?"

She shrugs and winces again, gently rolling her shoulders a few times before her grimace eases. "I don't know. Mom never asks me to stay so when she asked this time I did." She shakes her head. "I thought things might be different, but she wants to put me into rehab so she can control a problem she's not been able to resolve."

"She's your mom," I say, like that explains everything, when in fact I can't imagine living under the same roof as May.

Christine's right. She's domineering and overbearing, always needing to have the last word. Growing up rich does that to a person, I assume. When I initially targeted Trent and researched the Parker family I discovered May had been an heiress and wealthy in her own right before she married Percival Parker. And it shows. May has an air of entitlement no amount of money can buy.

"She won't like this." Christine points to her bruised face. "I'll face a lecture of epic proportions."

I want to point out she's forty-four and doesn't need to answer to anybody but I don't. "Do you want to spend the night? Trent's leaving early tomorrow and will be away for a night, so you won't have to see him. You can have a shower now, borrow some clothes, then I'll do a brilliant make-up job in the morning so May won't bombard you with questions? I've got an excellent essential oil blend that settles bruises like no other."

She visibly brightens, the tension creasing her forehead vanishing. "Thanks, that would be great. I'll text her, saying I decided to pop round and see how you were and decided to stay?"

A blatant lie but then, who am I to talk?

"Sure, go ahead, I'll leave a towel in the bathroom and clothes in the spare room."

I stand and sway a little, residual effects of whatever I'd ingested last night. Something niggles at the edge of my consciousness, something I wanted to ask Christine… I watch her struggle into an upright position and I remember what it is.

"So you weren't robbed?"

"No, which is weird, because why else would he beat me up?"

"How did you choose this dealer?"

"Actually, this dealer chose me. As soon as I entered the alley looking for the old crew he shoved me up against a wall and beat the crap out of me."

My half-baked suspicion starts to coalesce into something unsavory. "How did you escape?"

Her face contorts with fear before she swipes a hand over it. "He just walked away."

Christine shuffles to the end of the sofa and stands with difficulty. "I'd really love that shower now."

She's embarrassed so I drop the subject, despite the inkling that something to do with her assault isn't right.

"Do you need any help?"

"I'll be fine." She gives me a tentative smile. "I really appreciate this. You've been amazingly supportive and I can't thank you enough." The smile reaches her eyes. "Maybe once I get my head together we could catch up? Get to know each other beyond the obligatory Parker visits Mom makes us endure?"

Glad we've warmed to each other—after how many years?—I nod. "I'd like that."

While her gratitude gives me hope, I wonder if she'll be as supportive of me when the time comes. I doubt it. If I tell Trent the whole truth I doubt any of them will want to talk to me again.

CHAPTER THIRTY-SIX

RIA

Twenty-four hours later, I'm still in shock over Grayson's reappearance and his startling confession.

My ex-husband left us five years earlier because, if he's to be believed, he put us in danger.

It's infuriating, to think he didn't trust me enough to tell me back then. We could've talked it through. We could've worked out a solution. We could've done a lot of things… as a team.

I thought I'd got over him a long time ago but seeing him last night shot that down in a big way: because Grayson Parker is as attractive as ever. Not just physically, but on some deeper level that drew me to him in the first place. And now that I know he isn't the sicko I thought he was… after he'd left last night I'd studied that awful photo of him being dominated and felt like a complete idiot. It had been digitally altered like he said but I'd been too distraught by him leaving back then to look closely. I hadn't wanted to; one glance at that sordid photo and I'd seen enough.

Not that it would've changed anything if I had discovered the fake, I would've despised him anyway for leaving us without an explanation. And for staying away for five long years without a single word.

I should hate him for what he put me, and Shelley, through. I don't.

I haven't heard anything from him beyond a terse email saying 'he's looking into it'. It's disarming that he hasn't found anything out yet.

I met with Lars today, and got him to scour my laptop and run high security programs to ensure my safety is up to date. If Grayson hacked my PC it's possible my laptop is vulnerable too and I hate the thought of anyone else gaining access.

Lost in my musings I almost miss the turn-off to my street. I rarely walk but needed to clear my head today, so May picked up Shelley from school and is waiting at my place. Dusk streaks the sky mauve as the lights of Chicago cast a glow across the horizon. I like this time of day in bohemian Brunswick.

My cell rings and I fish it out of my bag. I glance at the screen. It's Shamira. As I'm about to answer I hear a footfall behind me. Not close, but loud enough that I notice. I glance over my shoulder and see nothing but shadows. It usually wouldn't bother me. I walk these streets at dusk or after dark many times, usually with Shelley, if we've been to our favorite vegan café for dinner or popped out for the best gelato in the area. But those threatening emails have made me jumpy and I shake off my momentary fear and answer the call.

"Hey, Shamira, how are you feeling?"

"Much better, thanks. Are you at home?"

"About two blocks away."

"Uh, good." She pauses, before rushing on. "Look, this is probably nothing and I don't want to scare you, but I think someone may be targeting the family and you need to be careful."

My breath catches and I instill calm into my voice. "Has something else happened?"

She hesitates again, before I hear a soft sigh. "This is confidential because she doesn't want anyone else knowing her business, but Christine landed on my doorstep last night in a bad way. She'd gone out to score drugs around the corner from here and a dealer attacked her."

I need to feign surprise, otherwise Shamira will ask how I know about Christine's addiction and I don't want to reveal the contents of those emails just yet.

"That's awful. Is she okay?"

"Yeah, but she's bruised so she stayed here last night because doesn't want any more lectures from May, and postponed her checking into rehab. The weird thing is, the guy who beat her up didn't rob her and might've deliberately targeted her. And if that's true, all the women in this family have had a mishap except you."

As the implication of what she says sinks in I think I hear it again. A footfall. Another. Like someone's following me. I dart a glance over my shoulder. Glimpse a shadow…

My blood chills. I pick up the pace, stopping short of breaking into a run as a surge of adrenaline makes my heart pound.

Shamira mistakes my silence for doubt. "Look, I could be way off base but I just thought I'd let you know—"

"I think I'm being followed." I see the lights from my living room spilling out onto my lawn. May has forgotten to draw the blinds. I'll chastise her later. Because right now fixating on that light and how close I am to it lends my feet extra speed.

"Ria, this is serious." She falls silent.

I don't want to look over my shoulder again. I make a beeline for the front door and all but fall against it, relieved when it opens almost immediately.

May is staring at me with blatant curiosity as I stumble in. "Shut the door," I say, lowering my voice with effort.

"Are you okay—" May asks at the same time as Shamira shouts in my ear, "Are you home?"

May is still staring at me quizzically, so I say, "Thanks Shamira, I'm home and I'm fine."

I hear her sigh of relief. "Please take what I'm saying seriously."

"Shall do." I hang up but hold onto the cell.

I drop my laptop bag near the front door and switch off the lights in the living room, before walking across to the window.

"What's going on?" May asks, sounding perplexed as she stares at me like I'm deranged.

"These need to be closed," I say, tugging on the cord for the blinds as I peer outside. I see nothing but a jogger—average height, dark hoodie pulled up, sweatpants—nothing out of the ordinary.

"Ria, what happened—"

"I thought someone was following me." I lower my voice and lift a finger to my lips. "I don't want to frighten Shelley."

"Of course." Her tone is brusque as I belatedly question my wisdom in telling her. Nothing fazes May. She's totally unflappable. Heck, even when that cyclist knocked her down she took it in her stride. "Are you sure you were being followed?"

And just like that, I decide to swallow my fears. May is too pragmatic to fathom someone is potentially targeting this family. Despite those emails only revealing Ashlin's, Shamira's and Christine's secrets, it looks like we're all in the firing line.

Besides, I can't articulate my theory, not without betraying how I know everything, so I take a few breaths and wait for my heart rate to slow.

"I could be wrong." I slip my cell into my pocket, needing the security of having it on me at all times after the fright I just got. "Let me wash up and I'll go say hi to Shelley. She's okay?"

May nods. "She's done her homework, had a shower and eaten dinner."

I don't even ask what she ate. May would've brought over one of her chef's meals, packed with protein and nutrients.

"Thanks, I won't be long."

However, when I enter my bedroom and close the door, the adrenaline wears off and I barely make it to the bed before collapsing onto it.

Something's not right. Did what just happen to me have something to do with Grayson's return and his vague explanation about being threatened years earlier and that danger carrying over to me?

I don't understand any of this. It makes my head ache and I feel vulnerable for myself and for Shelley. I hate to admit it but I need to talk to Grayson again. I need him to explain why I may be in danger and is that why he really came back. I need *him*… crazy, because I've been fiercely independent for the last five years out of necessity but having him back in Chicago, supposedly out of concern for me, is making me oddly vulnerable.

May hadn't mentioned him when I rang earlier asking her to pick up Shelley. Then again, she wouldn't. She saw how I fell apart when Grayson left and she's nothing if not diplomatic. She left me under no illusions she was appalled by her son's flaky behavior when he left and was one hundred percent on my side. Though why is Grayson staying with her if she's so supportive of me? Surely she would've told him to go elsewhere? Unless May isn't as trustworthy as I've assumed all these years?

Then again, maybe my recent scare is making me suspicious of everyone. May facilitated our divorce. She did everything she could to show me I was a part of the Parker family. Not such a great thing, taking recent events into consideration.

I stand, glad my legs have stopped wobbling, and pad to the door. I open it a fraction, to find May hasn't moved from the living room and is peering out into the darkness like I had moments ago.

"May, is Grayson staying with you?"

She jumps, like I've startled her, before turning toward me. "Yes. He said it's not for long." An embarrassed blush stains her cheeks. "I still don't approve of the way he treated you and Shelley. In fact, I'll never forgive him for it, but he's my son and when he asked if he could stay for a few days, I said yes."

"It's okay—"

"He also said he visited you?"

She's his mother, it's natural she's curious, but I have no intention of discussing any of this with her.

I nod. "It was all very civil but like you, I can't forgive him. But I do need to speak to him. Can you stay for another few hours?"

She opens her mouth, like she's going to say something, before closing it again. I'm glad. I'm not in the mood to justify my urgency in seeing her son tonight.

"Yes, I can stay."

"Thanks, I'll call him and be out in a sec."

She nods and turns away but not before I see displeasure downturn her mouth. I can't fathom it. Is she disappointed I'm deigning to speak to the man who abandoned me and that makes me shallow somehow? Or is she disappointed in her son and that manifests whenever he's mentioned, which is rarely these days?

I close the door and fish my cell out of my pocket. I stab at number one on speed dial, May's home number, and wait. It always annoyed me that I had no way of contacting Grayson after he left in the event of an emergency regarding Shelley. Until I realized if he gave a damn I would have his new cell number and that rammed home he obviously didn't care.

Am I being gullible in buying his excuse that he dabbled where he shouldn't have and left to protect us? Grayson had worked at Parker Partnership. What was the worst he could've discovered there?

I hate how discombobulated I feel. Nerves make my palms clammy, like they used to when we first met and I used to call Grayson. Back then, his family's wealth intimidated me and I lacked confidence. I'm a different woman now but it's been a long time since I called Grayson. The answering service picks up after the seventh ring.

Annoyed, I leave a brief message for him to call me and hang up. My cell rings ten seconds later, from the same number.

"Grayson?"

"Yeah." His deep voice zings my synapses as it always does. "Sorry for not answering. I'm laying low until I find out who's behind all this so thought it prudent I listen to the message rather than answering."

"Paranoid, much?" I mutter, hating the way his low chuckle makes me press the cell firmer against my ear, like I want to be closer to him.

"Everything okay?" His tone softens like it used to, like he kept a special voice especially for me, and I mentally curse my body's irrational response to it, my skin tingling with anticipation.

"Yeah, but we need to talk." It comes out a brusque order because I'm mad at myself more than him.

"Sure, when?"

I don't want him here, not if there's the slightest chance Shelley will see him. My daughter finally stopped asking about her father a few years ago and I don't want her upset if he's only in town for a couple of days. Morally, it's wrong to keep him from seeing her. But I'm the one who'll be left dealing with the aftermath when he breaks her heart again and I won't let that happen.

"How about I come over there? In an hour?"

I could've made it thirty but I want to spend some time with my daughter; and have a shower, which is more a necessity than a vanity thing.

"See you then."

I hang up before I'm tempted to linger like I used to. His deep voice is mesmerizing, always has been, and I pinch myself to stop from remembering. I open the door again and this time May is on the sofa flicking through a magazine.

"I'm taking a shower, spending a bit of time with Shel, then I'm going to see Grayson."

I say it almost defiantly, like I'm daring her to disagree. She merely nods. "That's fine, dear."

It isn't, because as I quickly undress and step into a scalding shower I can't help but think I'm doing the wrong thing.

I need Grayson's help. But if what he said about his rationale for leaving is true, how much of what's happening to our family is tied to him?

CHAPTER THIRTY-SEVEN

ASHLIN

I don't believe this. Shamira has landed on my doorstep with Christine in tow. They didn't call ahead. They've just arrived and rung the doorbell. Christine is half hidden behind Shamira and appears slumped. Odd. Then she moves to the side and I gasp. Her neck is bruised, her lip is swollen and she's sporting a shiner. I can ignore them but once I spy Christine's injuries I'm not that heartless. Besides, I'm curious why these two would pop in unannounced.

In a way it's good timing. I've been at a loose end all day, drifting through the house aimlessly, critically eyeing rooms from a design perspective, assessing how saleable the place is. I've been contemplating whether to sell this house or continue living a lie. Because that's what my marriage has been and if I stay here after the divorce comes through I'll be plagued by memories of a past I'd rather forget. Besides, with May cutting off access to the family fortune, my home is the only asset I have. I'll have no choice but to sell, invest the funds wisely and live off a meager income.

I shudder at the thought of cost-cutting and open the door. "This is a surprise."

"Sorry for turning up like this," Shamira says, sounding surprisingly forceful. "But Christine needs a place to stay for a night or two."

I bite back my first response, "Do I look like I run a hotel?" and open the door wider. "Come in."

"Thanks," Christine murmurs as she enters. She's limping, favoring her right leg, and wearing ill-fitting sweatpants and a loose T-shirt. She's make-up-less and her hair is pulled back in a low ponytail. I've never seen her anything other than immaculately groomed. Along with the bruises, she's a mess.

I take them through to the family room where the girls like to hang out. It's spacious, with floor-to-ceiling windows looking out over the infinity pool. Leather armchairs are placed strategically around the monstrous plasma TV, fitted out with every gaming console known to man. Not that the girls play much these days. Their noses are perpetually stuck to their smartphone and electronic tablet respectively.

"Can I get you anything?" I sound like a polite hostess entertaining friends when nothing is further from the truth. I have nothing in common with these women, never have, apart from our surname. "Maybe a steak for that eye?"

"Don't be a smart-ass." Shamira helps Christine into a chair and sits opposite me. Her chutzpah surprises me, considering the last time we spoke she was cowering in my hospital room, sucking up so I wouldn't tell Trent about her shitty past.

Maybe I'm feeling charitable, maybe I'm plain lonely, but I shelve my sarcastic comeback and settle for, "Do you want to tell me what happened?"

"Not really." Christine touches her cheek absentmindedly, where a blossoming purple bruise darkens the skin beneath her eye socket. "But I can tell you this much. I got tangled up with the wrong guy. He did this to me. And I can't go back to Mom's."

She eyeballs me with surprising clarity. "I was due to check into a private rehab facility but I've rung them and put it off for a few days because this"—she points at her black eye—"is only going to lead to endless questions I don't want to answer. If anyone sees me bruised in public, heading to a facility, we know what will happen to the precious family name and I'm not up to dealing with the resultant fallout from Mom."

I can't hide my surprise that she's seeing professionals for her addiction. "I'm impressed you're seeking help."

A faint blush stains her cheeks. "I got nudged into it by Mom and a doctor, but they're right, it's time I take back control."

"Good for you," I say, wishing I could take back control of my life as decisively.

"So can she crash here for a few days?" Shamira asks. "She stayed at my place the last two nights, which was okay the first night because Trent had already gone to bed, then he left early yesterday for an overnighter in St. Louis. But he'll be back today and Christine can't see him because he'll ask too many questions. So with your girls staying at May's, and Justin not at home either, we thought this would be the best place for her?"

I want to say no. I'm not a babysitter and the last thing I need while I figure out how to move forward is my husband's sister hanging around. But I'm not a complete bitch. I see the desperation in Christine's eyes and the doubt in Shamira's. They don't think I'll do this. Then again, I've never given them any reason to trust me. I'm standoffish at best, passive-aggressive at worst. I thrive on gossip and I love lording it over those it involves, like I did with Shamira. But there's power in being needed and they must be really desperate to ask me for a favor.

"Sure, you can stay." I try to sound welcoming but they're not buying my demure act. I don't blame them. I'm like a lion encouraging a lamb to enter my lair. They know I'll demand a price at some stage and they're unsure if they'll be willing to pay it.

Shamira appears uncertain, like she doesn't want to leave Christine alone with me. "You can't discuss this with anyone in the family."

I resist rolling my eyes at the obvious. "Your secret's safe with me." I mimic zipping my lips at Christine. "Though for what it's worth, you need to choose your hobbies more carefully in future."

"I knew this was a bad idea," Christine mutters, her glare malevolent but scared, like she doesn't know who to trust.

"You're always welcome to leave." I point to the door, my snide response something they're more familiar with and Christine's shoulders relax slightly.

"Phew, for a minute there you were freaking me out with your niceness." Christine mock swipes her brow and the corners of Shamira's mouth turn up.

"What about clothes?" My gaze sweeps her from head to foot. "Far be it from me not to be impressed with your choice of haute couture, but you could do with something better."

"Shamira kindly lent me something clean." Christine stares me down, daring me to make a remark. I don't. "I need a few things to tide me over until I'm locked away."

My eyebrows rise. "But isn't all your stuff at May's? Surely she'll know something's wrong if you avoid her completely before you check in?"

Christine waves away my concern. "Leave Mom to me."

Gladly. The last thing I need is another run-in with the busy-body matriarch.

"I'll go get that stuff you wanted and pop back shortly." Shamira stands, like she can't wait to get out of here. She turns to me out of politeness. "Anything you need?"

"A killer divorce lawyer."

There's an awkward silence and for the first time since Justin delivered the news I feel strangely vulnerable. I'll never be friends with these women but I'm glad they're here. I'm lonely. I've always been lonely, even when married.

"For what it's worth, I think you're better off without him," Christine says, bitterness lacing her tone. "Justin is a selfish prick."

I'm stunned. I thought the entire Parker clan doted on their eldest sibling and would treat me as the enemy as they always have. Shamira says nothing but her knowing expression means they've already discussed this.

I clutch my chest in mock shock, trying to make light of the situation in case I really stun them and start blubbering. I can feel the emotion welling in my chest, making me breathless, and the sting of tears behind my eyes. I'm turning soft and I don't like it. This divorce has thrown me off-kilter.

"Just saying it how it is." Christine shrugs and winces, making me wonder how far those bruises extend. "My brother thinks the world revolves around him. Always has. He's ruthless and will do whatever it takes to ensure he wins."

Shamira edges toward the door, obviously uncomfortable with verbally bashing Justin. She's always hated confrontation, which is why she surprised me so much by cornering me at the hospital.

She raises a hand in a wave. "I'll be back soon."

When she closes the door behind her, an uncomfortable silence descends. I don't do small talk and Christine and I have nothing in common: other than a mutual loathing for Justin, apparently.

So that's what I lead with. "I always thought you and Justin got along."

"We do, but that doesn't mean I don't see him for what he is." She touches her bruises, her fingertips drifting across them lightly. "He'd judge me for these, just like Mom. They're two peas in a pod. Money's their god, people come second."

"We all like money." I sound like I'm defending him when that's the last thing I want to do. "I guess being born into it ensures you want to protect it and see it grow."

She wrinkles her nose. "It's all they value. Everything and everyone who doesn't fit into their mold is deemed irrelevant."

I have no idea what's behind her acrimony but I'm glad to have an ally. I'll find out what Justin has done to bug her eventually but for now I take a different tack. "Don't take this the wrong way, but you look awful. Have you been checked by a doctor?"

She rolls her eyes and manages a half-smile. "Now you sound like Shamira."

"She's right every now and then."

Christine chuckles at my begrudging admission. "She came through for me in a big way and I won't forget it."

I have to ask the obvious question. "Why did you turn up on her doorstep?"

"Because I was in the neighborhood trying to score." Her eyes glaze for a moment and I glimpse pain.

I don't want to pry but I feel like she wants to talk. And while we'll never be BFFs I want to support her. She's my sister-in-law. She's family. I may not act like that means much most of the time but I do care.

"I'm guessing going in search of a fix isn't a one-off for you."

"I like the high so no, it wasn't a first." Her smile is self-deprecating. "But I'm guessing you already know that."

I hesitate for a moment before nodding. "I see you at May's parties. Some of the women I socialize with love a good party drug so I know the signs."

"I like getting high," she says, sounding wistful. "It's liberating."

"So May knows?"

She nods. "I guess I don't hide it as well as I think." She screws up her nose. "You probably noticed I don't have a great relationship with Mom, considering she's always been more focused on my brothers than me."

I don't respond because I have a feeling Christine doesn't expect one. Her eyes are unfocused, like she's lost in her musings, so I wait for her to continue. It doesn't take long.

"Having her ask me to stay on after the party for the first time, then having her talk to me like a real person, showed a caring side I didn't know she had. And when she called me out on my drinking she did it without judgment, so I ended up telling her about the drugs too." She points to her battered face. "I wanted one last high and I know she won't understand, she'll take it as a personal affront. And considering how far we've come lately, I don't want to risk her turning her back on me, not when I've finally got her support."

She blinks, refocuses and scowls, bearing a startling resemblance to May in that moment. "Not to mention she's on this weird 'avoid publicity at all costs' thing lately and I can't risk losing whatever money she's going to dish out. She's such a control freak."

I know the feeling, worrying about being cut off from the Parker fortune, but that's not the real issue here, as I wonder if that's what pushed Christine toward drugs in the first place; having a domineering mother she craved an escape from. May would be a downer to grow up with and I almost pity Christine for needing a chemical fix to cope.

"She'll guide Justin through every step of this divorce, that's for sure." I sound spiteful and don't care. It's the truth. Justin will do whatever May says. It didn't bother me so much in the early days of our marriage, when I assumed docility with my mother-in-law would earn more kudos. And it had for a while; she'd appeared to like me. But that waned as the years passed and even before Justin ended our marriage, May and I barely maintained a cordial civility.

Which I'd effectively ended when I threatened to spill Parker secrets to the competition. Not that I would, but I wanted to rattle her as much as this impending divorce rattles me.

"Don't let them push you around." Christine waggles a finger and that simple action seems like too much as pain tightens her features. "Stand your ground and don't back down unless you absolutely have to."

She's on my side and I'm flabbergasted.

"I didn't expect anyone in your family to understand," I say, searching her face for an ulterior motive and coming up empty.

Besides, what would Christine hope to gain by maligning her brother and mother to me? "Thanks for the support."

"Hey, you're letting me stay here, it's the least I can do." An odd expression flickers across her face... almost malicious, and I can't fathom it. "Besides, no one's infallible and I think Justin is about to learn that the hard way."

I have no idea what she's talking about. But I do know one thing. If Justin and May think they'll play hardball with me and I'll lie down and roll over, they're sorely mistaken. While I would never reveal secrets to Aaron and allow the opposition to get a foothold in Parker Partnership they don't know that and as a threat it could work wonders. It had certainly unsettled May.

I won't let them gain the upper hand. I must remain in control.

While inside I'm crumbling and wishing I'd done things differently.

CHAPTER THIRTY-EIGHT

SHAMIRA

After I drop off the clothes and toiletries Christine wanted at Ashlin's place, I head home. I need to speak to my husband.

I need to tell him: everything.

With Christine hiding out in the spare room yesterday before he'd left on his overnighter to pick up a rare guitar, I'd been skittish and he'd noticed. He kept eyeing me with suspicion, like he had after we bumped into that creep at the market, and I can't take it any longer.

The truth will hurt. It will probably end us. But I can't keep living a lie. Everything in my life seems to be escalating, like something bad is about to happen and I can't do anything to prevent it: the accidents to Ashlin and May, my poisoning, Christine's bashing, Ria being followed. It feels like things are spiraling out of control and if I don't take some of it back I'm in danger of doing something silly.

That's what the abortion had been about: taking back control.

I have to make Trent understand. But he won't. All he'll hear when I tell him the truth is he wants a child more than anything and I've ruined that for him.

I slip into the apartment. It's strangely silent. He must be listening to music with headphones in the den so I head to the kitchen, desperate for a glass of water. Like that will ease the tightness in my throat. It's like the truth is stuck there, wedged, unable to get out.

"Where have you been?"

I drop the glass in the sink and it clatters against the stainless steel. It doesn't shatter but a tiny crack appears down one side. I'm like that glass. A flaw fighting its way to the surface, soon to be seen by the one person I've tried to hide it from.

I spin around. He's snuck up behind me and I'm startled I didn't hear him. I blame it on my musings, refusing to consider that my husband is creeping around trying to scare me. And the doubts seep in again. If he poisoned me to give me a fright and teach me a lesson when I told him about my past, what's he going to do when he hears what I did to our baby?

"I popped into Ashlin's to see if she's okay." I settle for a half-truth. It's better than nothing.

His stare is disbelieving. "Why would you drop in to see her? You can't stand her."

Yet again, I have to summon more lies. "She's alone. I thought it was the right thing to do."

I hate that he believes me so readily. His expression softens and he reaches for me. "You're too nice for your own good. You know that, right?"

I don't answer, allowing him to drag me into his arms and smother me in a hug. His embraces usually comfort me. Today, it takes all my willpower not to squirm away.

I'm a bad person.

I've done a bad thing.

How can he ever forgive me?

I ease away, my heart pounding so loud I'm sure he must hear it too. "I need to talk to you about something."

Wariness clouds his eyes and I don't blame him. I've already shocked him once this week. I snag his hand and tug him toward the living room.

"Sounds serious," he says, holding onto my hand as we sit next to each other on the sofa.

I swallow the lump of foreboding lodged in my throat. "It is."

I've envisaged telling him the truth so many times in my head but now the time has arrived I'm speechless. I want to explain but my brain and mouth refuse to work in sync. My lungs constrict, making breathing difficult. Tiny spots dance before my eyes and I force myself to take steady breaths, in and out, so I don't faint. He squeezes my hand, conveying a silent strength I need but his understanding only serves to make me feel worse. When I don't speak, he squeezes tighter and tears burn the back of my eyes.

"Is this more stuff about your past?" He raises my hand to his lips and presses a kiss on the back, sweet and supportive, totally Trent. "Because if it is, you can tell me and I promise not to freak out."

Unlike last time hangs unsaid between us.

Dread seeps through my body, like every cell is swamped by some kind of drug that makes me shut down. I feel lethargic, like I can sleep for a month. It could be residual effects of the poison but I doubt it. It's my conscience overriding my sympathetic nervous system, insisting I'm an idiot for ruining the best thing that's ever happened to me.

After another deep inhalation forcing air into my constricted lungs, I finally manage to speak.

"I did something about fifteen months ago, something you may not understand, but I hope you'll hear me out and make an effort to work through it with me."

"You're scaring me." His brows knit into a frown and I stifle the urge to reach out a fingertip and smooth the deep groove away. "I already asked this last time and you said no, but have you cheated?"

"No." My indignation is warranted but what I've done is far worse and I know it. "I love you and I'd never do something like that."

He swipes at his brow in exaggerated relief while tightening his hold on my hand with the other.

He's going to be more than worried when I tell him the whole truth. But in order to make him understand, I need to explain what drove me to madness. He'll think I'm blaming him—his family— I'm not. The more background I give him, the more chance I have of convincing him of my motivations and ultimately saving us.

"Have you ever noticed how your family demand perfection?"

He's perplexed by my question and I don't blame him, it's so far left field. "Yeah, but what's that got to do with us? We've never conformed to what they want."

By 'they' he means 'May'. She rules the Parkers, the unacknowledged queen who bestows benevolence at will and can take it away as easily. We all know it; we just don't talk about it.

"I've never mentioned this to you but I feel the pressure of being a Parker. All the time."

His confusion increases as he stares at me like he doesn't know me at all. "Why didn't you say something?"

"Because I've always managed on my own since I was young, and I bottle all the bad stuff up in here." I tap my chest. "I internalize and it's not a good thing."

My convoluted way of leading up to the truth is pathetic but I have to continue. The words aren't coming any easier but now I've started to reveal the truth I can feel the tightness in my chest easing.

"One of the greatest pressures I've had to contend with is having a baby."

He releases my hand and I instantly miss his comforting touch. I'm not surprised. It's been a contentious issue between us for a while, his desire to procreate, my wish to wait. He's acquiesced to my viewpoint out of love, exactly like what I did was out of love. But he won't see it that way. He'll see it as evidence of me being a monster.

"I don't understand what the problem is. We've shelved the idea for now, like you wanted." His lips compress into a thin line I've seen many times before, whenever the topic of babies arises.

It eventually became so controversial between us that I agreed to a timeline: we'd start trying in twelve months. We rarely argued and I hated the tension after the baby discussions, the only flaw in our solid marriage.

A marriage in danger of falling apart, thanks to me.

I try to explain again, taking the circuitous route. "Remember that day last year when I went to a health retreat in Milwaukee for the night?"

"Yeah."

"I didn't go."

His forehead creases in confusion again. "Where were you?"

"In the hospital."

The groove between his brows deepens. "Why?"

I have to say the words. I have to force them past my lips. I have to trust my husband with the truth, knowing it may end us but powerless to keep living a lie.

"We got pregnant." I use 'we' because this is about us, even if I took the decision to terminate out of his hands. "I had concerns because of my past drug and alcohol use when I was… you know, doing all that stuff I told you about, so I had fetal testing done. Abnormalities were detected and the obstetrician advised me to terminate—"

"You had an abortion and you didn't tell me?" He leaps to his feet and stares at me like I'm an abhorrent freak. His lips are pinched tight, his eyes wide with shock and he's flexing his fingers, clenching and unclenching repeatedly, like he's lost all feeling. The shimmer of tears in his eyes reflects mine as he stares at me with something akin to loathing.

I get it, because I hate me too. He'll never know how much I wanted to confide in him before I went through the procedure that tore my heart in two. He'll never understand how utterly bereft I felt waking up in the hospital afterward, shattered and empty, like the doctors had scooped out more than my tiny growing baby.

And by the way he's glaring at me, with sorrow and regret and anger, he'll never see me the same way again.

"I don't understand," he murmurs, his voice quivering, as a lone tear trickles down his cheek.

That tear breaks something inside me; whatever's left to be broken. Sobs well in my throat, clawing for escape, but all I want to do is go to Trent, comfort him. I move toward him but he takes a step back, like he can't bear to be near me.

"Why didn't you tell me?" He shakes his head, the agony in his tone making me wrap my arms around my middle. "I should've had a say…"

Maybe he's right but I stand by my decision. It ripped my heart out but I made the tough call, like I always have. Prostituting myself to care for Mom, targeting Trent to care for me, terminating our baby to care for both of us. None of those things made me feel good about myself but I did what I had to do to survive.

I know confessing isn't going to change anything. My guilt will be ever-present, gnawing away at my self-esteem like always. I can't change what I did in the past to pay Mom's medical bills, and I can't take back the abortion, but if Trent knows everything about me then I have some chance of redemption.

"It tore me apart, having to abort the baby you wanted so much, but I couldn't face telling you about the abnormalities and having you go through the same heartache—"

"How thoughtful." His sarcastic retort echoes through the apartment that's the only real home I've ever known. "How do I know if any of this is true? You don't want a kid, you've made that perfectly obvious, so how can I believe you?"

Grief contorts his face as he sinks to his knees, his shoulders slumped, his head lowered, a broken man. I did this. Me. I want to curl up in a ball and die, the pain is that excruciating, like a cleaver hacking into my heart.

"I have the medical records if you want to see—"

"You killed our baby." He lifts his head slowly to stare at me and the hatred in his eyes snatches my breath.

The tears I'm battling fall then, sliding down my cheeks, pooling in the crevices of my mouth, and dripping off my chin. I have as much chance of stopping them as saving my marriage: absolutely none.

"I know you'll never understand this, but I'm going to try to explain anyway. I've never felt good enough in your family. I'm tolerated, not accepted. They demand perfection and I couldn't stand the thought of bringing a flawed child into that kind of environment." I shake my head and tears fly.

Swiping a hand across my eyes, I blink so I can see him. His hatred hasn't waned. His eyes glitter with it. He despises me but I can't stop now. I have to try to make him understand. "I'm a weak person and I'm terrified of having a child because of what I saw growing up. I know a child of ours won't face the same hardships, but I can't shake that fear. It's ingrained. A deep-seated part of me."

I press a hand to my chest, imploring him to listen. "Because of that fear it's going to be hard enough for me to cope with mothering a healthy child. So when the doctor told me the devastating news, I had no option."

He's staring at me in wide-eyed horror but the rigidity of his neck muscles has eased and I'm hoping his anger along with it. "We always have options, Shamira. Yours was to tell me what was going on so we could've decided together. You and me. The dream team, remember?"

Of course I remember. He'd called us that the night he proposed, the night I thought I'd finally left the horrors of my past behind and moved into a stable future.

And we have been the dream team, in perfect sync in all aspects of our lives, bar one. His desire to have a child and my inherent fear I'll fail at motherhood means it's going to take us a long time to get past this, if ever.

"It wouldn't have mattered what you said." I lay my hands out, palms up, like I have nothing left to hide. "I wouldn't have brought that damaged child into the world."

So now he knows all of it. I'm spent. My bones are jelly-like and I flop back into the cushions, feeling like I'll never be able to move again. I can't look at him. I can't see what I've done to the man I love. So I focus on his feet. He's not moving and after what seems like an eternity, he shifts toward me.

"I should've been there for you." He speaks so softly I'm sure I've misheard, because it sounds like he's not blaming me anymore and compassion has replaced fury in his tone. "You should've given me the option."

I can't defend myself any longer. There's nothing left to say. I could've confided in him when I learned the devastating news of our unborn child's abnormalities but I hadn't and I can't change that now.

"I could kill you for this," he mutters, and my gaze flies to his, the bitter words at odds with his audible pity a few moments before.

"Maybe you already tried?"

Even though it's the wrong thing to say if I'm trying to defuse the situation I can't help it. I need to know if the man I've always trusted implicitly has turned on me because I don't fit the image of his perfect wife. Who knows, maybe he's more like his family, particularly his judgmental mother, than I give him credit for?

His eyes narrow, not diminishing his contempt one bit. "You think *I* tampered with your drink?"

"I don't know what to think. But you were pretty mad after I told you about my past. Maybe you wanted to teach me a lesson—"

"Do you really think I'm capable of hurting you?"

He sinks to his haunches, bracing his elbows on his knees and dropping his head into his hands. His shoulders shake and I realize he's crying. I can't bear it. I go to him. I sit on the floor next to him and he raises his head. His visible anguish guts me, like someone has kicked me in the belly.

"I'm sorry." I lay a hand on his knee, grateful when he doesn't shove me away. "For everything."

He stares at me through reddened eyes, his tear-streaked cheeks softening the anger tightening his features. "I would never hurt you."

He straightens to a standing position, staring down at me. "I wish you could say the same."

He stalks toward the door, opens it and casts one last look over his shoulder. It's indecipherable and my heart aches for what I've done to us. This family has made me paranoid and sensitive and in that moment, I hate being a Parker. I wish I could say something, anything, to make him stay but when he slams the door behind him, I sag, like my chest has caved in on itself.

I don't move from the floor for ten minutes, twenty, maybe an hour. I doubt we'll come back from this. But the relief is liberating.

My husband now knows everything about me.

And if I believe him, I still don't know who tried to poison me.

It's like the bad old days when I didn't know who to trust, when my gut instincts were often way off and perps took advantage of my naivety. Not anymore. This time, my eyes are wide open and I have nothing left to hide.

If whoever has it in for me tries again, I'll be ready.

CHAPTER THIRTY-NINE

RIA

I'm almost at May's front door when I hear raised voices coming from the back. Grayson and Justin, arguing. I shouldn't eavesdrop, it's not right. But I find myself following the side path around the house regardless. Sensor lights lead the way but if the men notice they don't stop. It's only as I near the back garden I realize they're not outside; they're in the conservatory with the French doors open, hence their loud voices travel. I stop at the back corner of the house and listen.

"You shouldn't be here," Justin says, his voice barely above a growl.

Grayson laughs and I picture him leaning against something like he hasn't got a care in the world. He's always had a way about him, casual and laid-back, like nothing fazes him. I used to find it endearing, until I found out the hard way he's so cavalier he left me a single mother without a backward glance.

"Why not? I have as much right to be here as you do, brother."

"I'm not talking about this house and you know it." There's a pause, where I imagine Grayson's smug smile, goading Justin. "Ria doesn't need you back in Chicago screwing up her life again."

"How do you know what Ria needs?"

I hear the defensiveness in Grayson's voice but I also detect something else, an underlying protectiveness he doesn't have a right to, not anymore. I don't owe Grayson anything but in that moment I'm glad he doesn't know about my messed up attraction to Justin or that damn kiss.

"Because unlike you, I've been around for her." Justin's tone is silky and I mentally will him not to say anything about us.

Thankfully, he remains silent but Grayson has picked up on that hint of innuendo in his brother's voice. "I bet you have, you sleazy prick. You've always been the same, had to have everything you wanted." He lowers his voice to a hostile hiss. "Keep your hands off my wife."

"Ex-wife," Justin drawls and I hold my breath. I have to do something before he blurts it's too late and it's already happened.

I round the corner of the house and bound up the steps to the conservatory as Justin says, "What if—"

"Hey." I inject fake cheeriness into my voice, hoping my too readable face doesn't give away my guilt that not only has Justin had his hands all over me, he'd also had his tongue in my mouth. "How are you both?"

They stare at me with matching surprised expressions, like I'm the last person they expect to see. "I was about to ring the bell but heard you two talking so I came around the back."

"It's good to see you," Justin says, enveloping me in a hug. I shouldn't feel anything but I do, my body giving a betraying flicker of *something*. I know he's only doing it to rile Grayson and that annoys me so I shrug out of his embrace quickly.

"Ria called me earlier and said she'd be dropping in to chat, so if you don't mind leaving us alone?" Grayson's proprietary eyes glitter as he stares Justin down, his unexpected fierceness a side of him I've never seen. "Nice seeing you, big brother."

He makes it sound like he'd rather pet a rattlesnake and Justin gets the message. But I know him. He won't resist one last dig before he leaves.

"Are you sure you're okay if I leave?" Justin touches my arm and his hand lingers, his fingertips deliberately skating across my skin in a caress that hints at impropriety.

The action isn't lost on Grayson as I see his hands ball into fists but he doesn't move from his relaxed position against a high stool.

"I'm fine." I step away and Justin's hand falls, but his assessing stare sweeps over me, like he can't fathom why I'd want to be in the same room as Grayson, let alone talk to him.

I glare at him, willing him to get the message to leave us alone, and after a weird tense standoff that lasts a few seconds he shrugs and moves toward the door.

He ignores Grayson completely as he offers me an oddly intimate smile. "Call me if you need me."

Increasingly uncomfortable, I manage a terse nod, relieved when he leaves and Grayson closes the French doors before turning to me with raised eyebrows.

"Someone's got the hots for you." His upper lip curls in a slight sneer. "Is that why he left Ashlin? You two getting it on?"

"Don't be crass." I head to the kitchen to get a drink so he won't see the betraying blush heating my cheeks. I fill a glass with water from the tap and sip slowly, buying some time for my giveaway blush to ease before I turn back to face him.

"He's definitely got a thing for you." He follows me into the kitchen, the tread of his footsteps so familiar that I stop swallowing in case I choke. "I know I've got no right to tell you what to do these days, or offer advice, but stay away from Justin."

"Jealous?"

"Maybe." He shrugs but it's far from nonchalant, with his shoulder muscles bunching into knots. "I almost forgot how narcissistic he is. He has to have everything he wants, no matter the cost. Even when we were growing up he had to beat Trent and me at athletics, he had to score the most home runs at baseball and he hated that we threw more three pointers on the court than he did."

He takes a few steps closer, bringing him within touching distance. I can feel the heat radiating off him and grit my teeth against the urge to lean into him. "But this isn't about Justin," he says, as he rests his hands on my shoulders and I stiffen. "I care about you. I always have."

The sincerity in his steady gaze floors me and I'm so unnerved I shrug him off and my hand shakes, sloshing water over the top of the glass. I place it carefully on the bench top, wishing I hadn't when I'm tempted to reach out and trace the contours of his mouth like I used to. The urge is strong, the glint of reminiscing powerful in his eyes, that I curl my fingers into my palm and jam the resultant fist into my jacket pocket.

I need to wrestle back control of this situation and scorn is guaranteed to do it, because he always hated it. I roll my eyes in an exaggerated sweep. "Yeah, you care so much about me you left."

Frustration clouds his clear gaze, that unique blue so damn mesmerizing. "I've already explained why."

"Yeah, you stumbled onto something you shouldn't have and ended up being threatened, I get it."

If my sarcasm irks, he doesn't show it and his silence is as unsettling as his stare and its effect on me.

"Actually, that's why I called. I need to talk to you about that threat from the past and if it's followed you into the present."

He frowns and it does little to detract from his good looks. "What?"

"I think everything might be connected. What happened to you then and what's happening now. What if the same person who threatened you then is coming after the Parker family now?"

"This is getting out of control," he mutters under his breath, spinning away from me and stalking to the island bench where his laptop is charging.

Something in his tone alerts me that he knows more than he's letting on.

"What do you mean?"

He beckons me closer and flips open the lid of his laptop. "I'll show you."

I've made the right decision confiding in him but I can't shake the feeling I won't like what he has to say. The prospect of finally getting some answers is encouraging though, so I perch on a bar stool next to him and watch as he enters the cyber world with far more dexterity than Lars ever has.

"Wow, you really know your way around." I lean closer, watching his fingers fly over the keyboard. Sadness pierces my admiration: I always knew my husband was gifted with computers and if he'd stuck around we could've been a dynamite duo. He could've helped me with research and made my professional life a heck of a lot easier. Instead, I have no clue what he's been doing for the last five years.

"I love cyberspace, you know that."

"And by your deftness around the web you're better than ever."

He flashes me a bashful smile and I resist the urge to lean closer.

He moves around with ease, then does something that leaves me flabbergasted.

He hacks into the account of *that* sender, the one whose emails has turned my world upside down, twice.

"You found out who's behind this?"

"Not quite, but it's a start."

I'm flabbergasted he's done this with ease. "Whoever's behind this account is amazing at what they do because Lars couldn't get anywhere near them. How did you do it?"

"Advanced IP searches. Scouring the dark web for connections. That kind of thing."

He's being deliberately evasive and I call him on it.

"To know your way around the dark web, what exactly have you been doing since you left?"

"Odd jobs mainly, in remote towns, paid in cash so my location was untraceable." He shrugs, like emulating a ghost means nothing. "But I've also spent every spare second in Internet cafés trying to discover who drove me out of Chicago and threatened my family."

He eyeballs me and by the flare of pain I know he's talking about Shelley and me, not the Parkers.

"Did you find anything?"

He shakes his head, frustration pinching his mouth. "The initial threat came from a bogus email rerouted around the world many times over. I tried every trick I know and couldn't trace it."

He blows out a breath. "Then they emailed video footage of me at home, with you and Shelley in the background, so I knew they had the high-end computer skills to hack my laptop."

A chill sweeps over me. "They filmed us?"

He nods, anger creasing his brow. "Seeing that video scared the shit out of me and I knew they meant business insisting I back off so that's when I left."

He stares at the laptop screen, his frown deepening. "I still don't understand what I stumbled on years ago but it must've been big for them to force me out of Chicago and away from you."

There's so much pain in his voice I instinctively reach across and place my hand over his. He looks down and blinks several times, as if willing away tears.

"I would never have left you willingly," he says, his low tone fraught with anguish.

I want to say "I know" but I don't because deep down I still believe he should've stayed and we could've solved the big mystery together.

"I hate that I still don't know who's behind all of it and I'm hoping that coming back here hasn't put you and Shelley in jeopardy." He slips his hand out from under mine and drags it through his hair. "But when you reached out I had to come back."

"You don't think whoever you pissed off back then sent those emails to me now to draw you out? I mean, if you've stayed off the grid for five years, maybe they got to you through me?"

"But how would they know you'd reach out to me?"

"Because they know you're good at what you do?"

The corners of his mouth curl in amusement. "Glad you've finally admitted it."

"Shut up." I join in his soft chuckles.

"You know, maybe you're right. I did everything I could to stay off the grid after I left Chicago."

Sadness downturns his mouth. "I moved around a lot, not willing to take the risk of being tracked."

I glance at the screen. "And while you've been on the move you've been dabbling on the dark web trying to find these guys?"

"Yeah. I've had a good look at those emails and have tracked down this email account, but whoever's behind this, his identity is well protected."

"You've got a lot further tracking him than I have through my IT contact."

"When you called earlier and said you were followed…" He jabs a finger at the laptop screen. "Someone has upped the ante."

"Do you know who?"

"I'm getting close." His quick glance away tells me he knows more than he's letting on but I want to keep him talking and badgering him now will only result in him clamming up.

"How close?"

Two spots of color appear on his cheeks. "You'll have to trust me."

"Trust the guy who shut me out five years ago rather than tell me the truth?" I tap my bottom lip, pretending to think. "That's a toughie."

He ignores my snark. "I need some time to dig deeper."

"You better hurry because it's no coincidence May, Ashlin, Shamira, Christine and me have all had scares."

His eyes widen slightly. "What happened to Christine?"

I hate breaking a confidence but considering how serious this is we're way past the secretive stage. "She was attacked and bashed."

He shakes his head and runs a hand through his tousled hair like I used to. My palm tingles at the memory. "I don't believe in coincidences. Which is why I need to figure this out sooner rather than later. Another day should do it."

His gaze flickers to the screen and the scrolling code that makes my eyes hurt if I stare at it too long. "Once I crack the identity of this person we'll hand the whole thing over to the police."

I ask the obvious. "Why didn't you do that five years ago?"

He doesn't answer immediately. Instead, he pins me with a cool, assessing stare. "Why didn't you do it after you got those emails rather than reaching out to me?"

It's a good question and one I haven't pondered amid all the mishaps befalling the family. Now that I do I hate the obvious answer: I've become like the rest of the Parker family, desperately insular, overly-confident, overwhelmed with a desire to keep us all safe.

Sure, I'd initially justified it by telling myself I didn't want to drag the Parkers through any potential scandal because those emails had been so revealing. And I hadn't expected it to be so difficult to track down who's behind them. But the moment accidents started to happen I should've considered going to the police.

"Maybe I should've but I was trying to protect this family… and I thought I could solve it myself," I say, my voice trembling before I clear my throat. "You know me, I can never let a good story go untold and have to investigate."

"For what it's worth, I'm glad you reached out to me."

He slides an arm around my shoulders and squeezes. I lean into him, momentarily comforted, before giving myself a mental shake. Relying on this man for anything other than his cyber expertise won't end well.

I point at his screen. "Please get back to finding who's doing this."

"Okay." He releases me and refocuses; his fingers type at a speed I can never hope to emulate, despite my skill on a keyboard, before he shuts down the web. Only then does he turn to face me again.

"Is that the only reason you wanted to talk to me tonight, to find out who's behind this?"

"Of course. What other reason is there?"

He flashes his killer smile, the one that drew me to him in the first place that memorable day we met in a computer store twelve years ago. "You're still drawn to me after all this time and you can't stay away?"

"Yeah, keep telling yourself that." I stand, needing to escape because there's a glimmer of truth behind his question.

Even though it's been five long years since he gutted me, I feel that same pull when I'm with him. Especially now I know he didn't want to leave. He's easy to be with, always was. Our marriage had been like that too, only occasionally punctuated with arguments that all couples face but for the most part, stress free. I miss him. Miss this. This way he has of making me feel comfortable in my own skin, like he really gets me. Which is why I have to leave ASAP.

"Keep me posted, okay?"

I feel helpless, relying on him for answers, like I'm waiting for something to happen that I have no control over. I don't like it. I need to be proactive, not reactive. But what do I do now other than wait?

He stands too and steps toward me. "Stay safe."

Our gazes lock and a shimmer of excitement arcs between us.

I definitely have to leave. Grayson didn't trust me enough to tell me the truth when we were together yet I have to trust him now. It makes me increasingly nervous. What will he discover?

And what will be the repercussions, for all of us?

CHAPTER FORTY

MAY

When I gather my family regularly, I do it for them. I want them to know the value of commitment and those they can depend on. I won't live forever and being a Parker comes with responsibilities.

That's what today is about.

I've called a family meeting. They need to be prepared for change, especially now we can't trust Ashlin. Justin telling her he wants a divorce may set off a chain reaction that could have devastating consequences. She'll be hell-bent on vengeance, meaning she's a major threat to the family and I don't want her anywhere near us.

Christine hasn't come to the meeting either, considering she'll be ensconced in the private rehab center by now. She's spent several nights there now and I'm still annoyed she didn't say goodbye, preferring to sneak out of the house on the pretext of getting ice cream. I assume she didn't want to face any last-minute advice from me; not that I would've interfered, but I wanted to reiterate how proud I am of her for taking this monumental step to regaining control of her life. I've been tempted to call the facility several times to check on her but I have more important things to worry about. Losing doesn't sit well with me and managing the business in these troubling times within the family is taking all my attention.

I sit at the head of my dining table and note the curious glances cast my way. Justin, Trent, Shamira, Ria and Grayson. I hadn't invited my youngest son either but when he'd strolled into the dining room like he owned the place, I felt too uncomfortable to ask him to leave. Besides, he'll have no input in any of this so whether he stays to listen or goes is of no consequence. It's odd, seeing my youngest son at a family gathering when he's been absent for so long. I haven't figured out why he's returned after all this time but he and Ria seem on friendly terms, even though Ria appeared rattled when she'd arrived home last night after their discussion.

I hadn't bothered to ask my daughter-in-law if everything was all right. I saw it wasn't and besides, Ria wouldn't tell me if it weren't. So I'd planned on grilling Grayson when I got home but he'd already gone to bed.

"I need to be back at the office shortly so can we speed this up please?" Justin glances at his watch while the fingers on his other hand drum against his pant leg.

I like working with my go-getting son and admire his business nous but his impatience annoys me. I've tried to teach him the art of patience; that careful planning and a steady resolve ultimately win out. He impresses me most of the time and I wonder if his desire to escape has more to do with Ria being seated next to Grayson than any hunger to be back at work.

I'd seen the looks passing between my youngest son and his ex-wife, and they hadn't gone unnoticed by Justin either. He's grown considerably glummer in the few minutes they've been seated and served with coffees by the housekeeper.

Time to start.

I clear my throat, a habit I've tried to kick when I realized I begin all meetings like this. "I'd like to thank you all for coming here today on such short notice."

All eyes are fixed on me and I continue. "I mentioned at my party about access to the family fortune changing along with developments afoot in the company and I want to reinforce that today."

Grayson's eyebrows rise. "Wow, Mom's actually consulting the family on company business these days?"

I glower at Grayson and annoyingly, he smirks like he used to whenever he baited me.

"None of us are involved in the company, apart from Justin." Ria studiously avoids looking at the man she mentioned. Which tells me more than if I'd asked.

Something has happened between the two of them, something beyond the mild attraction they've always had. I'm not sure what to think about my oldest son turning to Ria for comfort so soon after his split from Ashlin. And by Justin's glower he feels Grayson's arrival threatens that. After this meeting concludes I'll make sure to speak to my youngest son and discover his intentions: why he's really here and for how much longer.

Trent has barely said a word since he arrived: in a different car than his wife. They're having a rocky time, I can sense it, but I won't interfere. Shamira has a gentle soul that matches my son's and they'll resolve their differences. She seems uncomfortable, like she'd rather be anywhere else than here.

"You're welcome to leave, Grayson, considering you gate-crashed this meeting. But you're a Parker too, maybe it wouldn't kill you to finally start acting like it."

Grayson relaxes back into his chair, smug. Justin's glower intensifies.

"I'm selling the company, and that means increased scrutiny for Parker Partnership and those associated with it." I eyeball each of them, determined to get my point across. "That means each and every one of you so I need exemplary behavior. No scandals. No photos in the press. Nobody talks about the situation with Ashlin. I'm not sure how many of you here know what's going on with Christine, but no one is to mention it outside of these four walls. And only Justin and I deal with whatever media attention comes our way. Is that clear?"

No one seems surprised by my announcement. Then again, they probably deduced the truth when I told them I'm closing the family account at my birthday. When it comes to money matters, the Parkers are very astute.

Everyone nods except Justin, who fiddles with his cell, tapping at the screen. He thinks he's above my lectures but I hadn't forewarned him about this little speech and rather than appear interested he seems bored. It doesn't sit well with me.

"Do you have any questions?"

Grayson raises his hand like a cheeky schoolboy in a classroom. "Do you always treat your family like ignorant subordinates or is this charade for my benefit?"

I had learned a long time ago to control my temper. Percival had tested my resolve daily and I soon became adept out of necessity at hiding my true feelings. He'd deliberately taunt me with the many failings he perceived. But our family fortunes had become intertwined the day I said "I do" and I knew that family always comes first, regardless of troubles behind the scenes.

Now, I muster my famed self-control to keep from thumping the table with a clenched fist as I glare at Grayson. "Family may mean nothing to you, as demonstrated by your ability to run away, but the rest of those here appreciate being kept in the loop."

My cutting chastisement has little effect on Grayson. If anything, his taunting smile reminds me so much of Percival my palm itches to slap the smirk off his face.

"Is that true, Mother? Have you asked them?" He gestures at the other occupants of the table. "Or are they too polite to say what they really think?"

I expect Justin to leap to my defense but the child I'm closest to remains obstinately silent. Trent and Shamira stare resolutely at the table and Ria glares at her ex-husband in wide-eyed shock.

"Grayson, you obviously have a problem with me that would be better addressed in private—"

"Do we all trust each other, considering what's going on?" Grayson glances around the table and I silently fume when my family members meet his eye when they hadn't met mine a moment ago. "Are you going to pretend we don't have our own motivations for toeing the line with Mom?"

Ria reaches across and pinches Grayson beneath the table and I bite back a smile. I like Ria's fearlessness and her ability to forgive and forget.

"I haven't got time for this." Justin stands so abruptly his chair bangs against the mahogany sideboard behind him. "I'll see you back at the office."

He storms out of the dining room and I don't call him back. He saw Ria reining in Grayson too and by his reaction he's jealous.

"We have to go too." Trent stands and Shamira does the same. "Don't worry, Mom, we'll be on our best behavior as always."

Shamira manages a nod before following her husband out, leaving me alone with Ria and Grayson. My son hasn't moved from his slouched position in the chair but Ria is standing, ready to follow the others out.

I want to ask her to stay. I never need a buffer but Ria has always had a calming effect on my son and I have no idea where his mood is coming from.

"Ria, can you stay a while—"

"Ria has to leave," Grayson interjects, shooting to his feet and laying a hand on her shoulder. "I'll see you out."

I don't like the desperation in his tone. I can't fathom his bizarre behavior but I'm assuming I'll soon find out without Ria acting as peacemaker.

"Thanks for coming, Ria," I say.

Ria appears as perplexed as me as she raises her hand in farewell and allows Grayson to propel her toward the hallway. As they reach the doorway Grayson glances over his shoulder and the venom in his eyes makes me reach for the table in support.

My youngest son has something to tell me and I have a feeling I won't like it. I don't like feeling out of control. I need to regain it.

CHAPTER FORTY-ONE

RIA

"What was that back there?" I cast Grayson a sideways look and jerk my thumb toward the house.

He glances over his shoulder, as if checking we're not being followed, and places his hand under my elbow to lead me further away from the house. "I wanted to rattle a few cages."

"Why?"

The moment the question tumbles from my lips I know the answer. Shock renders me speechless for a moment before I wrestle my disbelief under control. "You think one of *them* is involved?"

He shrugs, his somber stare filling me with dread. "I don't trust anyone in that room."

"You can't be serious." I glare at him. "You honestly think one of your own family is behind all this?"

He reaches out to me and I shake off his hand, his touch not in the least comforting. I'm scared, terrified in fact, that we're players in some kind of dangerous, twisted game that's bigger than the both of us. "Considering May, Shamira, Christine and I were targeted, that only leaves Justin and Trent."

Grayson eyeballs me. "We both know Trent wouldn't harm an amoeba."

I let the implication sink in that Justin is behind this.

Justin, the brother-in-law who has never been anything other than supportive to me, the man who has bestowed love and attention on my daughter as if she were his, the man who makes me feels things I shouldn't. It's unfathomable but…

The first email had incriminating photos of my three sisters-in-law but that second email targeted Ashlin only. And she was the first one to have an 'accident'. Being run off the road could've resulted in a fatality.

Having his wife removed would be a hell of a lot easier on Justin than going through a lengthy, acrimonious divorce or dealing with the repercussions of Ashlin's connections to the Parker Partnership's rivals and the threats she could make. He would be free. But am I seriously contemplating a guy like Justin could have his wife killed? It takes a dark, deranged mind to come up with a plot like that and Justin doesn't fit the image.

"I don't think Justin would do something like this."

"He's my brother and I hate to think it too, but it's all pointing to him." His lips compress in determination. "Though everyone has access to the family bank account and that means anyone with half a computer skill can get into the rest of the company's files, which is what I was doing when they threatened me to make me leave."

My head aches with the implication it could be anyone in the family behind this farce. "So you suspect everybody?"

His nose crinkles as he shakes his head. "My money's still on Justin but I need to find proof."

I nod slowly and he touches me, a glancing brush of his knuckles against my cheek. "Keeping you and Shelley safe is my priority. I left to protect you, and it's why I've come back. I hope you believe that."

He appears genuine but I'm still reeling so I bite back the obvious response, "I do," and say, "Please let me know as soon as you have anything definitive."

Not that I can do much to help. It's times like this I wish I could do more than write articles. Maybe if I had more interest in computers like Grayson, I could help him. Then again, about all I could manage was playing online games with him and I'd even sucked at that.

A small part of me wonders if my sudden interest in being able to help more has a lot to do with my ex-husband.

Hearing him admit he came back for Shelley and me sparks something within. Something that's been dormant, something I deliberately blocked out because he hurt me so badly.

But if I believe him, he left to protect us. He did the chivalrous thing because he cared. Would I have done the same?

Stupid questions I have no hope of answering when I should be focusing on discovering if Grayson is right and someone in the family is behind everything. Because I can't ignore the questions rolling around my head: is Justin doing this to be with me? In some warped way has he wanted to expedite the possibility of us getting together, even though it's never been a foregone conclusion?

He'd garner a lot more sympathy if he's a widower and waits the appropriate time before entering into another relationship. People will talk, yes, but they'll feel sympathetic toward us; him for being a widower, me for being abandoned years earlier. It would certainly smooth the way, if I was crazy enough to let anything untoward happen. I ignore my voice of reason that whispers I already have.

Maybe getting rid of Ashlin has been his end game all along and having the rest of us suffer accidents is his way of throwing off suspicion?

"Be careful." Grayson touches me again, resting his hand on my waist. "Don't say a word to anyone."

"Okay."

On impulse I place a quick kiss on his cheek. It feels so familiar, this bond between us. We never had proper closure and having him back is reawakening feelings long buried. Which ensures I need to get away.

He snags my hand as I turn to leave. "For what it's worth, leaving you was the hardest thing I ever did and if I could change everything I would."

My heart aches with what might have been for us but I don't reply. There's nothing I can say. Actions speak louder than words and Grayson's impacted my life long ago.

My car is parked on the road and as I head toward it I feel his stare boring into my back the whole way.

CHAPTER FORTY-TWO

ASHLIN

Surprisingly, my houseguest hasn't worn out her welcome. Christine is so quiet I barely know she's here and when we dine together she's not a bad conversationalist. But I'm glad she's made herself absent for now, hiding out by the pool to avoid Justin and give me some privacy.

By his abrupt tone on the phone earlier, he's in a foul mood. I don't care. I may have put up with his vagaries in the past, now I don't have to.

I hear a key in the front door. It reminds me I must change the locks. Though technically this house is his too and I don't want to antagonize him before we start the onerous divorce proceedings. It's going to be bad enough without adding further rancor to the mix.

I glance in the mirror over the glass-topped hall table, grateful I look well put-together despite the crap I'm going through: immaculate make-up covering the last of my lingering bruises, shiny hair, designer denim jacket over a red polo and white capris. I want him to see what he's missing out on. Then again, considering the infrequency of sex, let alone him looking at me, he won't care what I'm wearing or how much time I've spent blow-drying my hair.

The door swings open and I'm taken aback. He's wild-eyed and disheveled: top button undone, tie askew, shirt half tucked into the waistband of his creased pants. And the shadows under his eyes tell me insomnia is his new best friend.

"Are we alone?" He slams the door shut and strides up the hallway toward me.

I hesitate, not wanting to betray Christine's confidence, but she is his sister and he does care. "In the house, yes, but Christine is outside."

He glowers, like his sister being here is a personal affront. "Why isn't she in rehab?"

"Long story, but she's checking in later." I muster my best condescending smile. "Why are you here?"

"I haven't got time for your games," he says, dragging a hand through his hair and adding to his messy aura. "Do you have any idea what you've done?"

"No, what are you talking about?" I wave away his ranting, aware it's not wise to antagonize him when he's in this mood but way past caring.

"Your dalliance with Aaron could cost the company a great deal."

His voice is low and lethal. I think I prefer overt anger than this subtle fury and a frisson of fear skitters down my spine. Justin has never raised a hand to me but the way he's glaring at me, like he's hanging onto self-control by a thread, makes me increasingly nervous.

"I haven't told him anything—"

"Bullshit. Mom thinks I don't know but I did some digging and discovered they're sabotaging our potential sale by undercutting and swooping in for the kill." He advances toward me, a vein pulsing near his temple. "You need to stop."

I want to say "or what" but I see the malicious glitter in his eyes and I know he's hovering on the edge of losing it.

"I'm not your leak," I say, managing to sound calm and in control when in fact he has me rattled and battling an insane urge to make a run for it.

"You're pathetic, you know that?" His stare is scathing, like he wants to thump something and I hope it's not me.

At that moment, the doorbell rings and we both glance at the door like it leads to the fabled Oz.

"Expecting company?"

"Not with you here," I say, strolling toward the door like I don't care what he says when in reality I'm glad someone has interrupted our tense chat. "I wouldn't inflict your foul mood on anyone."

He swears under his breath as I open the door to find Ria on my doorstep.

"Hey, Ria." She looks as wild-eyed as Justin and I momentarily wonder if both of them arriving here at the same time means bad news and I swing the door wide. "Come in and join the party."

She hesitates when she catches sight of Justin, who does his best to appear relaxed, like our confrontation a few moments ago never happened. Bastard.

"Everything okay, Ria?" He moves toward the door to stand beside me and for a second I get the feeling he'd like to take my head and slam it into the frame.

He has an air of restrained fury about him, like he's capable of anything, and I wonder what Ria would think of the real Justin, the man behind the mask he presents to the world.

She stares at him with barely disguised hostility and I hide my surprise. "Did you have anything to do with Ashlin's accident?"

Shocked, my head swivels between them. Justin's jaw has dropped while Ria is practically bouncing on the balls of her feet, her body rigid with tension. She shoots me a concerned glance before refocusing on Justin through narrowed eyes.

A taut silence stretches before Justin shakes his head a little. "Of course not. Why would you think that?"

"Because you're online all the time at work."

I'm totally confused. What would being online at work have to do with my accident? But Ria must have good reason to confront him like this so I let her run with it. I have no idea why she thinks my husband was part of my losing control of the car and running off the road. Unless... now it's my turn to shake my head. Ria's online a lot for her job too. Has she stumbled across a hint of impropriety at the Parker Partnership or something more sinister?

Did my vindictive husband not want to settle for divorcing me but wanted to get rid of me permanently?

"Actually, Mom's the one with complete online control at work, not me." He folds his arms and glares at Ria like she's something nasty he's stepped in. I'm stupidly, irrationally glad he doesn't only reserve those disdainful stares for me. "She's in charge of the IT department, oversees major projects personally and is the only one with access to all files."

Ria blanches and sways a little. "May's in charge of IT?"

"That's what I just said," he snaps, thrusting his hands into his pockets. "What's all this about?"

"I have to go." She spins on her heel and sprints back toward her car, leaving us both staring at her, then each other, wearing matching frowns.

"What the hell was that all about?"

He shrugs. "I have no idea but I'm going to find out."

He takes out his cell and stabs at a few buttons. I don't care who he's calling but when I hear him say, "Mom, it's me," my curiosity is piqued.

I hate being privy to a one-sided conversation and it's a short one.

"Ria's in a tizz about you being our IT manager. Just giving you a heads-up she's in a strange mood and may be headed your way."

He pauses, nods. "See you later."

When he hangs up, I say, "Your family is a bunch of tattle-telling, manipulative, assholes."

"Which is why you fit right in but thankfully you won't be a part of us for much longer," he says, with a cryptic glare I have no hope of interpreting, before he marches out the door without a backward glance.

"Dickhead," I mutter, wondering if eleven is too early to fix sangria for Christine and me.

I've tried to curb my drinking since my boozy confrontation with Justin following May's birthday party precipitated our separation but after this latest bizarre confrontation, I need a drink, desperately.

CHAPTER FORTY-THREE

MAY

Grayson doesn't come inside immediately after Ria drives away. Instead, he stands at the top of the driveway like some lovesick puppy. I have no tolerance for that kind of behavior. It was his choice to abandon his family five years ago, he has to live with it and not stir up trouble now.

I don't understand my youngest son, never have. It had been a relief when he'd taken off. The only reason he'd worked at Parker Partnership was because he wasn't qualified to do anything else.

Now, as he trudges back inside, gaze glued to his cell, I wonder if he'll tell me the truth about why he's really returned home.

"You need to leave," I say, when he finally slips the cell into his pocket.

"Why?" He doesn't look surprised. In fact, his resignation reeks of a familiar meekness he's always shown, apart from that odd standoff at the family meeting earlier.

"Because you're messing with Ria and I won't stand for it."

"Ria's a big girl. She can take care of herself." He crosses his arms and leans against the door frame, like he doesn't have a care in the world. I always found his blasé attitude to life infuriating. "Why are you really trying to get rid of me, Mom?"

I flounder for a moment, unwilling to divulge the truth just yet. "You're upsetting family dynamics."

He barks out a laugh. "What's that supposed to mean?" He straightens and unfolds his arms. "Or should I guess?"

He knows. I can see it in his eyes. "Everyone was doing fine before you came home—"

"You mean Ria and Justin were doing fine." He shakes his head, anger pinching his mouth. "I'm not a complete moron. I see the way he looks at Ria, like he already owns her. And I get the feeling you'd be more than happy to facilitate that particular union."

"Don't be ridiculous, I'm not a matchmaker." I don't like anyone getting the better of me, least of all my youngest son who doesn't give a crap about anyone but himself. "But I want Justin to be happy after all he's been through and if Ria reciprocates his feelings, what's wrong with that?"

"You're delusional." He jabs a finger at the ornate sideboard covered in family photos. "According to you, Justin and Ashlin were a match made in heaven when they first got together but I guess that only meant her fortune melded well with ours. And now she's proven to not be a pushover, you don't care if she sticks around or not..." He trails off, a slightly startled expression making his eyes widen.

I've had enough. "If you're not leaving Chicago today, please find somewhere else to stay. You're no longer welcome here."

"Being kicked out of my childhood home. Nice."

I don't like the way he's staring at me, like he sees too much and it repulses him. "You'll always have a place here, Grayson, but now isn't a good time."

"It never is for you, Mom." A corner of his mouth kicks up in a sardonic grin. "You're the least maternal person I know. You've spent a lifetime treating your kids like possessions, trying to mold us into your vision of perfection. Only Justin is stupid enough to conform and even then you treat him like a lackey." He snorts. "All you care about is your precious company, your obscene fortune and the Parker name. Everyone else is merely an adjunct to that."

I don't respond to his accusation. Besides, what can I say when my youngest is right?

"I'll be out of here shortly," he says, and with one last shake of his head he leaves me standing in the living room, staring at the family photos, looking forward to rearranging them.

"Could you do me a favor?"

He pauses. "Only you could turf me out but want me to help you before I leave."

"My left knee is playing up and I need a prescription filled but the housekeeper has left for the day. Do you mind picking up my meds from the pharmacy? I'm expecting the gardener shortly, and we'd planned on having a discussion regarding new landscaping."

I expect him to refuse and I wouldn't blame him. But I'd instilled a sense of duty in all my children and he only takes a second before nodding, albeit reluctantly.

"Where's the prescription?"

"On the hall table, alongside my purse and keys. Take the money from it. Use my car."

He makes a pfft sound before stomping away. I wait until the front door slams before heading toward the front garden.

My visitor will arrive shortly and I need to be prepared.

I don't like surprises. Never have. Like the time Percival brought an escort home for his thirty-fifth birthday and forced me to join in their depravity. Or the time he'd deliberately pushed me in the pool despite knowing my fear of water. Or the time he'd belittled me in front of investors because I'd dared bar him from my bedroom.

No, I don't like surprises, not one bit.

I know what my visitor will say. After all, I've practically written this script.

I wish it hadn't come to this. When I started down this path I envisaged many scenarios but not this one.

It saddens me. I thrive on being in control of everything and everyone.

But at what cost?

Grayson has been gone two minutes when a car reverses into my driveway. Our eyes met in the rearview mirror. I'm right. My visitor knows.

It makes what I have to do all the harder.

Without waiting to see if my visitor follows, I turn and walk toward the back garden. This confrontation has to happen on my terms, where I can control the situation.

I know just the place to do it.

CHAPTER FORTY-FOUR

RIA

I have a bad feeling about this.

The moment Justin revealed his mother is the only one with access to all company files, I haven't been able to get it out of my head.

Is my sweet, supportive mother-in-law culpable in hurting her daughters-in-law?

I know she sees herself as the all-controlling matriarch, but there's a big difference between being the boss and wanting to injure her own family. It's ludicrous. Being head of the IT department in your own company and being able to create fake email accounts rerouted many times over are worlds apart. Not to mention the salient fact May has been targeted by whoever is behind this too.

I need answers. Grayson said he's close to finding the culprit but I'm not willing to sit around and wait for concrete evidence while my daughter is at risk. I'll do anything to protect her.

As I reverse up the drive I see May watching me. She's serene as always, elegantly unflappable. Our eyes meet in the rearview mirror but from a distance I can't tell if she's happy to see me or otherwise.

By the time I put the car into park, she's walking toward the back garden.

"May, wait up—"

"Grayson's calling for me, I think he's hurt himself," she calls out, glancing over her shoulder. "I asked him to re-plant a few shrubs and I think he's injured his back."

Grayson never had a green thumb but I guess May can coerce her children into doing anything if he's helping her plant. "Is he okay?"

"I don't know but he sounds bad." She's way ahead of me and I have to almost jog to keep up. She moves past the pool-house and follows the path behind the monstrous trimmed hedges that shield the back part of the garden from the house.

I never venture past the hedges because of the bees. For as long as I've known her May has been a keen apiarist. When I first started dating Grayson she'd bore me silly with tales of her honey, beeswax, propolis and royal jelly. I couldn't fathom why anyone would want to be around the vile things. It wasn't until Grayson told her I'm allergic that she shut up about her bees. She's always been understanding about my anaphylaxis, ensuring her hives are well away from the house I regularly visit as part of the Parker clan.

I pause at the hedge. I can't see her but I'm increasingly nervous about stepping past the border that separates me from her bees.

"Ria, come quick! Grayson's hurt badly." Her frantic tone, coming from behind a garden shed, has my feet running before I can contemplate the wisdom of venturing past the hedge.

It isn't until I round the corner of the shed that I know I've made a mistake.

Possibly a fatal one.

May is standing beside a box less than five feet away, her hand resting on the top. Her smile is as guileless as ever but there's a hint of something else in her eyes. It chills me to the bone.

"Do you know this is called a Langstroth hive? It opens from the top and the frames are vertical." She drums her fingers lightly on the top, her tone well-modulated and calm, like it's perfectly normal she's duped me into coming near the insects that can kill me—and she knows it. "Clever things, bees. And totally under appreciated."

Her grin widens and it creeps me out. Goosebumps rise on my skin and the nape of my neck prickles with trepidation. "Want to come closer and take a look?"

I'm close enough, without a hope of outrunning those bees if she lets them loose. I don't want to antagonize her and I need to play dumb so I can buy some time. Grayson must be inside the house and if I can back away slowly then make a run for it I may stand a chance. There must be thousands of bees in that hive and if she opens the lid on that box I'm in serious trouble, considering my EpiPen's in my bag in the car.

"Is Grayson okay?" I pretend to glance around, forcing a confused frown.

"We both know he's not here, dear, so please don't patronize me."

The drumming of her fingers matches the pounding of my heart as a cold sweat breaks out over my body.

"I don't understand—"

"Of course you do, otherwise you wouldn't be here. Justin called and told me about your bizarre little conversation so being the intrepid investigative journalist you are I knew you'd come straight here." She tut-tuts and waggles a finger at me. "You're a very intelligent woman but you're extremely predictable."

I have to keep her talking, have to give Grayson a chance to find us. Because I know exactly why she has led me here.

Injecting false enthusiasm into my voice, I say, "Justin and I discussed the IT at the company. He keeps pushing me to write an article for you as good publicity." I force a laugh, when in fact I want to scream. "But you advised us not to garner unwanted attention because of the upcoming sale, so I refused. But he won't take no for an answer and it's starting to bug me. So I'm sorry if he rung you about it but I'm sure we can sort it out ourselves. Unless he keeps persisting."

Doubt flickers in her eyes and I mentally score one to me. I continue, desperate to confuse her so I have a chance to escape.

"He mentioned you head-up IT so I thought I could get you onside when he asks me again? I imagine your department is state of the art but if you're selling, do you really want me writing an article?"

"Ah, well… yes, you're right, I'd prefer we didn't draw attention to the company at this point in time." Deep lines of confusion crease her brow, as if she's buying my fabrication, and I take a step back.

It's a mistake. I realize it the moment her brow clears and she fixes me with that maniacal stare again.

"Nice try, dear. I almost believed you." Her lips pull back in a sinister smile that bares her teeth like a feral animal. "But you know, don't you?"

I'm dead. I knew it the moment she lured me here under false pretenses. But I'll keep fighting. It's what I do, what I've always done. If I can stretch this out in the hope Grayson will come out of the house… "Know what—"

"You're doing it again. Patronizing me." She rattles the top of the box and the humming increases, filling me with dread. "This could've been simple if you hadn't poked your nose into my business. But now that you've figured out I'm the only one with full online control at the company, you've left me no choice but to get rid of you."

I gulp, swallowing my dread. I'm petrified and totally stunned that the mother-in-law I trusted is actually a madwoman.

"This all started with that stupid Ashlin." She tut-tuts. "That vain woman ruined the sale I'd negotiated thanks to her affair with Aaron, her pillow talk sabotaging my company, and she had to be removed before she inflicted further damage. So I arranged that car accident with a contact of mine who'll do anything for a fast buck, and thought the problem was solved."

Her face crinkles in consternation. "But the world is full of incompetence and they didn't get the job done. So I had to buy some time and prevent anyone looking too closely into her so-called accident, so I diverted suspicion with a few more." A sly smile curves her lips. "I enjoyed watching you all buzzing around like my beloved bees, not knowing who would be targeted next. And in the meantime, I used the distraction to continue siphoning funds from the company before the sale, ensuring my grandchildren are well provided for and never reliant on their wasteful parents."

She's crazy. Absolutely round-the-twist. She instigated all the deliberate 'accidents' in the family as a distraction to protect her precious money? Before I can formulate a response that doesn't articulate exactly how nuts that is, she continues.

"Slipping ground-up painkillers into Shamira's drink was easy, her head is always in the clouds. And paying some kid to pretend to run me over was a cinch." She winces and rotates her wrist. "Though taking a tumble and spraining this wasn't part of the plan."

She fixes her surprisingly clear gaze on me and that clarity scares me the most. She's lucid and talking about murder like she's planning her next shopping expedition. "Then there's my pathetically addicted daughter Christine, who can't keep off the drugs. Rather easy paying someone to teach her a lesson."

Bile rises in my throat. She paid someone to beat her own daughter? I can't fathom the depths of her madness, made worse by the calm, controlled façade she presents.

"As for you." She jabs her finger in my direction. "Jumping at shadows. Always looking over your shoulder. Having you followed by a PI on the pretext of an investigation into your private life was a breeze."

She looks sad, like she's perpetuated this madness reluctantly. "I had high hopes for you, dear. You could've joined Parker Partnership and been a great asset to our PR department, writing all our copy, making us look amazing until another sale opportunity came along. Just imagine, you could've worked alongside Justin and who knows what may have developed between the two of you." Her tinkle of laughter sends ripples of alarm down my spine.

"He likes you, you know. It's obvious. And with time you could've reciprocated his feelings and made a powerful couple, capable of anything." She shakes her head. "It's a shame that won't happen now, because you're the only one who knows any of this and for that, you have to die."

I want to yell "you're crazy, Grayson has almost figured this out," but I see her grab the top of one of the hives and my throat seizes, in the same way it will if one of those bees stings me.

"It's a shame you'll have an anaphylactic reaction to my bees and won't be around to tell anyone what you know. And they'll think it was a weird accident, you coming down here looking for me and getting stung." She lifts the handle an inch and I swear I stop breathing.

Fear floods my lungs and my muscles lock, making movement impossible. I'm on the verge of emptying my bladder in terror and there isn't one damn thing I can do about it.

I think of Shelley, my darling daughter: her faintest lisp, her penchant for unicorns, her unswerving belief that all is right with the world.

If only.

I can't die this way. I won't.

"May, you've been under a lot of stress lately. You said as much when you called the family meeting this morning, so maybe all this is a way of dealing—"

"You know, Percival was like this at the end." She mimics talking with her free hand. "He blathered too, begging for forgiveness for yet another indiscretion, saying he'd have me investigated for costing the company money, before flinging a separation in my face."

Her eyes glitter with malice. "He actually thought he could leave me and get away with it."

Her calm grin is chilling. "So many ways to cause a heart attack by ingesting untraceable concoctions." She pats her chest, over her heart. "My only regret? I didn't kill him years earlier. But I could put up with his sadism and his infidelities, I couldn't tolerate being ousted from the company."

She snaps her fingers. "He thought he was smarter than me when he stumbled on my little scheme to siphon money from the company. As bad as his nosy son Grayson." She snickers. "It was too easy getting rid of Grayson by threatening harm to you and Shelley, but when Percy picked up where he'd left off… I stopped him. And became a wealthier woman in the process."

I'm shell-shocked. She'd been behind those threats forcing Grayson to leave? I thought she'd sent those emails to me and caused our accidents. But learning she murdered her husband means I have no chance. She's revealed too much. Nothing will save me bar a miracle.

"So you see, dear, while it pains me to do this, you've left me no choice."

I want to yell that Grayson has almost figured this out. But I can't put him in danger. For I have no doubt, if she killed her husband she'll kill her son without hesitation. And I have to think of Shelley, I have to protect her. If I'm not around, she'll need her father.

"Think of it this way. Your death will be surprisingly painless and fairly quick. You'll get stung, your throat will constrict and you'll pass out. Simple." She grasps the handle tighter and lifts the lid, sliding a frame out of the box.

Bees swarm the air and the instant adrenaline surge makes my legs move. I turn and run. Long strides that cover the ground but not fast enough. My thighs cramp and my calves burn but I keep running without looking back.

The buzzing fills my ears and I panic, swinging my arms in a wild attempt at swatting, making contact with nothing but air.

I hear a strange hissing behind me and smell smoke.

"Nooo…" May's anguish almost stops me but I keep running, needing to clear the hedge before I can risk a glance back.

My lungs are thick with smoke and I cough, making a desperate lunge when I reach the hedge, and I'm through.

Only then do I peek over my shoulder to see Grayson, brandishing a smoker, while May attempts to lift more frames.

She's tugging at the hives, hunched over, oblivious to everything but killing me. I see Grayson lift the smoker overhead and bring it down on the back of her neck. Her fingers relax and she appears to grasp at air before she slumps to the ground, unconscious.

"Run!" he yells and I do, not stopping until I reach the front of the house.

Another adrenaline burst propels me at a pace I never knew I'm capable of and my legs are wobbling when I finally reach my car. I fumble for the remote in my pocket, stabbing at it several times before the thing unlocks.

I wrench open the door, tumble into the driver's seat and slam the door shut, hitting the lock three times until it clicks.

Only then do I finally allow myself the luxury of bawling.

CHAPTER FORTY-FIVE

ASHLIN

We're on our second sangria each when Christine's cell rings. She glances at the screen and wrinkles her nose.

"It's Grayson."

"What does he want?" I tip my glass back to catch the last few drops with my tongue. My head feels fuzzy and I'm enjoying the wine buzz before midday. It blurs my run-in with Justin nicely. Hopefully, after a few more glasses, I'll forget him altogether.

"Probably doing Mom's dirty work. She must be dying to know how I'm doing in rehab but rather than calling herself she's getting a minion to do it."

Christine stares at the blaring phone, clearly dithering.

"Just answer it already," I say, reaching for the sangria jug. "I'll top you up after you do."

"Deal." She tosses back what's left in her glass with two gulps before answering. "Hey, Grayson, what's up?"

I hear the deep murmur of his voice, followed by Christine easing the phone away from her ear for a moment. She's pale and the glass slips from her hand, landing on the grass beside the sunlounger.

I lean forward and touch her thigh to get her attention, mouthing, "What's wrong?"

She shoos me away, pressing the phone to her ear again. "I don't understand."

I hate being privy to one-sided telephone calls and resort to topping up my glass. She'll tell me what's going on when she's done.

"Mom did *what*?"

Christine's ashen, making the bruises on her cheekbones pop and her shiner resemble an eye-patch.

I wonder if she'll want to stay with my girls coming home today. I'm looking forward to picking them up from school later and spending some time with them. I adore my girls and with the impending custody battle I need to make sure I do everything right. I know Justin. He won't give in easily and he'll use every dirty trick at his disposal to make me look like a bad mom.

"Do you need us to come down there?" She fixes me with a glare I have no hope of interpreting. "Okay, I'll be there soon."

She disconnects and the cell falls into her lap, as if her fingers have turned numb.

"What's your mom done this time?"

She stares at me, wide-eyed, and shakes her head. "I can't believe it."

"What?"

"Mom tried to kill Ria." Christine leans down to pick up the wine glass she dropped while I try to process what she's said.

I press my fingertips to my temples. "I'm not that drunk, yet I could've sworn you said—"

"Mom tried to murder Ria."

I can't understand any of this but before I can interrogate Christine she pushes slowly to her feet, shaking her head. "I have to go."

"Do you want me to come—"

"No," she yells, and I wince. "Sorry, but this is something the Parkers have to do on our own."

I let her go, trying to clamp down on my irrational fear that this family is capable of anything.

CHAPTER FORTY-SIX

SHAMIRA

"I can't believe this." Trent is shaking his head, his pallor scaring me. "Mom tried to kill Ria?"

He's repeated this twice already, and Justin obviously loses patience on the other end of the line, because Trent says, "I'll throw a few things together and be there as soon as I can."

His eyes are wide when he hangs up. "Mom's lost the plot. She's been behind everything, including trying to poison you."

I kind of figured that out from snippets of his conversation just now, but I can't worry about his psycho mom when there are more important issues between us.

"I need to go and be with my family."

"Okay," I say, but he's already turned his back on me and is heading for the bedroom.

I follow, watching with a heavy heart as he packs, haphazardly stuffing random items of clothing into a duffel bag. I'm oddly dispassionate. Empty. Aching. None of this feels real but it is, a living nightmare where the man I love finds me abhorrent and is leaving me.

Because that's the real reason he's packing. Spending time with his family while they sort out this mess with May is the last thing he'd do if he didn't want to get away from me.

"I'm sorry," I say, for the umpteenth time.

I've lost count of how many times I've apologized: for the abortion, for the lies, for the paranoia.

He wants space, some time apart to think. He says he still loves me, for what it's worth, but I believe in the old adage 'actions speak louder than words.'

He zips up the bulging overnight bag and turns to face me. "That's it, then."

I avert my eyes from that bag, wishing I could unzip it and re-hang all his clothes. "Will you keep me posted?"

His sigh is heartfelt and I ache for what he's going through, his mother's lunacy on top of my confession. "I have no idea what's happening but for now I need to go see my crazy family so we can face this together and I'll probably stay on for a while."

"Good plan."

I can't fathom that May is capable of murder. She's too refined, too dignified. We don't know why she did it and I don't want to know. All I'm hoping for is that Trent has time to think about us while he's getting a handle on his loony mother with his siblings. I understand his need to be with them and I'm hoping that living with that motley bunch will have him coming home sooner rather than later.

"There's going to be a lot of media coverage for the family." His eyes darken with pain. Pain I caused. "They're going to dig, to try and come up with whatever dirt they can. Are you prepared for that?"

I eyeball him so he can see I'm not afraid, not anymore. "The most important person knows everything about me now so I don't care what they print."

Surprise widens his eyes. "But the shop? It could affect your business."

Even now, when his world as he knows it has been obliterated—first by me, then his mother—he's concerned about me.

I cross the short distance between us and lay a hand on his chest, relieved when he doesn't pull away. "Nothing is as important to me as you and our marriage. So whatever happens, we'll face it and we'll get through it." My hand slides up to cup his cheek. "It's what we do."

He allows my hand to linger a moment before gently removing it with his. "I need time, okay?"

I believe him. I have to. Because from the first moment I realized he meant more to me than a meal ticket out of my old life, I believed in this man. He's loyal, dependable and supportive. I wasn't lying when I said the business means nothing to me, the money too. He's all I want.

But there's something that's niggling at me and I know if I don't ask him now, I'll obsess.

"How did your mom know which bottle of mine to poison?"

He stiffens. "What?"

"That night at my launch, how did she know which bottle I used for my usual pick-me-up blend?"

He glares at me, affronted I've had the audacity to ask such a question, because he's not stupid and he knows what I'm implying.

"You think *I* had something to do with her poisoning you?"

I take a steadying breath and blow it out. "Did you?"

"After all you've kept from me and all we've been through…" He shakes his head, then drags a hand through his hair. "Fuck, Shamira, surely you can't believe I'd harm you?"

I don't know what to believe, that's the problem. I trust my gut and when it comes to my husband, I know he's ultimately on my side. But he'd been so disgusted by my revelations and I have to know whether he had any part of his mother's lunacy.

"You were so mad at me and I just want to know—"

"I had nothing to do with Mom poisoning you." He hoists the duffel higher on his shoulder, sadness clouding his eyes. "She's been to every one of your launches and could've seen you drink from that damn bottle any time. But the fact you think I had something to do with hurting you…"

He swivels abruptly and heads for the door, leaving me heart-broken and lamenting the yawning gap between us. If I hadn't already shattered his trust in me by keeping the secrets of my past, I've irrevocably damaged it now by implying he was an accomplice to my poisoning.

"Is it okay if I call you—"

"I need time," he says, his hand resting on the doorknob. "Leave me alone to sort this mess out with my family."

I should've known that when things get tough, the Parkers would rally around each other. It's what they do. And it leaves me feeling more of an outsider than ever.

"Okay," I murmur, as I watch my husband walk out the door and I pray to a god I don't believe in that he'll come back.

CHAPTER FORTY-SEVEN

RIA

I'm still shaking, locked in my car, when Justin's SUV screeches into the driveway. He swerves next to my car, kills the engine and flings open his door before making a beeline for me. I shudder as a fresh wave of nausea rolls over me. I came close to dying several minutes ago.

Justin bangs on my window and my fingers tremble as I unlock the car door. He wrenches it open and reaches for me.

"My God, are you okay? Grayson told me what happened…" He trails off when I burst into tears again and he hauls me out of the car and holds me close against his chest. Grayson is still in the house with May; he texted me to say he's okay, that he's calling the family for back-up, but now I know what May's capable of I'm exceedingly nervous that he's alone in there with her.

I sob, great gut-wrenching cries that make my head ache, oblivious to his murmured platitudes but grateful for the comfort nonetheless.

His cell rings and he reluctantly releases me to slide it out of his pocket.

"It's Grayson," he says, before answering it. "What's going on? I've just arrived."

A frown furrows his brow as he glances at me. "Ria's okay, I'm with her now."

He pauses and his frown deepens. "Are you sure that's wise?"

After several moments where I struggle to hear what Grayson's saying, he nods. "Okay, we'll come in."

I inadvertently take a step back. No way am I going anywhere near their psycho mother.

Justin hangs up and says, "Grayson says Mom's groggy from him knocking her out, and he's restrained her, but he wants us in there with him—"

"I don't care what he wants. I'm waiting out here until the police arrive."

His gaze darts away, sheepish. "Grayson has called Christine and Trent. They're both coming over too, but he wants us to be in there until they arrive." He swipes a hand over his face. "And I don't blame the guy. Why should he be the only one to deal with her?"

"Fair point." I gesture at the house. "Why don't you go in and I'll wait out here for the others?"

He reaches out to touch my hand and I flinch. "Ria, Grayson and I won't let anything happen to you."

I refrain from responding with "you almost did."

He tries to take my hand again and I yank it away. The last thing I need is for Grayson to see us walking in hand in hand. Not that it would mean anything. The moment my ex-husband returned I haven't given Justin a second thought. I'm not fickle but Grayson and I always had something special and while I know we can never go back, I'm hoping that now we've uncovered who threatened him all those years ago he might have a chance to be part of our lives again.

"Okay." I take tentative steps toward the house, hating that I'm still shaken up. I'm not this woman. I'm strong and independent, but coming face to face with crazy May, no matter how groggy she is, isn't high on my to-do list right now.

Justin unlocks the front door and we enter, treading lightly as we walk down the hallway to the back of the house. My heart is

thumping with fear, until I spy Grayson standing in the doorway
to the conservatory.

Without a second thought I cross the short space between us
and fling myself into his arms. He wraps his around me, holding
me tight, and at last I feel some sense of calm. I'm all cried out
from a few moments ago but I cling to him, inhaling his familiar
scent, comforted.

When we ease apart, he places a finger under my chin and tips
it up. "Are you sure you're okay?"

Mute, I nod.

He gives a little shudder. "I can't believe… I mean, if I'd lost
you—"

"Ssh, it's okay." I press a finger to his lips and am startled by
the intimacy of it.

Justin clears his throat behind us and in that moment I realize
how much Grayson means to me, because I'd forgotten my
brother-in-law was even there.

Clutching my hand tight, Grayson says, "She's in here."

I balk for a moment and he squeezes my hand, infusing me
with his silent strength, and I will my legs to move. The three of
us enter the conservatory, where May has presided over so many
family gatherings. Where she entertained with aplomb. Where
she lavished her granddaughters with attention.

A lump swells in my throat at the thought of what I'll tell
Shelley, who adores her grandmother.

I spy May sitting on the sofa near the French doors leading to
the patio. She's half slumped and her hands are bound at the wrist
with what looks like gardening twine.

We lock gazes across the room and I clamp down on the instant
flare of pity, because May isn't some frail, broken old woman.

My mother-in-law is a murderer.

She killed her husband and was about to do the same to me.

"Justin, how nice of you to join us," May says, like we've all come to pay her a visit.

"You're sick." Justin shakes his head as the three of us take a seat on the sofa opposite. "What the hell is wrong with you, Mom?"

"Absolutely nothing." She eyes us with defiance. "I protect what's mine."

"By killing Dad? By trying to murder Ria?" Justin's face reddens with anger. "Not to mention trying to hurt Chrissie, Shamira and Ash."

May scoffs. "Like you don't want to hurt Ashlin yourself."

Justin's lips thin and he looks away. His hands are clenched into fists and Grayson lays a comforting hand on his shoulder for a moment before removing it.

"I hope you haven't called the police," she says, sounding imperious as always. "I want to talk to you all before I'm taken away."

"Trent and Christine are on their way, then the police will be contacted," Grayson says.

May's brow furrows. "I should've known Christine wouldn't check into rehab. My daughter is a total waste of space."

Grayson and Justin both stiffen but neither says a word. I don't blame them. How can you converse with a madwoman?

May's fanatical gaze focuses on Justin. "I hope I can count on you." She bestows her usual proud smile on Justin, the one that makes him straighten his shoulders even if he doesn't know it. He's always been her golden boy, doing exactly as he's told.

"Let me guess, this is about your precious company." He avoids her eyes, his discomfort evident in every line of his tense body.

"Of course. You're exactly like me, and don't you forget it—"

"I'm nothing like you," he spits out, half-rising off the sofa before Grayson placates him again.

May grins and steeples her fingers as if oblivious to her restraints, resting her hands in her lap.

"All I need you to do is keep the company running as smoothly as possible because another sale is imminent." Her chilling grin widens. "Whatever charges are leveled at me, they won't stick. I'll accentuate the poor helpless grandmother act, and considering the healthy yearly donation I make to the pension fund of most cops in this city, I'll be well looked after until I'm released."

"You're delusional," Justin mutters, bitterness lacing his reluctant response, as if he can't bear talking to her.

"No, I'm remarkably sane." Her gaze glitters with malice. "I value what's rightfully mine. I fight for it. I protect it. I make the tough calls for the sake of the company and you do too."

Disgust pinches his mouth. "But you're forgetting one point. I don't kill to get what I want."

"Don't you?" May leans forward and fixes Justin with a maniacal stare. "You killed your marriage years ago because you had the hots for your brother's wife."

I feel Grayson lean into me and I lay a comforting hand on his thigh, while Justin recoils. I know May, she likes nothing better than one-upmanship and no one, not even her favored eldest son, will get the better of her. "The minute Ria became available five years ago you started retreating from Ashlin. Subconsciously at first but it spiraled and I watched your obsession grow." Her smug smile makes his eyes narrow. It does little to hide his hatred. "Face it, son, you hoped your marriage would end so you could go sniffing around Ria."

Justin's jaw clenches, like he's struggling to hold back a response, as May gives an exaggerated tut-tut designed to taunt. "Seriously, Justin, you should be thanking me. I was trying to do you a favor by expediting your wife's departure, ensuring she wouldn't sabotage another sale with her whoring, saving us a fortune in alimony, preserving more money for your daughters who will ultimately carry on the Parker tradition with Shelley—"

"Shut up," he growls, leaping to his feet. The muscles around his clenched jaw bunch as he struggles to get himself back under control, and I finally speak.

"She's pushing you for a reaction, Justin. Don't give her the satisfaction."

May's gaze swings onto me as Justin sits. "So, finally found your voice, dearest daughter-in-law?" She shakes her head. "You were always my favorite. Pity you had to be such a nosy-Parker." She laughs at her own joke, a cackle devoid of amusement.

"I can't believe you were behind everything." I shake my head. "Those threatening emails, the accidents—"

"I don't know about any emails, but yes, I already told you I had a hand in the rest." Her offhand shrug infuriates me, like she doesn't give a damn how much she hurt her family. "Everyone can be bought and I have contacts everywhere who will do anything for a price."

May likes toying with people, always has, to see if they have the mettle to match wits with her. She's picked the wrong person this time.

"So you really think your contacts will get you out of this?"

"Of course." May has never been short on confidence. "I'll never confess to anything. And it's my word against you and Grayson, and I'll tarnish you both if I have to. Besides, there's little evidence, circumstantial at best. Plus I have the Parker fortune on my side. I can buy anything and anyone." Her eyes glitter with triumph. "I've done it before."

I don't bother responding to her ridiculous claim. Instead, I ask the one question I need an answer to.

"Why did you do it, May? All of it?"

She eyes me with respect. "For my grandchildren."

Grayson, Justin and I are stunned into silence by her bizarre proclamation.

"I know my own children only speak to me because I control the money. It's why I cut them off and wanted to sell the company, to invest for Jessie, Ellen and Shelley." Her expression softens. "They're innocent, untainted by the greed that drives the rest of you. Plus they're young and pliable. I can mold them into strong, independent women who won't be duped by usurpers."

She lets out a soft sigh. "They're my one chance at redemption considering I failed my children…"

"But you're forgetting one thing, May." I glance across at Justin and he gives the slightest nod, as if he knows what I'm about to say. "After today, you'll never get to see your grandchildren ever again."

May jerks as if prodded and I swear her eyes roll back in her head. "What did you say?"

"You heard her, Mother." Justin's tone is low and menacing. "You will never be allowed anywhere near your granddaughters after this."

May's shoulders straighten, outrage puffing her chest as she stares at us in disbelief. "You can't be serious. Everything I've ever done has been for them. They're good girls. They deserve to be looked after." She starts to bluster, her face reddening. "They need to be instructed on how to be proper Parker women. They need guidance on self-reliance and money management and company policy and—"

"Shut up." Grayson's cell buzzes and he takes a quick glance at it. "Chrissie and Trent are almost here, so it's time I rang the police."

May ignores him and continues to stare at me, the strange glint in her eyes beseeching me to understand something I have no hope of fathoming. "I need to see my girls. They need me—"

"It's over, Mother." Justin sounds plain weary now. "You are never seeing Jess, El and Shelley ever again. Your precious attorneys that you keep on retainer will draw up the necessary legal documents to ensure it once they hear what you've done."

May deflates before our eyes, appearing to shrink in on herself. Her shoulders slump, her head falls forward and she's plucking at invisible threads on her skirt.

"Can I use the bathroom please?" It's a soft, subservient tone I've never heard May use, a plaintive plea from a defeated woman.

"Fine," Grayson says, waiting until May stands and not offering a hand to help. "But I'll be right outside."

The fact she doesn't snap back with some wisecrack about him being her prison guard is telling. Maybe she's finally accepted it's over for her?

May shuffles from the room, with Grayson tailing her, leaving Justin and I to stare at each other in dumbfounded silence. After a few moments, Justin swipes a hand over his face and says, "She's wrong, you know. I wouldn't have wished anything bad to happen to Ash no matter how I felt about you—"

"It's over, Justin."

I eyeball him so he'll understand I'm referring to everything. Him, me, the forbidden attraction.

Understanding sparks in his eyes and he nods. "Okay."

Relief filters through me, but it's short-lived when I hear Grayson's frantic yell.

CHAPTER FORTY-EIGHT

MAY

I can't believe it's come to this.

Hiding in my own bathroom, buying some time, trying to gather my wits.

My chest is tight, anxiety robbing my lungs of air.

I've done all this for my granddaughters. I won't be deprived of the chance to help them, to make them true Parkers and better than their sniveling parents.

I'm trying to stay calm. I know what will happen. The police will charge me with one count of murder—that had been a dumb move, taunting Ria with my smugness about getting rid of Percival—and one count of attempted murder. Though if they really want to throw the book at me, they'll try to pin Christine and Shamira's 'accidents' on me too. It's silly, because I never intended to murder them, just throw the focus off Ashlin so the hit-man I hired could try again while I used the distraction to continue siphoning company funds for my girls. Annoyingly, if Grayson hadn't shown up, Ria would be dead and I wouldn't be in this predicament. I curse the vagaries of fate.

As for the other charges that will come to light, embezzlement and fraud, I can fight those. Grayson thought he was so damn smart stumbling across my siphoning company money years ago but it didn't take much to scare him off. Threatening his wife and child put paid to his interference. He's weak and afraid, like his father. I counted on it and he proved me right. He fled, enabling me to stash away hundreds of millions of dollars without Percy knowing. I'd initially done it to spite my asshole husband, for all the years I'd put up with his emotional abuse, later realizing the money would protect my granddaughters from the harsh lessons of life. Then not long after Grayson left, Percy started digging where our youngest son had been and I couldn't have that. Percy discovered my secret and threatened to oust me from the company. So I'd killed him. I thought I'd gotten away with it too, until now.

With my admission to Ria, the police will reopen the case. Not that it matters. Justice moves slowly and I'll be a model prisoner. I'll get privileges because of my age, my social standing and my money. I can buy anything and anyone.

I envisage the whole scenario: paying exorbitant sums to the corrupt guards to protect me, biding my time, planning the untraceable crime.

Because I will walk out of prison a free woman.

I'll send a message to my online contact, the man who can do anything and maintain my anonymity, to take out the two people who are the only witnesses to my confession.

I won't miss my son Grayson. He was dead to me years ago.

As for Ria, she has proved to be a major disappointment.

I thought she might console Justin after his marriage imploded, the only potentially good thing to come out of this farce. But he's recalcitrant and bitter, and Ria could've helped him through it. She should stand by him and support him, not be making goo-eyes at Grayson.

I can make it happen. Once Grayson and Ria are gone, there'll be nothing standing in my way. The prosecution will drop the charges and I'll be free.

But then I remember Justin and Ria's threats, that regardless of what happens I'll never see my beloved granddaughters again… they'll keep them from me… I'll have no access at all…

I stare at my reflection in the mirror as my bravado fades.

I can't go to prison. I can't face a lifetime of being deprived of the only thing that matters to me anymore.

Everything I've done has been for Jessica, Ellen and Shelley. And if they'll never know it, what's the point?

A loud banging on the door makes me jump. "Hurry up, Mom," Grayson yells and I flip him the finger.

He's an idiot, the twine binding my wrists already loosening. They think they're so smart, my family. I bet they imagine incarcerating me then enjoying the spoils I've worked a lifetime to build.

But would they enjoy it as much if dogged with guilt?

I'm not a weak woman, far from it, but I'm exhausted. I'm going to be dispossessed of the only thing worth fighting for, my granddaughters. I know Justin, he's as stubborn as me, and Ria is a protective mom. She won't let me near Shelley no matter how much I grovel, not after what I did to her.

So there's only one way out.

I hook the twine over a gold tap and tug, over and over. It bites into my wrist, the pain sharp, and a few drops of blood trickle into the sink. I don't care. In a few moments I'm free and I flex my wrists several times before opening the bathroom cabinet, instantly spotting what I'm looking for.

The untraceable poison I doctored Percy's whiskey with is on the bottom shelf, hidden in a misnamed bottle for an old muscle relaxant. The faintest shimmer of fear makes my hand shake as I fill a glass with water, unscrew the cap and tip the powder in. I stir it with my index finger, staring at the colorless liquid that will end all this.

My regret is fleeting as I take the first sip, before forcing myself to gulp the rest. My head swims and my eyes blur as I slide toward the ground, grasping at the sink for support. There's a loud crash as I knock over the expensive soap holder and the last thing I see is Grayson's stricken expression as he flings open the door and stares at me in open-mouthed horror as I take my last breath.

CHAPTER FORTY-NINE

RIA

The funeral is small and private, the resultant media furor isn't.

May would be proud that she's as notorious in death as she was when she lived.

The memorial service at the cemetery is brief. We're not hypocrites. We disperse as soon as the ceremony is finished, seeking refuge in black limousines with dark tinted windows to avoid the news cameras. Only Justin faces the media scrutiny. He has to, being CEO of one of the biggest financial companies in the state. After only three weeks in his new role as sole boss at Parker Partnership, he's thriving. He's not selling the company and after recovering the hundreds of millions May siphoned, he's using the money to expand and consolidate all assets. He's fair too, insisting all family members have a seat on the board and individual trust funds. Thankfully, he's too busy to visit or contact me beyond the family meetings he calls. Our attraction has fizzled out and I'm relieved.

I'm growing closer to Ashlin too. I guess everything that happened has brought us together. With Christine moving back to Chicago and postponing her rehab until after the funeral, the four of us—Shamira, Ash, Chrissie and I—have caught up for dinner a few times. We'll never be best friends but more than our surname bonds us now. We closed ranks after May's suicide a month ago, relying on each other because we can't trust anybody else. Ironic, that her death solidified our bond when she tried so hard to make us a cohesive unit when she was alive.

Everyone's secrets are revealed and we're all closer for it. We accept each other for who we are in a way May never did.

We're catching up at May's mansion later for a wake. A celebration of the loving grandmother she'd been because the kids deserve to remember her that way. Maybe we all do.

But for now, I have somewhere I need to be.

I give the limo driver directions then raise the glass between us to ensure I have complete privacy. I need to read the letter Grayson pressed into my hand at the end of May's service, with a whispered, "Meet me at our place after you read this."

It's all very cryptic and I'm over the mysteries of this family, but as I slide a sheet of paper covered in Grayson's familiar scrawl out of the envelope I can't help the flicker of excitement that zaps through me.

He used to leave me notes when we were married all the time. Cutesy, love notes mostly, tacked onto the cookie jar or on top of the butter in the fridge or in my lunch bag. He'd said emails were too accessible by anyone and words meant more when written down so he preferred the personal pen touch. I used to accuse him of being a romantic goofball but considering that anybody can be hacked for a price, and after what we've all been through, I tend to agree.

Memories of his past notes bring tears to my eyes and I blink several times before I start reading.

Dear Ria,

I'm writing this the old-fashioned way not as some lame attempt to recapture our past but because you know as well as I do that emails aren't safe.

I owe you an explanation.

May was telling the truth about not sending those emails. I did.

I gasp out loud and reread that last sentence. Twice. What the… He can't be the one who sent them.

Why the hell would he have sent me that incriminating photo five years ago?

But as I mentally pose the question, I know. He wanted to ensure I didn't try to find him.

I continue reading.

I'll explain everything when I see you shortly and I hope you'll hear me out.

But I want you to know that everything I did has been out of love for you and Shelley.

Leaving you both was the hardest thing I've ever had to do and once you hear the truth, I hope you'll find it in your heart to forgive me. And maybe, just maybe, we can move forward together? Recapture the life we once had?

I love you, Ria.

Always have.

Grayson x

(This will self-destruct in five minutes.)

A guffaw bursts from my lips. He always used to sign off that way when we emailed each other. It's so quintessentially Grayson I find myself pressing his letter to my chest with one hand and swiping at the tears trickling down my cheeks with the other.

I have no idea what he's going to say but it doesn't make what he put me through any easier to accept. I understand his rationale to protect Shelley and me five years ago but I can't help but wish if he'd been more open, none of this would've happened.

He's re-bonding with Shelley and I've facilitated that. My daughter needs to know her father and vice versa. They've regularly met over the last four weeks and he's taking it slow, like I insisted. But it's obvious how much they love each other and I'm glad my daughter has a chance at a real relationship with her father.

As for letting him back into my life… it's too soon.

I need to tell him that, in person.

The limo stops outside my place and he's waiting out the front, hope lighting his eyes as I step out of the limousine.

He glances at the letter in my hand. "You read it?"

I nod and shove it into my handbag. "We need to talk."

"I was hoping you'd say that." He takes a step forward and I hold up my hand.

"I don't know how I feel about you or if I can forgive you…" my voice quivers and I clear my throat, "but if I gave Ashlin a second chance it's only fair I do you the same courtesy."

That lopsided grin I once loved lights up his face. "However long it takes, I'm okay with that."

He takes another step forward and this time I don't stop him. "Maybe you can write an article on our crazy family? Or better yet, pen a novel and win a Pulitzer?"

"None of this is remotely funny—" He crushes me to him in a bear hug that snatches my breath.

I don't resist. I enjoy being held by him too much.

When he releases me, I point at the house. "Time to tell me everything."

Solemnity fills his eyes as he nods and follows me. I unlock the door and wait until we're both inside before closing it. "Do you want a drink?"

He shakes his head. "No, I need you to know everything so we can start moving forward."

I don't tell him that may never happen, that my trust in him and this family is shattered. But I will hear him out and I gesture at the sofa, where we both sit, a yawning gap between us.

There's an awkward pause, before he rushes in. "So I guess you figured I sent that ridiculous photo so you'd end our marriage hating me and expedite our divorce."

I nod, fixing him with a dubious stare. "Stupid."

"I know, but at the risk of sounding repetitive, I had to because the danger to you and Shelley was real. I received death threats, along with footage of you and Shelley at home, and photos at school, at the supermarket, everywhere." He drags a hand through his hair and the urge to smooth it is strong. "I had no choice because they told me to leave or they'd make good on threats so to keep you safe I ran. I figured if I stayed off the radar and resumed investigating what I'd discovered at the company remotely I could get proof and ultimately get my life back, with you and Shelley in it."

He sounds genuine but I need to hear all of it before I make any kind of decision that will affect my daughter's future.

"So May was behind the threats?"

He nods, anguish twisting his mouth. "Back then, I noticed an anomaly in Parker Partnership's finances. Millions being siphoned out. Mother must've flagged it because a day after I discovered it, I received the threats."

"This is bizarre." I press my fingers to my temples and massage them. "So why did you send those emails to me?"

He glances away, sheepish. "After regularly trying for years to infiltrate the company online to get proof of who's behind everything, I discovered a flaw in their latest software program about two months ago and realized only five people have complete access to the program, three of the IT managers, Mom and Justin. But anyone who had access to the family's bank account could hack into the program if they knew what they were doing."

He shakes his head. "I couldn't believe someone in the family could be responsible for stealing hundreds of millions, let alone getting me to stop investigating by threatening you and Shel, but I had to consider all possibilities so I needed to come home in order to delve deeper. But I know you trust everyone implicitly and would hate me after I abandoned you, so if I'd come to you, you wouldn't believe a word I said. That's when I sent those emails appealing to your investigative side, knowing you'd eventually reach out to me."

"That's awfully cocky of you." Annoyed he knows me so well, I glare at him. "What if I'd gone directly to May after receiving those emails? Or Justin?"

"You'd never do that because you've always been protective of this family, but I knew you'd want to investigate because that's who you are. And ultimately, you'd reach out to me."

I shake my head. "There were so many potential flaws in your dumbass plan."

"Yet I'm here and we now know the truth."

It's a sobering thought, the extent of May's treachery, and we both know it.

"Do you think your reappearance rattled her and that's why she lost the plot?"

"No, it didn't faze her, because she probably thought I'd given up." His stare is filled with concern. "I'm so sorry I inadvertently put you in danger again."

I shrug, like his mother's depravity means little, when in fact I'll have nightmares for the rest of my life about those last few moments when she'd lifted the top of that beehive.

"She was a desperate, delusional woman," I say, sounding surprisingly calm. "It's rather terrifying to think she wanted to mold our daughter, along with Jessie and Ellen, like some twisted puppet-master."

He shudders and reaches for my hand. "It's over and now you know the truth about me."

He scoots closer and I let him take it. "I know you must think the Parkers are more trouble than we're worth, after all you've been through. But I love you. I want to come home, be a husband and a father again." He raises my hand to his lips and presses a kiss to the palm. "I want to make our marriage work."

I want to believe him, I really do. His eyes radiate sincerity and his expression is guileless.

But I can't ignore the fact this man lied to me five years ago and what's to say he's not doing the same now?

When I remain silent, he says, "I don't expect you to take me back overnight, but I'm hoping we can start rebuilding trust and see what the future holds?"

Hope blooms in my chest but I squash it. I'm not the same naïve, trusting woman I was when I married him and into the almighty Parker family. I'm wiser now. Time to start acting like it.

"I need time," I eventually say, and he seems appeased by that, bundling me into his arms for a hug.

Being a Parker has taught me one thing.

Who to trust.

And for now, the only person I completely trust is me.

A LETTER FROM NICOLA

I want to say a huge thank you for choosing to read *The Last Wife*. If you enjoyed it, and want to keep up to date with my latest releases, please sign up at the following link. Your email address will never be shared and you can unsubscribe at any time.

www.bookouture.com/nicola-marsh

The idea for *The Last Wife* came about in a most interesting way... at a child's birthday party of all places! With kids cavorting among rides and building blocks, I discovered that a fellow parent had an unusual occupation: ethical hacker/penetration tester.

What followed was an intriguing conversation about the intricacies of the cyber world and the dark web. Fascinating stuff for an author whose imagination runs wild!

It made me wonder... what if the least likely person used this cyber knowledge to control and intimidate her family? And how far would she go?

I'm also intrigued by the behind-the-scenes machinations of families, particularly in-laws, and how often mismatched people are forced to socialize, all in the name of family. I loved creating the unique Parkers and I hope you have as much fun reading about their tribulations as I did creating them.

If you enjoyed *The Last Wife* I would be very grateful if you could write a review. I'd love to hear what you think, and it makes such a difference helping new readers to discover one of my books for the first time.

I also love hearing from my readers—you can get in touch on my Facebook page, through Twitter, Goodreads or my website.

Thanks,
Nicola

 @NicolaMarsh

www.nicolamarsh.com

NicolaMarshAuthor

@nicolamarshauthor

ACKNOWLEDGEMENTS

Bringing a story to life takes a team and I'm so lucky to have a great one.

With thanks to Jennifer Hunt, my fab editor at Bookouture, who has a keen editorial eye and makes the entire process as smooth as possible. Jen, it's such a pleasure to work with you. Your insight and professionalism makes this writing caper a lot easier. Thank you!

With gratitude to my agent Kim Lionetti, I love having you in my corner. The Ryan Gosling pics you send me? An added bonus and invaluable writing inspiration!

Thanks to Kim Nash and Noelle Holten, PR whizzes at Bookouture. Your passion for books and unswerving enthusiasm makes me eternally grateful that I have you to champion my books too.

To the entire Bookouture publishing team and its authors, I'm so thankful for the support with every single book published. Bookouture sure is a great place to be.

Thanks to Michael Connory, for answering my cyber questions and alerting me to the intricacies of the Web. Fascinating stuff.

With eternal gratitude to Soraya Lane and Natalie Anderson, who always listen, encourage, support and are there for me. You are the best.

Thanks to Martin, for making me laugh, even through the endless edits.

For my boys, you are the loves of my life. Thanks for being you.

And for my readers, you buying and reading and reviewing my books makes this all possible. Thank you so much!

Made in United States
North Haven, CT
17 June 2022

20356158R00190